"One of those people is me," she said, her voice chilly.

"Yeah, I know. I thought you were different, but you're just another outsider, coming in and telling folks who've lived here all their lives how to manage their own affairs."

She let out an exasperated sigh. "That's not— Dirk, don't you see? Like it or not, the newcomers are here to stay. Sooner or later, you're going to have to come to terms with that. If you want to save your ranch, you're going to have to adapt to a changing world."

A rush of heat flooded his face. "That's right, explain it to me. Poor Dirk Hager! He's just another benighted Southerner, toiling away on his failing ranch, too dumb to realize what he really needs!"

"You're not being fair."

"No, you're not being fair. You expect me to do all this adapting and changing and be willing to take a chance and trust people, when you refuse to do the same."

"What are you talking about?"

"I'm talking about us, Macy. You and me. That's why I thought you wanted to come over, because you'd decided I was worth the risk. My mistake."

Dear Reader,

The name *Texas* comes from a Caddo word meaning *friend*. Friendship is our state motto, and in my experience, Texans do tend to be friendly, neighborly folk.

And the neighbors keep coming! Down the road from our place, an old ranch has been carved up and sold to people who want a country place of their own. I used to walk that road without seeing another soul, but not anymore.

Early in 2021, a major snowstorm hit Texas. For days, Texans struggled to keep warm and fed and care for property and livestock. But for country folk, being prepared is a way of life, and so is neighborliness. We helped each other through the storm, and afterward, when hardware stores ran out of plumbing supplies, two men gave us what we needed for our repairs. One was a new neighbor from down the road. The other was someone we'd never met before. We gave him a jar of homemade salsa.

Change isn't easy, as Dirk Hager knows. But it's a chance to grow and expand our definition of *neighbor*.

I hope you enjoy Dirk and Macy's story.

Kit

HEARTWARMING

Snowbound with the Rancher

———

Kit Hawthorne

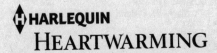

HARLEQUIN
HEARTWARMING

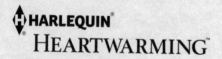

ISBN-13: 978-1-335-58468-7

Recycling programs
for this product may
not exist in your area.

Snowbound with the Rancher

Copyright © 2022 by Brandi Midkiff

For questions and comments about the quality of this book,
please contact us at CustomerService@Harlequin.com.

Harlequin Enterprises ULC
22 Adelaide St. West, 41st Floor
Toronto, Ontario M5H 4E3, Canada
www.Harlequin.com

Printed in U.S.A.

Kit Hawthorne makes her home in south-central Texas on her husband's ancestral farm, where seven generations of his family have lived, worked and loved. When not writing, she can be found reading, drawing, sewing, quilting, reupholstering furniture, playing Irish penny whistle, refinishing old wood, cooking huge amounts of food for the pressure canner, or wrangling various dogs, cats, goats and people.

Books by Kit Hawthorne

Truly Texas

Hill Country Promise
The Texan's Secret Son
Coming Home to Texas
Hill Country Secret

Visit the Author Profile page
at Harlequin.com for more titles.

To the people of Kingsbury:
neighbors, friends, family.

ACKNOWLEDGMENTS

Thanks to all those who helped me get the horse and ranch stuff right—my husband, Greg, my daughter, Grace, and fellow authors Nellie Krauss and Janalyn Knight—and to my brother-in-law Bryan Gillaspie for his inside knowledge on how to remove a tree after it falls through your roof. Thanks also to my critique partners: Mary Johnson, Cheryl Crouch, David Martin, Janalyn Knight, Willa Blair, Nellie Krauss, Anne Dietz and Ani Jacob. And thanks to my editor, Johanna Raisanen, for her unerring taste and judgment.

CHAPTER ONE

DIRK HAGER SCANNED the northern horizon as he made his way along the fence, keeping his horse at an easy walk. Thick gray clouds covered the sky, heavy with the threat of snow. The bleached buffalo grass rippled in a breeze that was getting colder by the minute.

Monte's flaxen mane stirred against his thick, copper-colored neck. He was a big horse, over sixteen hands, with a good bit of Belgian Draft mixed in with his quarter horse ancestry.

Not for the first time, Dirk wished there was a way to truly and permanently coyote-proof a long fence—although, nowadays, it wasn't so much coyotes he was worried about; it was dogs. A coyote didn't normally want to come too close to the house, but a dog didn't care. And with all the newcomers in the area, there was bound to be an uptick in the local population of marauding dogs. He'd seen it before. People moved to the country and thought it was fine to let their dogs roam all over, with never a thought as to the havoc they'd wreak on nearby poultry or livestock. Problem was, folks like that didn't think of their dogs as *dogs*—predator animals with the capacity, suppressed but never wholly bred out of them, to hunt. They didn't believe their family pets could ever steal chickens or kill calves. Once the inevitable happened and their dog got shot by some rancher defending his livelihood, they wrote aggrieved letters to the editor of the local paper, casting themselves as the innocent victims of barbaric, trigger-happy cowboys eager to relive the days of the Wild West.

It was all a matter of respect—for other people's property, and for the dogs themselves. The same qualities that made a vicious, undisciplined dog into a menace also made an asset of a good, well-trained dog— like Fletch, Dirk's old Aussie–border collie mix, with his tireless work ethic and almost intuitive grasp of what Dirk wanted him to do at any given moment. Fletch was smarter than most hired hands, and far better company.

Some wild turkeys had gathered around a concrete watering tank just beyond a dip in the land. Dirk saw them fan their tails, then did a double take. Amid the subdued spreads of brown-and-chestnut feathers was a brilliant semicircle of turquoise, purple, royal blue and gold.

"Huh," he said aloud. An actual *peacock* was out there in his pasture, hanging out with the wild turkeys like a city slicker on a dude ranch. A newcomer's pet, no doubt. Dirk was no expert on peafowl but seemed to recollect that they weren't especially cold hardy. That fancy bird had better skedaddle on home if it didn't want to freeze to death come nightfall.

All that was assuming the Extreme Winter Weather Event that the weather folks kept yammering about didn't turn out to be so much hot air. Dirk didn't trust weather forecasters, always piling on the drama with all their fancy talk. But he'd heard at the feed store that a lot of hunters and trappers had reported seeing unusually thick fat reserves on game animals this fall, and in his experience, that was usually a good indication of a hard winter to come.

So he was hoping for the best while preparing for the worst, which was pretty much business as usual. He hadn't bought a gas generator or made a panicked grocery run to H-E-B, but he'd laid in a good supply of feed and checked that his pantry was full. For country folks, being prepared was a way of life. Stuff happened. Roads and gravel driveways got washed out, power failed. And when it did, official help wasn't always close to hand. Country folks had to rely on themselves, and take care of their neighbors.

The word *neighbor*, though—that was a relative term. Alex Reyes, now, over on Corbett Road, was a terrific neighbor and friend. He and Dirk, and their grandfathers before them, had helped each other out loads of times over the years—and worked together to help other folks, for that matter. Just yesterday, the two of them had gone to check on Miss Ida, who lived alone a mile or so down the road and didn't get around so well anymore. They'd brought some hay for her horse, Peaches, and spent an afternoon splitting firewood, stacking it on the front porch, recaulking some windows and replacing a rotten porch step. Miss Ida had fed them on cornbread, turnip greens and pot liquor and sent them both home with thumbprint cookies packed in slightly battered vintage tins with snowy landscapes printed on the lids.

That was good old-fashioned neighborliness, on both sides.

But the horde of outsiders currently overrunning Limestone Springs and the surrounding countryside—that was another thing entirely. Those weren't neighbors; they were an infestation.

Dirk halted his horse and dismounted. A dead tree branch had fallen onto the fence, stretching the space between the strands of barbed wire. He pulled the branch free and set it by the fence post, then used his fence tool to crimp the slack out of the wires.

As he walked back to Monte, he automatically looked around for Fletch. He had his lips primed for a whistle before remembering.

His heart seized up with a sharp pang. He wouldn't ever again see that lithe body, with its long blue merle and copper coat, weaving its way through the grass toward him. In a year that had been full of losses, that one was the most recent and the most fresh.

He swung himself into the saddle and checked the sky again. Still no snowfall, but those clouds were looking thicker and heavier.

And away to the north, a dark smudge rose up from somewhere behind the tree line.

Dirk frowned. Wood smoke—and from the look of it, coming from not too far off, in one of the new lots in Masterson Acres. A cozy fireplace blaze in one of the newcomers' houses? Or the early stages of a grass fire heading his way? That'd be real cute, if a devastating fire swept through the area just ahead of the Extreme Winter Weather Event.

Probably just chimney smoke, he told himself. But he'd go take a look to make sure. If he had to guess, he'd say the smoke was coming from Lot Eight, but he wasn't yet familiar enough with the new houses to be able to mentally place their chimneys from across the creek. He wasn't even sure they all *had* chimneys. In this climate, most folks didn't bother with fireplaces.

It had been a dry fall in Seguin County, and a dry summer before that. All the weed stalks and parched grasses amounted to so much tinder, ready to catch in a spark from a passing car. Dirk hadn't forgotten the fire that had threatened the Ramirez ranch, La Escarpa, a few years back. It could have been catastrophic, if Tony Reyes, who was both a volunteer firefighter and intimately familiar with that particular ranch, hadn't seen the fire in its early stages, called Dispatch and gotten the Ramirez cattle to safety.

Dirk followed the trail to the spot where, for decades, he and his father and grandfather had forded the Serenidad Creek into the old Masterson place. The banks sloped gently here, angling the trail down to a dry creek bed littered with fallen leaves. On the far side, he opened the gate without dismounting his horse.

The Masterson ranch hadn't actually been lived on in decades. Generations of teenagers had partied on the deserted property since the seventies at least; Granddad used to keep a plastic trash bag tied to his saddle horn for all the empty beer cans that got left behind. In those days, and going back before that as long as Dirk could remember, his family, the Hagers, had leased the Masterson place for their own cattle. It was a good deal all around; the Mastersons got to keep their ag exemption, and the Hagers got to increase the size of their herd without having to buy more land.

Not that the Hagers were opposed to owning more property. Far from it. Buying the Masterson place outright would have more than doubled their acreage, providing additional grazing and water and road access. Eventually, once Granddad had built up enough capital, he'd made an offer.

The Mastersons had turned him down, saying they weren't quite ready to part with the old family homestead. The following year, he'd offered again, and had again been turned down, in what soon became an annual tradition. The problem was that the property was jointly owned by the dozen or so descendants of the last Masterson who'd actually ranched. Whenever one bunch was ready to sell, another bunch wasn't, and by the time the reluctant ones came around, the others had changed their minds. But they'd always said that once they were all in agreement, the Hagers would be their first call.

That call had never come. When the Mastersons finally did decide to unload their property, they'd gone a different route altogether, carving up the old ranch into parcels of mostly twenty acres or so, and selling them off piecemeal.

Dirk could still taste the bitter disappointment. He'd had to watch as a whole parade of people came through—first the Mendozas with their earth-moving equipment, followed by the surveyor, and then the Realtors, showing the land to dewy-eyed city folks in shorts and flip-flops. Within an unbelievably short period of time, the lots had all sold and construction had gotten underway. The houses had been finished and occupied for a while now. Dirk's grandmother would be appalled that he hadn't yet gone to welcome his new neighbors with a covered dish in hand, though not as appalled as she'd be by what had happened to the place.

In fact, Dirk *had* met some of the new folks—a family called Hansen, with a spindly, pasty-faced teenage son who looked like he'd been raised in a basement and never seen sunlight before. But the encounter hadn't been a social call, and it sure hadn't been friendly.

Anger churned hot in his belly at the memory, ready to boil over if he let it, but he pushed it down. No sense in getting worked up all over again.

Used to be, Dirk knew how most everyone in this town was connected to everyone else. His own family of hardworking German immigrants had been on their land since before the Texas Revolution, and an ancestor of Alex's had been among the Tejano freedom fighters under Juan Seguin. True, Alex's wife was some sort of hippie from one of the northern states, but she'd never made a nuisance of herself—besides which, she was the one who'd found the missing will that had saved the Reyes place from being carved up and sold off, just like the Masterson place, so Dirk supposed he ought to feel grateful to her.

But he didn't have the energy for gratitude. The truth was, he was fed up with outsiders. He was worn out from trying to hold on to his own place, much less defend it from encroachers.

Nobody said life was fair. That's what Granddad used to tell him. But Granddad was gone now. Just about everyone and everything he'd ever cared about was gone.

For the past year Dirk's life had been one blow after another. No sooner had Granddad's will been read than Granddad's second wife's grandson—Dirk refused to call him his cousin—had driven down from New Jersey to claim his inheritance and try to insinuate himself into the ranch where he'd never truly belonged to begin with. Not long after that, the last and biggest parcel of the Masterson land had sold, crushing Dirk's hope that he might manage to buy at least that much for himself, and raise hay on it if nothing else, and not be forced to reduce the herd he'd been building up with such tender care over the past several years.

Then Kyra had left him. Well, technically he supposed he'd left her, since he was the one who'd moved out, but that was only after she'd served him with divorce papers. She'd made herself out to be the injured party, claiming he had no room in his life for anything but his unhealthy obsession, by which she meant the ranch, but they both knew that was just an excuse. By that point, though, Dirk hadn't cared enough to fight back. So he'd packed up the few belongings that mattered to him, and he and Fletch had left the house in town where he'd never truly felt at home anyhow, and moved into the old stone house that had been in his family for the past hundred and seventy years.

Fletch had died a little over a month ago, and in all honesty, Dirk missed his dog a whole lot more than he missed his ex-wife.

Another quick stab of hurt passed through his chest, almost taking his breath away, and for an instant the grief felt almost like panic. He was stretched to the breaking point already. He couldn't take another disaster.

Please, God, please don't let it be a wildfire.

He had almost reached Lot Eight. The smoke was thicker now, blue-black against the overcast sky. He could just make out the shape of a house, with a length of shiny new steel pipe, topped with a metal cap, rising from the back of the roof. Chimney pipe.

But the smoke wasn't coming from there. Up ahead, he could hear something crackling, and a flash of orange flame showed through a break in the trees at ground level.

Dirk's mouth went dry as he and Monte rounded the last turn in the trail and emerged from the woods.

What he saw was not an uncontrolled fire racing through the grass and brush. It was only a cozy little blaze, ringed with stones.

A *campfire*. A picture-perfect campfire, complete with Adirondack chair.

Dirk hadn't known just how scared he'd been until now, when it was evident that there was nothing to be scared of. His legs went weak and his stomach felt queasy.

The house on this lot was on the small side, probably not even fifteen hundred square feet. Raw as it was, it didn't look as jarringly out of place to Dirk's eyes as most of the new construction in Masterson Acres. Give it five years, and it might pass for an authentic old farmhouse. A Kia Soul was parked around back, near a pair of French doors.

He took in all this in an instant. Then his gaze went back to the fire.

There was a woman curled up in the Adirondack chair, a slender, pretty woman with her hair gathered into a loose bun. In her oversize plaid shirt, skinny jeans and weird, chunky, fleece-lined ankle boots, she could have been a model in an ad for winter clothing. All she needed was a steaming mug of hot chocolate. Maybe she had one. Maybe she was getting ready to roast hot dogs and marshmallows, here at her festive little fire that had nearly stopped Dirk's heart.

Her eyes met his. They were almond-shaped eyes of some dark color beneath softly rounded brows. They opened wide at the sight of this stranger on horseback who'd turned up without warning in her backyard, but surprise quickly gave way to suspicion and possibly hostility. Dirk could see it in the vertical crease that formed between the eyebrows and the sudden tightening of the mouth. Her whole face seemed to close off as if she'd just slammed a door shut.

Quickly she got to her feet. She was tall, long-limbed and broad-shouldered.

"Can I help you?" she asked, in a tone that really meant, *Get out*.

Dirk didn't answer. It wasn't that he didn't trust himself to speak. At that point he simply wasn't capable of it.

A garden hose stretched from the hydrant at the side of the house all the way to the campfire, and judging from the way the sprayer nozzle was quivering, there was plenty of water pressure built up inside. Dirk walked Monte over to it and dismounted.

"Sir," the woman said, "this is private property. I'm going to have to ask you to leave."

Still Dirk didn't answer. He picked up the sprayer, aimed the nozzle into the cute little campfire and pulled the trigger.

A broad cone of water shot out of the nozzle and into the flames. Clouds of steam rose with a hiss.

Behind him, he could hear the woman saying, "What…? What…? What do you think you're doing?"

Still dousing the fire, Dirk said over his shoulder, "I'm doing you a favor, ma'am. If that fire of yours was to spread, you could end up in jail, and I reckon you'd stay there a mighty long while, cause none of the folks at the local bail bonds companies would spot you the money to get out, seeing as you'd've burned down their houses, along with half the county."

She made a huffing sound. "I wasn't burning down anyone's property! It was just a little fire."

There was something in her voice that he didn't like, a sort of northeastern sound to the vowels. He glanced again at the Kia Soul. New York plates—he might've known.

"Yeah," he said, "most fires are, to start

with. But the thing about fires is, they spread. Seguin County hasn't had a drop of rain in five weeks. The entire landscape around here isn't much more than a bunch of kindling right now, ready to go up in flames at the tiniest spark. That's why the county commissioners declared a burn ban. That means no bonfires, no burning of brush piles or household trash, no fire pits, no open burning of any kind—not even cute little campfires like this one of yours. Nobody wants another Bastrop."

There was a pause. Then she said, "Another what?"

A hot coal of anger burned in his chest. Even now, over a decade after the Bastrop County Complex Fire, the memory was enough to make him sick. Fifty-five days of raging wildfire, thirty-four thousand acres burned to the ground, sixteen hundred houses lost, along with ancient pine forests, innumerable wildlife habitats, four human lives and untold horses and cattle.

And Little Miss Don't-I-look-cute-in-my-plaid-shirt-and-fleecy-boots? She'd never even heard of it.

He released the nozzle's trigger and turned to face her. "Oh, of course. What was I thinking? You wouldn't know about Bastrop, would you? You're not from around here. Well, how about California and Australia? You've heard of those places, haven't you? You've seen videos of fires there, right?"

A violent struggle showed itself on her face. It was a strong face, the kind that stuck in your memory a long time, with those broad cheekbones, that firm jaw, those piercing eyes.

Something shifted in her right hand. It was a two-by-four, and she was holding it like a potential weapon—as if Dirk was the one who posed a threat in this situation.

She drew herself up tall. "I've already said this once. I won't say it again. *Get off my land.*"

Exactly what he'd have liked to say to her. But in the eyes of the law, she was the one who actually had the right to say it.

Dirk turned back to the fire. It was thoroughly extinguished by now, but he gave it one more blast with the spray nozzle, more for show than anything, before dropping the hose.

"Happy to," he said.

He stepped back over to Monte and swung himself into the saddle. Looking down on the woman from his superior height, he pointed back the way he'd come.

"See that line of trees back there? That's the

Serenidad Creek. Just across that creek is my ranch. That makes us neighbors. I don't like that any more than you do, and nothing would please me better than for the two of us to never speak or lay eyes on each other again. But I will defend my property against anything or anyone that threatens it. So do us both a favor, and don't give me a reason to come back."

At that exact moment, a swift dark blur came racing around the corner of the house and planted itself in front of the woman. It was a dog—a huge, deep-chested dog with a black-and-gold brindled coat and tiny yellow eyes in a broad head. Facing Dirk, it let out a barrage of booming barks that matched its appearance.

Dirk could feel Monte shift into a high state of vigilance, but the horse held his ground. The dog stayed in a low crouch, with tail tucked, ears back and hackles raised.

An aggressive dog—of course the new Yankee neighbor had to have an aggressive dog.

Dirk pointed at the animal. "Another piece of advice. You get that dog under control, and put up a fence to keep him contained. If he goes onto other people's land and kills their stock, he will be shot."

The woman lifted the two-by-four a little higher. "Is that a threat?"

"It's the truth. You're in the country now, ma'am, and around here, people defend what's theirs."

He turned Monte and rode away. The dog didn't come after them, but its barks followed them to the Serenidad.

All the earth-moving, tree-clearing and fence-reconfiguring had broken up the lines and contours of the landscape. Everything once familiar to him was now reshuffled or gone.

Dirk didn't feel the cold anymore; his anger heated him through. But before he'd reached the cover of the trees, the first flakes of snow began to fall.

CHAPTER TWO

SMOKE ROSE FROM Macy Reinalda's quenched
fire as she stood rooted to her spot, watching the cowboy ride away. Every line of him
radiated hostility, from the gray felt cowboy
hat on down to the tough-looking canvas field
coat, past the well-worn, thigh-hugging jeans
all the way to the brown Ropers resting in the
stirrups.

The marvel of it was that he hadn't raised
his voice—at least, not until Gunnar had
started barking, and then only loud enough
to be heard. His manner had been almost def-
erential, with all those *ma'ams*, and no snark
in the tone, but he'd managed to communicate
what he thought of her all the same. Genuine power didn't have to be showy. It simply
was. He'd said his piece, then gone on his
way, leaving her gripping a weaponized two-
by-four and staring at his retreating back.

It was a well-made back, lean and strong in
the saddle, broad through the shoulders and

narrow at the waist. He'd come riding up like a cowboy out of an old Western, with that stern, square face, all angles and planes, and narrow eyes that looked as if they spent a lot of time squinting, or scowling.

Now that the encounter was over, Macy's stomach churned with postadrenaline nausea. Her heart raced and her hands shook. She hadn't felt that way in a long time—not since Andrew.

She dropped her two-by-four and took a deep breath.

Had it really been only minutes earlier that she'd been sitting by her nice cozy fire, reveling in the wide-open space of her Texas acreage, congratulating herself on putting that constant low-grade anxiety behind her for good? Twenty acres had seemed enormous when she'd taken her first look at the plots for sale in the newly designated Masterson Acres. The idea of neighbors hadn't entered her thinking at all. Anyone who might share a boundary with her would be too far off to matter. And when she'd started her fire, it had never occurred to her that anyone else could possibly be affected. It had seemed an entirely private matter, here in the blessed security and solitude of her vast estate.

But she'd been wrong. She'd escaped her New York problems only to land in a whole new set.

The worst thing about it—even worse than the shattering of her illusion of solitude—was that the cowboy's points hadn't been at all unreasonable. Now that the heat of confrontation was over and he was riding away from her, she had an uncomfortable conviction that he was right and she was wrong. It made sense that there would be regulations governing outdoor fires. This wasn't the open range of the nineteenth century, after all. Had they had burn bans in Upstate New York? She couldn't remember, but she'd been just a kid when she used to visit her aunt and uncle at their semirural home there, too young to pay attention to such things.

Gunnar stood firmly planted in front of her, hackles raised, still barking his head off. What would have happened if he'd attacked the man's horse? She shuddered. She wouldn't think about it. There was no need, because it hadn't happened. Gunnar had only been defending her. He knew his job—had known it from the start on an intuitive level, from the moment she'd first laid eyes on him a little over a year ago in that kennel at the shelter.

She'd seen the way he'd watched her—wary, but not vicious, and with a kind of childlike hopefulness in his golden eyes. This was a dog who'd learned to be cautious, who knew the world wasn't always a friendly place, but wasn't bitter about it. A dog who needed a chance to start over, in a secure home where he could relax and be loved.

All that, and he was a big, intimidating dog, with a frame that suggested he'd get bigger still before he finished growing. Exactly what Macy needed. She'd chosen well. She was a good judge of character in dogs, if not in people.

But the world had dangers for dogs and people both, and willing as he was, Gunnar couldn't protect Macy from everything.

"Gunnar, hush," she said.

He hushed, then circled around to Macy, plopped his hindquarters onto her foot and turned his face up to her with that eager, trusting look that always went straight to her heart.

"Good boy," she said, rubbing his ears. "The scary man is gone now. You barked him away."

She barely had to stoop to reach his head. Gunnar had filled out a lot over the past several months, losing that lanky adolescent look he'd had in the shelter. They'd both been pretty cramped in her San Antonio rental house, with its almost nonexistent yard, and in spite of Gunnar's obvious gratitude at being rescued, she'd always felt uneasy about not providing more space for him to play. She'd done her best, taking him for walks and to the dog park, but it wasn't the same. During the week since they'd moved here, it had been a pleasure to watch him stretch out his legs and run, and to see his dawning joyful realization that this was no park; this was home now.

She saw the cowboy's face again—his hard mouth, square jaw, steely eyes.

You get that dog under control, and put up a fence to keep him contained. If he goes onto other people's land and kills their stock, he will be shot.

If Gunnar had crossed that creek into the cowboy's place, and hurt his cattle…

Well, he hadn't. And he wouldn't. From now on she'd keep Gunnar indoors, or else on a leash—at least until she could get a fence built. How fast could she make that happen? Should she enclose a yard-sized portion to begin with, and then fence in the rest of the acreage? She'd seen some sort of wire grid fencing while out on her walks; maybe that was what she should use. How should the yard fence be laid out? And how should she go about finding someone to do the work?

Enough. Those were problems for another day.

The long-foretold snow was coming down at last, landing on Gunnar's black fur.

"Come on, boy," she said. "Let's go inside."

Gunnar lolloped ahead of her in that comical way of his, turning now and then to look over his shoulder and make sure she was still coming. He reached the French door and sat on his haunches, waiting politely for her to let him in.

Through the living room window, the white lights of her Christmas tree shone like tiny stars. Macy felt her heart rate slow down. The second she walked inside, the tension in her neck and shoulders melted away, and her spirits lifted.

She loved this little house.

She'd taken her time coming up with the floor plan, wanting to get it exactly right. She'd started by poring over plans she'd found online, comparing the ones she liked, brooding over them, analyzing what appealed to her and why. Then she'd experimented with combining different elements—altering, refining and sometimes starting over completely, before finally distilling it all down to a simple penciled sketch on a sheet of graph paper, which she'd presented to the contractors, Alex and Tony Reyes. They'd passed the paper back and forth between themselves, made a few minor alterations and said, *Yep, we can build this.*

Now, a mere four months later, it was all done, and she was actually living in her perfect little home, specifically designed to meet her needs and satisfy her taste.

Just inside the French door was Macy's work room. It opened to the kitchen in the front, and in more conventional house plans would have been called a dining room, but in Macy's mind it had been a work room from start to finish, and labeled as such on her graph paper sketch. The old pine harvest table, with its turned legs and honest patina, was not for meals, but for a commercial-grade sewing machine, currently being serviced at a place in town. Beneath the table stood two storage carts on wheels, easy to pull out and push back in again. A shallow-drawered wooden chest, originally an architect's cabinet, held tools and supplies, next to a tall shelf unit neatly fitted with canvas-covered bins and other organizational aids. Right beside the door leading to the garage, a small stack of flattened moving boxes waited to be taken to Goodwill.

A hand-quilting frame ran parallel to the table, along the boundary between work room and living room. It held an in-progress Irish chain quilt in shades of ivory, turquoise, coral, green, red and gold. She might sell it when it was finished, and she might not. Financial independence gave her a lot of freedom.

Beyond the quilting frame, in the living room, two back-facing windows flanked a biscuit-colored enameled wood-burning stove on a tiled platform. A gigantic ottoman, slip-covered in heavy-duty, dog-proof cotton duck cloth, stood near the stove. Gunnar headed straight for the ottoman. He climbed up easily, folded his long limbs and flopped down with a contented sigh.

Macy hadn't lit the fire yet, but she'd prepped the stove earlier in the day, building a teepee of tinder, kindling and small logs. An old jadeite washtub held larger logs ready to be added as needed. She had a full cord of firewood just outside on the back deck, surely more than enough to get her through any Texas winter weather event, however extreme.

Of course she could have burned Andrew's old letters right here in the stove, and saved herself the whole unpleasant episode with the cowboy, but she hadn't wanted to pollute her bright, shiny new Vermont Castings Intrepid FlexBurn with them. It had seemed fitting to do the deed outdoors, under the sky, on the last day of fall—a final purging of her connection to the old life.

Oh, well. The outdoor fire had been fun while it lasted, and she'd accomplished her primary goal of watching Andrew's toxic words turn to ash.

She opened the front doors of her wood-burning stove, struck a match and held it to the tinder. Tongues of flame flared up and caught the kindling. Before long, a bright blaze was shining through the sparkling clean glass doors into Macy's living room.

"Back to work," Macy said aloud. Gunnar thumped his tail without raising his head.

She turned to the built-in bookcases that lined the living room's interior wall. Several open boxes full of books stood along it at intervals. Such a luxurious expanse of shelves! She'd spent the whole afternoon blissfully arranging and rearranging the books. It was engrossing, happy work. So many decisions to make! Should Patrick O'Brian be shelved with British naval history, or with Jane Austen? Did *The Vinland Sagas* belong with Scandinavian history, or American? Which

section made more sense for books on herbs—
gardening, wellness or food? Should the big
volume on Chinese landscape painting go with
the book on the history of the Tang dynasty, or
should all art books be grouped together, regardless of continent and era? Should all the
David McCullough books go together, or be
dispersed according to subject matter? Extra-
large or oddly shaped books presented special problems. Alternating uprights with stacks
took care some of these issues, and made the
shelves look pretty, too.

Then she'd delved into a box of reference
books and found the antique document box
that held Andrew's letters. Instantly the joy of
arranging her library had withered and died.

She shook her head hard. The letters were
gone now. She'd erased all physical evidence
of the hold Andrew had once had on her. She
could go back to shelving her books with a
light heart.

But first, she had some googling to do.

She pulled her phone out of her back pocket
and started typing.

It took less than a minute for her to learn
that Seguin County was indeed under a burn
ban. All open burning was prohibited, just as
the cowboy had said, and violation of the ban

could lead to penalties including steep fines and jail time.

Then she looked up Bastrop.

What she found made for a sobering read. The Bastrop County Complex Fire had been a devastating event; over a decade later, the affected area—a few counties over, east of the Hill Country—had yet to fully recover. The blaze had been started not by a careless individual, but by downed power lines during a drought. Nevertheless, Macy could see how locals—and Texans in general—would be sensitive to outdoor burning, and rightly so.

"Stupid," she muttered, meaning herself. That was always her first response to any miscalculation, to blame herself for letting her guard down, for failing to foresee every possible angle and outcome—in short, for not being omniscient. Her stomach tightened in the old familiar way. It was exhausting, constantly thinking ahead and trying to predict the future.

Well, she knew now, and she wouldn't make the same mistake again. No more outdoor fires for her without proper governmental clearance. And no more unrestrained runs through the countryside for Gunnar, either.

The wood-burning stove was starting to

put out heat. She opened the top, added a mid-size log and settled it in with the poker.

Outside, a thin blanket of snow had accumulated, blurring the harsh stubble of parched grass and defining the limbs of the dark oaks and elms along the Serenidad Creek. The Extreme Winter Weather Event had begun at last.

It was funny how worked up people seemed to be getting about it. Where Macy came from, weather like this wasn't extreme, or much of an event. It was just winter.

She started toward the box of reference books, then dropped onto the sofa and curled up under a cashmere throw she'd knitted a few years back. She pulled it over her head, covering herself completely. When she was a little girl, she used to snuggle down under her covers exactly this way, pretending she was a tiny woodland animal tucked away in a warm burrow for the winter. She liked to imagine people walking by outside her hollow tree, or underground den or whatever, without ever knowing she was there.

That was basically what she'd created here, with her snug comfy house stocked with everything she needed. All those filled jars standing in neat rows in her canning pantry were like so many nuts stowed away for the winter.

Solitude, independence and comfort. That was what she'd been seeking in her new home. To be in complete charge of her environment without having to answer to anyone else. The freedom to set her own schedule, to work into the wee small hours and then take a nap at eleven in the morning if she wanted. Not that she was really so Bohemian as all that; she was regular and methodical in her work and life habits. But she wanted to be able to do it if she chose to, and not be criticized for it or have her motives scrutinized and questioned for every single action of her life.

How many acres would it take for her to have the isolation she craved?

MACY HAD THE dream again that night, the one where she'd inexplicably married Andrew after all, with no memory of how it had happened or what had become of her exquisitely plotted scheme to get away from him. For whatever reason, she'd done it, she'd married him, and now she was trapped.

She lay on her back for a full minute, frozen with horror, staring up at the ceiling, before realizing it was the ceiling of her new house in Texas, which Andrew had never seen or set foot in or known about. The heavy breathing she heard was only Gunnar, asleep on his slipcovered dog bed in the corner of the room.

Slowly, cautiously, she stretched out both arms, feeling the empty mattress on either side of her. She ran the thumb of her left hand over the ring finger. It was bare. She'd taken off Andrew's diamond and sealed it inside the envelope that held her parting letter to him. The letter had been a short one—no accusations, no attempt to justify why she was breaking off their engagement, no parting shot. By then she'd accepted that Andrew couldn't be reasoned with or persuaded. There was nothing to tell him beyond the bare facts that she was leaving, she was finished and she wasn't coming back. She didn't owe him an explanation. She didn't owe him anything.

Taking off that ring and dropping it inside the envelope had felt daring and irrevocable, even more so than selling her house had done. Again she felt that wild, exultant rush, like a plunge on a roller coaster. She'd done it. She'd escaped Andrew's bullying and belittling forever.

Macy rolled around on the bed, reveling in the empty space. This was real—her little house in Limestone Springs, the scent of lavender linen spray, the soft tickle of her thick, fuzzy blanket against her neck, the warm hug of flannel sheets, the pale moonlight coming through the curtains she'd made herself.

She got out of bed and slipped on her fleece-lined thick-soled house shoes. Gunnar went right on snoring on his enormous foam cushion. Outside the master suite, a short hallway contained the closed doors of a compact laundry area, a second bathroom and two additional bedrooms. One of the bedrooms held a few rolls and bolts of fabric, along with one future reupholstering project, an old wing-back chair with great lines, which she'd gotten for a song because the seat cover was torn. The other held nothing at all.

Feeling like a queen, she walked past this luxurious extravagance of space, through the foyer and into the great room.

The books were all unpacked and shelved now, and the impact of the floor-to-ceiling library was every bit as striking as she'd hoped. Her Christmas tree stood along the bookcase wall. It was an artificial tree with built-in lights, pencil slim and easy for her to set up and move around. No ornaments, just a simple white velvet skirt. She loved the elegant simplicity of it, loved the vast expanse of books behind it. Her heart swelled with well-being, contentment and pride. She held on to the feeling. She wouldn't let Andrew into her head.

She walked over to the windows. The wood-burning stove was still putting off a modest heat. Before going to bed, she'd closed the damper almost completely shut. The big overnight logs were glowing well and holding together; in the morning, she ought to have some good-sized coals to start the day's fire.

Outside, the moonlight shone an eerie blue on the snow-covered Texas landscape. Near the remains of Macy's campfire, the Adirondack chair had a big drift of snow in the seat and puffy snow cushions on the arms.

Macy frowned. The snow on the deck boards didn't have the pristine smoothness of an undisturbed fall. It was marked all over with what looked like a lot of partial asterisks.

Bird tracks. Disturbingly large ones.

And standing on Macy's deck, just outside the French door, was a dark shape that looked like a similarly large bird.

She flipped the switch for the outdoor light. The bird flared into vibrant color—cobalt blue, emerald green, turquoise and gold. A long sweep of tail curved around behind it like a train on a royal robe. The bird's head was topped by a crest of stiff feathers tipped with tiny furry blue fans. A mantle of snowflakes coated its back. It stared at Macy through the glass, looking as outlandish as she herself had probably appeared to the cowboy whose name she'd never caught.

Macy didn't know much about peafowl, but it was a fair bet that the national bird of India wasn't well suited to cold weather. The bird seemed to think so, too. Its feathers were all fluffed up, and it was shaking, actually shaking with cold. It kept trying to draw its feet to its body, first one and then the other.

There was no way of knowing whose bird it was or how far it had come, but it was tame enough to recognize a human habitation and see it as a place of refuge, and it clearly wanted in.

Hadn't she read something once about it being bad luck to bring peacock feathers into the house? Supposedly, their presence would doom any unmarried women in the household to lifelong spinsterhood.

But Macy didn't believe in luck, any more than she believed spinsterhood to be a calamity.

She opened the door and told the peacock, "Come on in."

CHAPTER THREE

DIRK LIFTED THE three sizzling strips of bacon out of the skillet, laid them on his plate and poured the bacon grease into a wide-mouthed quart-sized Mason jar. The amber-colored fluid mingled with the waxy-looking congealed grease already in there, re-liquefying the top layer and making dark specks swirl. He put the lid on the jar and set it back in the fridge, next to another grease jar that he'd filled up a while back. Dirk didn't know what he was supposed to do with all these jars of chilled bacon grease, and he didn't care. His oma had always saved hers in the fridge, and so did he. Kyra used to think this was cute, or said she did, but somewhere along the way it had turned into one of the many things about Dirk that she wanted to change.

He set the skillet back on the stove burner without washing it or even wiping it out with a paper towel. What was the point? He'd just use it again tomorrow to fry more bacon. The heat would kill the germs.

He ate the bacon in the kitchen, standing up, holding his plate at chest height. It was delicious. His one and only kitchen skill was his ability to make perfect bacon.

He was halfway through his second slice when something sharp dug into one of his knees. Taffy was climbing his jeans like a little mountaineer, baby claws hooked into his flesh, stripy face peering earnestly up at him, tiny pink mouth opened in a soft mew.

He balanced his bacon plate on a stack of paperwork, detached the kitten from his leg and cuddled her against his chest. She purred rapturously, shutting her eyes to slits and kneading his flannel shirt with her paws. Then he set her down and poured out a big bowl of kitten food.

Taffy dove in greedily, meowing and gobbling kibble at the same time. Dirk filled her water bowl while he was at it. He'd already filled several pitchers and jugs with drinking water in preparation for the Extreme Winter Weather Event. Not that he expected his pipes to freeze; he'd been not just dripping but flowing his water from all the faucets in the house, hot and cold both. He sure didn't need the trouble and expense of damaged plumbing in an old house.

The various mismatched water receptacles jostled for space with stacks of dirty dishes, stacks of clean dishes, empty food containers and random trash. For the better part of a year, ever since splitting with Kyra, Dirk had been living in defiant squalor, a reaction against the overdecorated discomfort of his former married life. Kyra would have been repulsed, and that was half the fun.

While Dirk was finishing his bacon, Taffy took a break from scarfing her cat food and wandered over, licking her chops and giving Dirk an expectant look. Dirk picked up the toy he'd made her—a wad of paper tied to a stick— and started flicking it around. Taffy loved it. She crouched and pounced in rear-waggling, whisker-twitching delight, all four paws wildly extended.

Miss Ida's cookie tin sat unopened on the counter, looking bright and festive among all the clutter and trash. Dirk had decided to wait until Christmas to start on the cookies. That was the full extent of his holiday plans.

The house was crammed with an odd assortment of furniture, sort of an early-farmhouse-meets-late-bachelor aesthetic. No more slick surfaces, sharp points, glitter or fluff for Dirk. Only shabby comfort.

So here he was at age thirty-six, sleeping in an ancient twin bed in his grandparents' old house, piling up pizza boxes like monuments, reveling in disorder like a hog in mud. In the evenings, he sat in Granddad's old club chair, which exactly fit all of Dirk's angles and kinks and was covered in some worn fabric that might have been green during the Eisenhower administration. He ate his dinner there, and when he was done he wiped his greasy hands on the arms of the chair.

Fletch used to lie down on a worn rug up next to the chair on the left side, right in range for Dirk to reach down and give him a pat. Sometimes Dirk would call him up onto the chair with him, but Fletch knew this was a breach of protocol and always looked disapproving when it happened. He'd go ahead and snuggle, but with an air of humoring a small child, and was always clearly relieved to get back down to his spot on the floor when Dirk let him. Dirk hadn't yet lost the habit of trailing his left hand down to rub Fletch's soft floppy ears.

A loud click sounded in the kitchen. The LED displays on the new-to-Dirk oven went dark, and the refrigerator's hum went quiet. The brownouts had started last night, as predicted, making it hard for Dirk to get a good night's sleep. Whenever the appliances shut down or came back up, he'd wake up and check the time on his phone. The outages were only supposed to last fifteen minutes at a time, but Dirk was sure they were going longer than that. He'd been tempted to get out of bed and unplug every appliance in the house, just to stop all the beeping, but instead he'd stayed bundled up in his warm bed. Now he felt all bleary-eyed. Should he make some extra coffee to get him through the morning? Well, no, he couldn't, not with the power out. Oh, well. Maybe he'd just come on home after feeding cattle and take a nice long nap.

He downed the last of his coffee and balanced his plate and mug on top of some other dirty dishes. Then he carried Taffy back to her food bowl and gave her a pat.

"I'll see you soon, Little Bit. Eat your kitty food and snuggle down in your fluffy bed if you get cold. When I get back, we'll light a fire in the fireplace, and you can learn how to curl up in front of it and stare into the flames like a grown-up cat."

The house was chilly, but tolerable. The old

furnace didn't work well enough to bother with; Dirk relied on the fireplace for heat. And there wasn't any point in lighting a fire until after he'd finished feeding and was ready to stick around and keep it going.

He put on his coat and hat and went out into the morning.

Outside was like a winter wonderland. The snow lay thick and heavy, softening all the rough edges and prettifying everything. The cold air stung his face, but he had his thermals on under his jeans and button-down, and he was wearing his insulated boots. Their rubber soles squeaked against the snow. It was a pretty deep fall, coming almost to his knees in a few places. Shadows looked blue against the stark white. Everything was extra quiet, as if the world had been wrapped in insulation.

Over in the horse pasture catty-corner to the feed barn, Monte gave a long whinny and started prancing along the fence, steam puffing from his nostrils. Cold weather never bothered him. It just gave him a little extra sass—as if he needed any.

"Good morning to you, too, knucklehead," said Dirk. "I'll go get your breakfast ready."

The thermometer outside the feed barn

registered an even ten degrees Fahrenheit. A mite chilly for this part of the state, but at least there wasn't any wind.

The barn felt positively warm compared to outdoors. Dirk filled a bucket with oats and took it outside, along with two flakes of hay. He put the hay in the rack at the top of the feeder, scooped the snow out of the trough and poured in the oats.

Monte started right in on the oats, chomping away with his big strong teeth.

"You're welcome," Dirk said. He gave Monte a few pats on his thick neck.

Next, he loaded up the cab of the truck with bags of cubed cattle feed until there was hardly room for him to climb into the driver's seat. Then he drove the truck into the west pasture, along the hard-packed earthen road made by decades of truck use, and honked the horn. The Black Angus cows and calves came running, their hooves sending the snow flying behind them. The heavy chuffing sounds of their breathing carried through the still air.

There was a certain finesse to pouring cattle feed in a steady stream out the window of a moving truck while simultaneously driving that truck. He had to drive slowly and pour fast. The goal was to leave an even stripe of feed for the cows to line up at so they could all get enough to eat without crowding or hogging. It'd be a whole lot easier if he had a hired hand to do it with him, or instead of him, but hired men never seemed to last very long.

The feed cubes weren't really cubical in shape. They were hard cylinders, something like sausage links, or cigars. They dropped through the snow, leaving a dark trail. The cattle had no trouble nosing out their breakfasts.

The blades of the windmill over by the concrete water tank were covered with frost. Dirk used a five-pound sledgehammer to break the layer of ice that had formed at the top of the tank. He picked up some of the bigger ice chunks and tossed them out of the way, in the direction of the pond. Then he looked over the cattle to make sure there weren't any sick or injured animals needing attention.

Up ahead and across the fence to the left, Dirk could see the east pasture of the Reyes place, stretching back toward the old stone German-built house that Alex's ancestors had been living in for the last century and a half or so. Farther still, the Reyes ranch continued to the Serenidad. On the other side of the creek lay two hundred acres of good bottomland grazing where Dirk used to run his cattle. Now it was home to the Hansens. What a waste.

He'd been inclined to dislike the Hansens from the start, and his first dealings with them had done nothing to change his mind. What happened was that somewhere in the whole process of tearing down old barbed wire and T-posts and putting up the new fencing, some of Dirk's cattle had ended up cut off from the rest of the herd in Lot Nine, which no longer shared a boundary with his land. Dirk had been mildly irked that no one had bothered to give him a heads-up so he could clear his animals out before the fencing had been reconfigured, but the real shocker had come when he'd gone over to see about getting them back, only to discover that the new owner of Lot Nine had knocked down all the cattle pens.

"What exactly did you think you were doing?" Dirk had asked the citified Mr. Hansen. "Didn't you *notice* the half dozen of my cows inside your fence?"

"Of course I did," Hansen said huffily. "They're kinda hard to miss. Their manure is everywhere, and one of them nearly attacked my wife while she was trying to take a picture of it. Our Realtor assured us that you'd get them out."

As a matter of fact, the Realtor had had no business assuring them of any such thing, but Dirk let that pass for the moment. "And just how did you expect me to do that?" he asked.

Hansen shrugged. "I figured you'd bring a—a trailer. A cow trailer. Head 'em up and move 'em out. That's what you cowboys do, right?"

Then he grinned. The guy thought he was being jovial.

Dirk made himself count to ten before answering. "Well, Mr. Hansen, that's what my pens were for, to load them into the trailer. They don't just hop in like a bunch of Labradors going for a car ride."

Hansen looked taken aback for a moment but quickly recovered. "Oh. I see. Well, I... I'm sorry it worked out that way, but after all, this is my property now, and I can do with it what I want. And those cows need to go."

"And how do you propose we make that happen? Are you going to buy or rent me some more fencing for a new crowding pen and loading chute?"

The last of Hansen's smile melted away. "I really don't see how any of that is my responsibility. Like I said, the property belongs to me now. Technically, your cows are trespassing."

"*Technically*, Mr. Hansen, you're in violation of the law. In sales of rural property, when the seller has prior lease agreements in place, the buyer is under obligation to honor them, whether they're written contracts or handshake deals."

Hansen swallowed. "I, uh—nobody told me that. That wasn't disclosed in the sale."

Dirk narrowed his eyes. "Well, I'm sorry it worked out that way, but I really don't see how any of that is my responsibility."

It gave Dirk a grim satisfaction to throw Hansen's own words back in his face, but that was the only pleasure the situation had provided. He'd been sorely tempted to get a lawyer, just on principle. He knew he was in the right, legally speaking, and he'd have enjoyed watching Hansen squirm, and making an example of him to the rest of the newcomers.

But the price of six cows couldn't really justify the potential legal fees, not to mention the time suck. Revenge was a luxury Dirk couldn't afford.

In any event, things had worked out all right in the end. Alex's property overlapped a bit with Hansen's, so it was simple enough for Dirk and

Alex to get Dirk's cows over to the Reyes place and use Alex's pens to load them into Dirk's trailer.

But the idiocy of the Hansens' behavior, their sense of entitlement, had infuriated Dirk. He'd seen them in passing on a few occasions since, still wearing shorts and flip-flops in spite of all the brush, thorns and snakes on their property. They were just the sort of people Dirk couldn't stand, who moved to the country thinking it was all sunshine and daisies, without having the slightest idea of what rural life was actually like.

Alex was feeding his own cattle. He had someone helping him today, a man in the bed of the truck who was pouring the feed out while Alex drove, snug and warm in the cab. Dirk didn't recognize the guy, but he appeared to be doing a decent job.

Dirk waited for Alex to finish feeding and drive over. They often met at the fence this way during their morning cattle feeding. Decades earlier, their grandfathers had hung a gate there so they could drive onto each other's property when they needed to.

Alex parked his truck, gave some instructions to his helper and walked over to the gate where Dirk was standing. He was a big strong guy, several years younger than Dirk, with long black hair pulled back in a ponytail. He'd been ranching full-time for a few years now, when he'd inherited the property from his grandfather. Before that, he'd worked a variety of jobs, including construction and car-and-tractor repair. He'd briefly returned to construction, acting as general contractor, along with his brother Tony, on the houses at Masterson Acres.

"I see you've got yourself a helper today," Dirk said.

Alex glanced back over his shoulder. "Yeah, that's Nathaniel. He's a cousin of Lauren's from back east. He's staying with us while he gets some stuff sorted out."

Getting stuff sorted out could mean a lot of things—credit card debt, trouble with the law, a sticky situation with an ex. Dirk didn't pry.

"He appears to have some giddy-up in his step," he said.

"Yeah, he's a good worker, and pretty quick on his feet. You should have seen how fast he moved the other day when that mean bull of mine came after him. Got him treed in the bed of the truck." Alex chuckled. "Too bad I didn't get video. You should have seen Nathaniel's face."

"I don't blame him. Your Brahmas are scary. I like my Black Angus better. Excellent beef quality, mild temperament. They put on weight better, too. They aren't constantly burning off calories chasing hired men into trucks."

"Well, I like my Brahmas. They're long-lived, resistant to insects and incredibly heat hardy. Plus they're just handsome animals, a pleasure to look at."

Dirk squinted at one loose-skinned Brahma with a hump over its withers at the back of its neck. Like camels, Brahmas used their humps to store water. They did have a striking appearance, but knowing what he did about their temperaments made them a lot less attractive in his eyes.

"Handsome is as handsome does," Dirk said. "Anyhow, that heat hardiness isn't doing them much good today."

Alex waved a hand. "Ah, this is a hundred-year storm. Come summer, it'll be as hot as blazes again, and my herd'll barely notice. But you know, we could always do a little crossbreeding, combine the best qualities of Angus and Brahmas. It'd be fun, getting the proportions right, seeing how they do."

The Brangus cross was considered a desir-able breed, and would probably tolerate heat better than Dirk's cattle, with their Scottish origin and dark hides.

"Maybe next year," Dirk said. "Right now I've got way too much on my plate to go experimenting with bloodlines."

"Get yourself a hired man like I did," said Alex.

"Oh, yeah, cause it's that easy. Where is this Nathaniel staying, anyway? At the house with you all?"

"Nah, he's staying in Lauren's van that she used to travel the country in before we were married. It's actually a pretty nice setup— running water, composting toilet, kitchenette, light and heat. Speaking of cousins, have you heard from Roque lately?"

Dirk felt his jaw stiffening. "First of all," he said, "he is not my cousin. Second, no, I have not. I hope that fool gave up and went home and isn't still running around pretending to be a cowboy."

"I don't think he has. I saw him in the feed store again not long ago."

Dirk winced inwardly. "Was he all duded up like a drugstore cowboy again?"

"He's dialed it back some. Still wearing the duster and hat, but not the chaps and spurs. He was getting hay and horse feed, so I guess he's still got that horse your grandfather gave him."

"He gave him a nice horse trailer, too, and a hefty chunk of change." The memory still rankled, but Dirk knew he had a lot to be thankful for. Granddad could have left Roque some land, too, either by willing him some acres of his own or by leaving all the land jointly to Roque and Dirk, which would have been such a hassle that even thinking about it made Dirk queasy. As it was, Roque had been fairly easy to get rid of—from the ranch, if not from town.

"I heard Juan Mendoza is letting him stay on that acre lot of his on the outskirts of town," said Alex. "Let him put up some fencing and pasture his horse there. He's sleeping in the trailer Mr. Mendoza used when he did rodeo, back in the eighties."

Just for a second, Dirk felt a pang of—not concern exactly, but curiosity as to how well Roque was weathering the cold. Then he put the thought out of his mind. Roque was a grown man, not the skinny little loudmouthed kid he'd been when Granddad first brought him to the ranch. He wasn't any responsibility of Dirk's, and anyway he was from New

Jersey, which meant he was probably used to far worse as far as winter weather went.

"Speaking of people who don't belong here," said Dirk, "do you know if any of the newcomers in Masterson Acres own a peacock?"

Alex rubbed his chin. "Hmm. Might be the young couple on Lot Six. They talked about getting one. They were pretty pumped about moving to the country."

"Aren't they all," Dirk sighed. "Are you even a little bit embarrassed about the part you played in getting all these folks out here?"

"Hey, I didn't sell the Masterson land. Those houses would have gotten built with or without me. At least this way, some of those dollars go back into the local economy, by way of my pocket."

"You wouldn't happen to remember the buyer of Lot Eight, would you?"

As he spoke, Dirk fiddled with a bend in the wire fencing that covered the gate. He didn't meet Alex's eyes, but he could feel Alex watching him.

"I do, actually. Northern woman. Kind of quiet and intense. Didn't say much about where she came from—played it pretty close to the vest. Paid cash for the land and the construction."

"Huh," said Dirk. "Another rich northerner coming to the South to buy up land."

"Financial solvency is a fine quality in a human being. She was a good-looking woman, too, as I recall."

Dirk looked at him. "Are you *matchmaking*? You're starting to sound like Tony. Anyhow, don't waste your time. Lot Eight and I have already had words."

"Oh, I see. And I take it those words were not perfectly courteous and reasonable on your part?"

"She deserved it," Dirk said.

Time to talk about something else.

"So how are things at your place?" he asked. "How's Lauren doing?"

Alex smiled. "Doing great, actually. She's pregnant."

Something that might have been envy clutched at Dirk's chest, but Alex was his friend, so he made his voice as cheerful as he could. "You don't say? Well, congratulations to you both."

Lauren and Alex already had a two-year-old girl called Peri, a golden-haired little charmer. Alex wasn't Peri's biological father—Lauren had already been pregnant when they'd gotten together—but her ex-husband wasn't involved at all, and Alex was the only father Peri had ever known.

"Thanks. We're pretty excited."

"How about Miss Peri? What does she have to say about the news?"

"I don't think she really gets it. She asked if she could have a kitten instead."

Dirk chuckled. "She's pretty young herself yet. She'll figure it out."

"Yeah. She's at such a fun age right now, you know? Follows me around outside when I'm doing my chores, and climbs up on that old tractor in the front pasture, playing rancher, just like I used to do when I'd visit my grandparents out here when I was little. She makes everything exciting and interesting. I'm so grateful to have all this—" he stretched out an arm toward his land "—and be able to share it with her."

"You're a young father on a ranch," Dirk said. "That's a blessing, all right."

"Yeah." Alex shot him a keen glance. "Sure you don't want to change your mind and join us for Christmas? We aren't doing anything fancy, just dinner and presents. Ordinarily, we'd get together with the extended family at La Escarpa, but with the roads like they are, we'll be staying home this year. We'd love to have you."

"Thanks just the same, but I've already got plans."

If Alex suspected how scanty Dirk's Christmas plans were, he didn't let on. They said their goodbyes, and Dirk drove the truck back to the feed barn. Monte had finished eating and was standing in a relaxed posture with one hip canted, his hoof edge resting lightly on the ground.

The old stone house looked all snug and cozy beneath the overarching boughs of the pecan trees. A feeling of deep contentment spread through him. All the creatures he was responsible for were fed and healthy. All his equipment was put up where it belonged. Everything was squared away and taken care of, here in the two thousand acres of his dominion.

If only he could keep it that way.

CHAPTER FOUR

DURING HIS TIME in the Army, some of Dirk's fellow soldiers, while sitting around one day cleaning weapons, had held a heated discussion about where they'd all go in case of a zombie apocalypse. Shopping malls, armories, grocery stores, state and national parks and other locations were put forth and debated in terms of defensibility, access to weapons, comfort, proximity to food and water and other features. When Dirk's turn had come around, he'd said without hesitation, *I'd just go home.*

And home was the ranch. The ranch had it all—ample space, water access, weapons and ammunition, plenty of timber for fuel and construction purposes, habitable structures, room for gardening and protein on the hoof. If worse came to worst and the zombies managed to take out all the cattle, Dirk reckoned he could set up one of those round corral traps for feral hogs and get his meat that way. He'd back a feral hog against even the toughest zombie any day.

Yep, if the world ever went completely out of whack, the ranch was the place to be—and when things finally did hit the fan and nothing made sense anymore, Dirk had in fact gone straight to the cozy old limestone house beneath the pecan trees.

It had to be admitted that the house wasn't at its spiffiest right now. It looked as if an actual zombie apocalypse might be currently in progress. The structure itself wasn't falling apart; it just needed a whole lot of minor work—tree trimming, drywall repair, a little carpentry, some fresh paint. Seemed like he was always fixing something or other, but he never seemed to get ahead. It was a "one step forward, two steps back" sort of a deal—just like the rest of his life.

From inside his coat pocket, Dirk's phone went off—"Desperado" by the Eagles.

He smiled as he answered. "Hey, kiddo. What's up?"

Ava's voice came through clear and sweet. "I can't believe Texas is having a heavy snowfall and I'm not there to see it. How could you do this without me?"

"I wasn't consulted in the planning or scheduling of the event," Dirk replied.

His little sister was always worked up about something, in a positive or negative way. She was the most enthusiastic person he knew.

"Well, I'm gutted about it," she said. "Absolutely devastated."

"Yeah, I can tell. You're so distraught you can hardly speak. Hey, where are you, again?"

She gave a gasp of feigned shock. "You don't remember?"

"That would be why I asked," he said.

"Take a guess."

He started crunching his way back toward the barn. "No."

"Oh, come on," she said in her best wheedling tone. "I'll give you a hint. It's somewhere in the southern hemisphere."

"Greenland."

"That isn't… Oh, you're just messing with me. Guess for real."

"Latvia."

She let out one of her vehement sighs. "Honestly, Dirk. I don't know why you have to be so difficult. New Zealand! I'm in New Zealand."

"Oh, yeah. That was going to be my next guess. Isn't it pretty late there?"

"Or early, depending on your point of view. I couldn't sleep."

"I guess it's high summer in your part of the world, huh?"

"Sure is. I've been invited to the beach for a Christmas barbecue."

"That doesn't sound very Christmas-like to me."

She sighed again, a softer, sadder sigh. "To me, either. No doubt that's very Americentric of me, but it's how I feel. I think I've been here too long. The whole place is starting to look stale. I'm getting a hankering for snow and Baroque architecture. Maybe I'll go to Dresden next. See the old ancestral home."

"As far as I'm concerned, the ancestral home is right here."

Dirk worried about Ava sometimes. She claimed to love traveling, but there seemed to be a restlessness behind it all. Would she ever find a place she loved well enough to stay there and put down roots? These phone calls were all well and good, but he wanted her close by. She was the only family he had left, and except for Granddad's funeral, he hadn't seen her in person in years.

"So what about you?" she asked. "What are your holiday plans?"

"Uh, well..."

"You don't have any, do you?"

"Not really, but I don't care. It's fine."

"Uh-huh. Are you seeing anyone?"

Dirk made a scoffing sound. "Are you kidding? That's the last thing I need right now. I'm doing just fine on my own, thank you. I'm turning into a regular hermit, and I like it."

"No, you don't. That whole hermit thing of yours is a put-on. I mean, don't get me wrong. I'm glad you're free from Kyra. Glad she initiated it, because you never would have. You took a vow, and you meant it, and you'd have followed through no matter how rough things got. You're a faithful man, and I love that about you. But that woman is grasping and shallow and mean, and believe me when I say you are well rid of her. I get that you'd need some time on your own to decompress and get your head on straight. But you're not a loner, Dirk. You're not a genuine introvert. You're just a cranky extrovert who's a bit gun-shy at present. If you go on keeping to yourself, it's going to warp you."

"Thank you for that analysis of my temperament," said Dirk.

"No problem," Ava said cheerfully. "It's a service I provide free of charge. So how's it going with the whole winter storm thing? They're saying it's a hundred-year storm."

"Are they? Good. I'd just as soon go a hundred years without having another one."

"Oh, come on. You're not bothered by the cold, surely."

"Not by the cold itself, but the rolling brownouts are getting on my nerves. The entire state is having unusually low temperatures at the same time, so the power grid is stressed from everyone running their heat nonstop. Luckily I don't depend on electricity for heat, but I like it for other things. I couldn't even make myself a second pot of coffee this morning."

"I keep telling you, you need a French press."

"Well, I still would've had to heat the water, wouldn't I?"

Ava laughed. "That's true, isn't it? We're all too dependent on our modern conveniences. But tell me about the snow. Is it beautiful?"

Dirk took a long look at the blue-shadowed smooth whiteness. "It is, actually."

"I want to see! Take some pics and send them to me."

"Maybe later. I need a nap before I do anything else. Anyhow, I'm no photographer."

"Oh, it's not that hard. You have a good

eye. Just remember what I told you about the rule of thirds and you'll do fine. I'll bet the Masterson house looks magical in the snow."

Dirk chuckled. "If by magical you mean deserted, dilapidated, creepy and liable to fall down, then sure."

"You've seen it?"

"Mmm-hmm, lots of times."

"I mean today."

"No, of course not today. How could I have? I've been feeding cattle, not traipsing around the countryside."

"Will you please ride down there and take some pictures of it? Please, please, please?"

Dirk rubbed his chin. "Well, I might ought to ride on down the road and see how Miss Ida's getting along, and then maybe I could cut across and take a look."

"And take pictures?"

"Yes, I'll take pictures."

"Thank you! You're the best big brother in the world."

"If you say so. Why is this so important to you, anyhow?"

"I just love it, that's all."

Figured. The one place in Texas that Ava loved was that run-down old Victorian monstrosity. How much money would it take to buy the place, much less restore it, assuming the family could be persuaded to part with it?

After they hung up, Dirk spent a moment staring down at his phone screen, feeling a lot lonelier than he had before Ava had called.

Then he put his phone away. He'd reached Monte's pasture while they were talking.

"Looks like we're going for a ride," he told his horse. "If this really is a hundred-year storm, I reckon we ought to make the most of it."

ORDINARILY, MACY LET Gunnar out first thing in the morning, right after she got up, so he could go potty before breakfast. By the time she was dressed and had her coffee brewing, he was ready to come back inside for a bowl of kibble. All this typically happened very early, usually before sunrise. But last night's confrontation with the cowboy, and the nightmare about Andrew after that, had made her a lot less eager than usual to spring out of bed and start her day.

She woke to see snow outside her window. The thermometer in her bedroom said fifty-nine, but her bed was warm. She snuggled down under her blankets and quilts and reveled in the fact that she wasn't married to Andrew.

Gunnar kept coming over to her and sticking his muzzle in her face. After she rolled over, he pawed at her back and whined.

"Go lie down," she told him, eyes shut.

She heard him pad over to his dog bed and settle down, but within a few minutes he was back again.

Besides getting a late start, she had some additions to her morning routine today. First there was the fire to see to, followed by the peacock that she'd herded into her garage last night. According to the internet, in the absence of their usual diet, peafowl could happily get by on dog or cat food, as well as kitchen scraps, so she'd given him some leftover rice and vegetables along with some of Gunnar's kibble. Macy was happy to see he'd eaten most of it. He'd also managed to dirty the water she'd put in a shallow cake pan, and was now roosting up on a storage shelf, his tail curled around him, staring at her.

Freshening his water was tricky with Gunnar tailing her so closely. Gunnar hadn't yet seen the big fancy bird in the garage, and Macy intended to keep it that way. She managed to hurry through the door and shut it quickly behind her without letting Gunnar follow her or get a glimpse into the garage, and without sloshing more than eight to ten ounces of water on herself.

"There you go," she said to the bird, setting the pan of clean water on the damp floor. "Drink up. And try not to be such a slob."

By the time she had her snow gear on, Gunnar was visibly antsy. *All the better*, she thought. He'd get his business done right away and they could both go back inside the nice, safe, snug house.

Gunnar loped expectantly over to the French door, but instead of letting him out, Macy clipped his leash to his collar. He gave her a quizzical look. The leash wasn't part of their morning routine, and Gunnar was a dog who liked his routine, but he was beautifully leash trained. No doubt he'd miss his off-leash rambles, but he'd manage until she could get that fence built.

She took him outside. He padded cautiously through the snow, stopping every few steps to look questioningly at her over his shoulder.

"Go ahead," she said aloud. "Go potty."

But he wouldn't. He just kept giving her that bewildered look. She led him around a wider and wider area, hoping he'd find a site that suited him, but no luck.

"Fine," she said at last. "We'll go inside.

When you need to go bad enough, you'll co-operate."

Back in the house, she unclipped his leash and took it to its hook in the entry closet. By the time she returned to the living room, Gunnar was sitting at the French door, staring longingly through the glass.

"Tough luck, buddy," she told him. "You're going to have to learn. From now on, until we get a yard fenced in, you're going to have to do your business on the leash. I can't risk letting you loose. I know this isn't what you're used to, but you'll adjust."

He didn't look convinced.

For the next hour or so, he kept trotting over to Macy, staring hard at her until she made eye contact and then running to the French door in an exaggerated lope. He was like a stereotypical American tourist abroad, speaking English loudly and clearly in hopes of being understood.

She tried again with the leash. Again Gunnar refused to do his business. Again she brought him back inside.

He planted his haunches at the French door and gave her an aggrieved look.

"I know you think I'm being obtuse," she

said. "But I have my reasons, and this is how things have to be now."

He gave a lugubrious sigh and went back to staring sadly outside.

They repeated this routine a total of five times, with Macy putting on and taking off her outdoor gear every time. The power went off, and came back on, and went off and came on again. The floor of the work room was soon covered with dirt and melting snow, Macy's nerves were strained and Gunnar was growing more agitated by the minute.

Macy had just brought some towels to soak up the slush when Gunnar suddenly started whining and doing a little dance. There was a new urgency in his behavior this time. Macy hustled into her coat and pulled on her boots.

When she clipped on Gunnar's leash yet again, he gave an audible groan.

She led him outside, reached into her pocket for her gloves—

And lost hold of the leash. Gunnar took off like a hairy cannonball in the exact direction the unknown cowboy had ridden off in last night.

"Gunnar!" she shrieked. "Get back here!"

She tried to run after him, plodding through the knee-deep snow, but he quickly outstripped her. Plumes of snow sprayed out from his churning feet. It was as if he was flying over the ground. Within seconds he'd reached the line of trees that marked the Serenidad Creek, the border between her place and the cowboy's, and disappeared into the herbage.

Her own progress was slow. The even white surface of the snow hid the rough terrain below. By the time she reached the creek, Gunnar was long gone. She stood a moment, catching her breath, staring down first one side and then the other of the wooded, winding creek bed. The creek was mostly dry, but in a few low spots, the white gave way to smooth gray ice.

Until now, Gunnar's trail had been plain enough—not that she'd needed it, since she'd watched him run here. But the creek bed was rough and uneven, and the rocks and dried grass and weeds made it harder to see tracks.

After studying the ground awhile, she found a few distinct dog prints leading to the left and headed that way. She hoped and prayed that he would keep to the creek bed and not cross over to the cowboy's land. Maybe he'd double back soon. Maybe she'd see him trudging her way, any second now, all played out, bladder emptied and ready to go home.

The Serenidad. She'd loved that name when she'd first seen it on the plat. It had seemed like a good sign.

But she was anything but serene now. Stomach in knots, heart pounding, legs shaking, she made her way along the bank, careful of her footing, searching for her dog, her best and only friend.

A raw sob tore loose from her throat. She had to find him. She had to.

CHAPTER FIVE

As Dirk rode Monte down the driveway toward Darnell Road, he made himself a mental checklist of tasks. It was about time to regrade the driveway and trim back some of the spindly mesquite limbs so they wouldn't scrape his truck. The electric gate at the entrance was getting slow to start, meaning it was time to replace that big battery again.

Always something to do around this place. Never enough money or time.

He took the horse gate that stood off to one side of the electric gate and went on through to Darnell Road. The narrow country road was coated with snow and free of cars. Overhead, the bare branches of oaks and elms met in a continuous arch. The only sound was the steady thud of Monte's hooves on the packed snow.

They followed the road a half mile or so down to Petty Road, where they turned left. Dirk kept an eye on his fences all the while and made occasional stops to clear ice balls from Monte's feet.

Miss Ida's place was about a mile up Petty on the right. A thin trickle of smoke rose out of her chimney, and Peaches, her palomino pinto, was munching hay out of the feeder.

"Well, good morning, neighbor!"

Miss Ida waved to him from beside the chicken coop. She had on a man's hunting cap, a wool plaid coat and old cowboy work boots with what looked like fleecy pajama pants loosely tucked into the tops.

"Morning," said Dirk. "How're you this fine day?"

"Can't complain. I slept pretty good until about four in the morning. The electric blanket helped, when it was running. I just got the chickens fed and gave Peaches her hay. Now I need to get the ice broke in her water so she can drink."

"Let me do that for you," Dirk said.

"Well, thank you, hon. You know where the axe is."

The axe was in the shed where he'd left it after he and Alex had split the firewood when they'd been here last. Dirk used it to smash the ice, then returned it to its spot, leaving

Monte tied at the pasture fence so he and Peaches could visit together.

The level on the firewood stack hadn't gone down by much. Dirk gathered up an armload and took it to the kitchen door. Miss Ida saw him coming from inside and let him in.

The house wasn't very warm. "Did your fire go out?" Dirk asked.

"No, I've still got some coals left from my overnighter log. I just haven't put on any new logs this morning."

Dirk carried his load of firewood to Miss Ida's old wood-burning Earth Stove in the corner. The fire was holding on, but barely. The few remaining coals were almost smothered in ash. Miss Ida knew better than that. Was she worried about running out of wood?

Dirk scooped out most of the ash into the ash can and put in some more kindling on top of the coals. Once the flames were good and strong, he added some midsize logs.

"Keep that fire fed," he said. "Don't skimp on wood. It's there to be burned, not to look at. Don't worry that you're using too much. You ought to have plenty in that stack to get you through this storm, and once you use it all up, we'll get you some more, me and

Alex. The main thing is to stay warm. You hear me?"

Miss Ida nodded and waved her hands. "I hear you, I hear you. Now come sit down and have some biscuits and butter."

"Thank you just the same, but I'd best be on my way," said Dirk. He didn't want to be eating up all Miss Ida's food.

"Well then, I've got a little something for you to take with you," she said.

The little something turned out to be an unopened bag of San Antonio Blend coffee that he strongly suspected had been gifted to her. It had a red-and-green-plaid gift wrap bow already stuck on the front, and he was pretty sure he saw her rip off a gift tag before handing him the bag.

"San Antonio Blend," he said. "My favorite. Thank you."

He tucked the coffee bag into one of his coat pockets. He didn't like to always be taking from Miss Ida when she had little enough for herself, but he couldn't very well refuse when she made such a point of giving him things.

He got back on Monte and kept going along Petty Road. On his right were several smaller properties, like Miss Ida's, with houses dating back to the middle of the last century or earlier—comfortable-looking places with mellow old barns. The land on the left was all his, right up to the Serenidad. He crossed the bridge to the far side of the creek, then turned Monte off the road and down a shallow slope toward the creek. Monte knew exactly where to go, and halted on his own when they reached the gap.

The gap was an informal gate, invisible to anyone who didn't know what to look for. On the back of a stout cedar post, the barbed-wire strands ended in small loops hooked onto nails. Dirk unhooked the strands, took Monte through, and fastened them back behind him.

Now he was riding along a level track through a tunnel of creek, trees and sky that divided the old Masterson land on his right from his own land on the left. All the colors were stark—the glaring white of the snow, the dark brown of bare oak branches, the deep green of cedar, the smattering of red berries on the smooth gray leafless limbs of possum-haw holly. Cardinals flitted back and forth across the creek, hawks glided overhead and a herd of whitetail deer stepped lightly through the snow. Dirk stopped and took pictures once in a while but didn't bother sending any of them yet. Once back home, he'd cull out all the blurry or not-so-good ones and maybe do a little photo editing on the ones that made the cut.

The Masterson house was a sixteen-room Victorian mansion, built by Zeke Masterson back when he was a big-time rancher in Seguin County, and situated between Lots Two and Three of Masterson Acres. It was built on a hill, and Dirk's path rose in a steady climb from the road as the creek banks got higher and steeper. At last Dirk reached the fork-trunked elm tree that signaled the turn-off to the house.

If Ava had been here, she'd have gone right over to the house, poked around all the porches and maybe gone in through a broken window. Dirk did not share her casual atti-tude toward property rights, so he stuck to the creek, which was public land, and took his pictures from there. The creek curved around behind the big old house, and a thick stand of oaks stood up behind it. It was a nice setup, well thought out. Probably it had been a real pretty place back when it was lived in and cared for.

When he'd finished taking pictures, he

got back on Monte and continued along the creekside trail, past the house, skirting Lot Three on his right. He had his second wind now and wasn't all that eager to go home. It had been a while since he'd ridden this way; he'd forgotten how pretty it was. There used to be a tree that had fallen across the creek without losing its root system, then shot up vertical branches from the now horizontal trunk. He wanted to see if it was still there.

Something rustled faintly farther along the bank of the creek. Dirk waited to see if anything would emerge, but nothing did. Maybe it was just a possum or an armadillo, but it didn't sound right for either, somehow. He kept his eye on the area as Monte stepped closer.

Whatever the thing was, it was black, and bigger than an armadillo or a possum. A feral hog? A young Black Angus calf? It seemed about the right size for either. He approached cautiously, ready to go for his gun if necessary.

It was a dog. And not just any dog—the Yankee woman's dog from last night, lying still except for an occasional twitch.

Dirk dismounted. He ground-tied Monte and crept close.

The dog was hopelessly caught in a tangle of barbed wire and nylon leash. He was alert enough, and not hurt bad as far as Dirk could see.

The dog's attitude had changed completely since he and Dirk had last met. Ears low, eyes drooping, he looked as sad and sorry as a dog could be. Scared, too.

"What happened to you, knucklehead?" Dirk asked. "You got yourself caught, didn't you?"

The very tip of the dog's tail, the only part of him that was free, thumped against the ground.

It was easy enough to guess what had happened. The dog had been running along, trailing his leash behind him, and gotten caught by the leash and his collar. Once a few barbs were stuck, he'd started struggling, which only made things worse, until he'd found himself pretty much hog-tied.

A confused trail led from the dog to a deep snowdrift against a fallen log, now all churned up. Probably the wire had been hidden there beneath the snow, loosely coiled.

Dirk turned and walked back to Monte. Behind him, the dog let out a low whine.

"Don't worry," Dirk said. "I'm not leaving

you. I'm just getting something to cut you loose with."

He took his fence tool out of Monte's saddlebag and brought it back to the dog. He crouched down. The dog couldn't move his head, but his eyes followed Dirk's every move.

It looked as though the dog hadn't been stuck for long. He wasn't stiff with cold or anything. He wasn't snarling, but that could change fast.

Slowly and carefully, Dirk snipped with the wire cutters until the dog was free.

Dirk wouldn't have thought a dog that big could move that fast. In a fraction of a second, he lunged—not to attack Dirk, but to thank him. He planted his huge paws on Dirk's chest and gave him a slobbery kiss on the face.

Dirk fell backward, down the edge of the steep creek bank. He was aware of a confused motion, a sort of spinning of earth and sky, followed by a stab of pain, and then everything cut out.

"Gunnar!"

Macy's voice went out through the clear cold and vanished, swallowed up by the snow.

No echo came back to her, and no answering bark.

Why, why, why hadn't she put up a fence to begin with, before she and Gunnar even moved in? How could she have been so stupid? Just because her property was big didn't mean Gunnar could run all day and never reach the end of it, or that it was a good idea for him to have complete run of the property itself.

She'd loved seeing him run loose, so happy and free after all those months of confinement in a small yard. With all its little hills and motts and remains of old outbuildings to explore, Gunnar's new country home must have seemed to him like a doggy paradise. Before today, he'd never gone far, and always come back quickly whenever she'd called him.

But last night's encounter with the angry cowboy had changed everything.

If only she could have communicated the facts of the matter to Gunnar in language he could understand. If only she could have looked into those trusting amber eyes and said, *Listen here, buddy. You can't go running off wherever you like for as long as you want. You need to stay within the boundaries of our property and not linger outdoors. Do your business fast and hurry back to me, or your hiney could be in serious danger. And never, ever cross that creek.*

She kept her ears focused, straining to hear a bark…or a shotgun blast.

With his heavy build, Gunnar was definitely more of a sprinter than a distance runner, but after a morning's confinement, he'd had energy to burn. In trying to protect him by keeping him on the leash, Macy had only made things worse.

She had no idea how much time had passed—five minutes, ten, an hour—or how far she'd walked. The creek bed kept curving and twisting, and she didn't have any landmarks to guide her. She might not even be on her land anymore. And Gunnar could be anywhere on or off her twenty acres. He could be cavorting with the cowboy's livestock this very minute.

It was inconvenient, not knowing the cowboy's name, but she thought she had part of it figured out. If his place backed up to hers, then it must be the one on Darnell Road that she'd passed on her walks. A sign above the metal gate said Hager Ranch in big letters, with a smaller sign underneath reading, Since

1856. It was a good bet that the cowboy was a Hager.

She'd liked the look of the Hager Ranch, with its tidy fences, rolling fields, scattered trees and contented-looking black cows. Her long, rambling walks were deeply restful to mind and spirit. So much land, so few houses.

Something caught at her foot for what felt like the millionth time, nearly tripping her. She stopped to free herself. Another tough, thorny vine, hidden beneath the snow. This place had a lot of hidden menaces.

She wished she were home right now, safe and warm by her wood-burning stove with a mug of coffee in her hand and her dog lying safely at her feet, both of them watching the snow fall from behind the window. There was something special about the quality of light on snow, the feeling of being all wrapped up and muffled against the world. She didn't mind being snowed in; she liked it.

This would be her first year to celebrate the holiday entirely on her own, free from other people's rules and expectations. She'd left New York, and Andrew, last November, but hadn't had time or energy to celebrate properly. This year, she meant to do it right, with Christmas CDs, the BBC *Pride and*

Prejudice and gifts for Gunnar's stocking—
a plush squirrel that made a crinkle sound
when squeezed, and some new beef-flavored
chew strips.

She stopped in her tracks. Was that a bark?

Yes. Yes! A whole barrage of barking, getting louder, growing closer. Her heart leaped
into her throat.

"Gunnar!" she called. "Gun—"

And here he came, running toward her,
full tilt, faster than she'd ever seen him run,
trailing his leash behind him. She knelt down
and opened her arms, and he catapulted into
them, licking her face and nearly knocking
her down before racing around her in circles,
still barking.

"Oh, Gunnar! Where have you been? You
were a very naughty boy. Don't you ever run
away like that again, do you hear me? Never
ever, ever."

He put his paw on her shoulder and licked
her face again.

He didn't seem scared, just excited. But
there was blood in the snow at his feet, and
stretching back in a trail behind him—not
heavy, but distinct.

She tried to get him to settle down while
she checked him for wounds, but he wouldn't

stop wriggling, so she figured he couldn't be hurt too badly. She couldn't find any animal bites on him, or bullet wounds, just minor cuts and punctures.

She took his leash in her hand. Both collar and leash were a bit worse for wear, scarred and scratched, but still functional.

"What happened to you, huh, boy?" she asked him. "What sort of trouble did you get yourself into?"

Slowly, carefully, she followed Gunnar's bloody trail, keeping him close behind her and holding tight to his leash. He seemed perfectly willing to go back that way, so whatever happened, it must not have spooked him much.

She rounded one last bend and stopped. A saddled horse stood several yards ahead, ground-tied.

He was a big, handsome fellow, sorrel, with a flaxen mane. There was a quarter horse look to his head, with its flat profile and broad forehead, and to his sturdy, muscular build, but he was bigger than a typical quarter horse, with something in the length and shape of the neck, and the set of the shoulders, that put her in mind of draft breeds. His muzzle was lighter in color than the rest of his face, and his forehead had a small marking like a crescent moon.

He gave Macy a shrewd, cynical look, as if he'd seen it all and nothing could shock him anymore.

He was a distinctive-looking horse, and Macy knew exactly where she'd seen him before.

Gunnar let out a sort of raspy bark that he used whenever he saw something he wasn't sure about. It sounded like he was saying *merf.* The horse turned away, showing his profile again, unimpressed.

"Hush," Macy said, and Gunnar hushed.

She fastened his leash to a tree trunk and cautiously approached the horse. He kept one eye on her but stayed calm.

Gunnar's bloody trail led to the edge of the steep creek bank. Some short lengths of wire were lying there, looking freshly cut. Macy walked over, looked down and saw her neighbor at the bottom of the creek, glaring up at her.

CHAPTER SIX

HE WAS WEARING the same canvas field coat she'd seen on him the night before. His jeans were ripped and bloodstained, but not heavily so. His face was set with pain, with the jaw flexed and the lips flattened out.

The memory of their last meeting hung heavy in the air. Clearly this was no time to air past grievances, but what should she say? Everything that came to mind was either painfully redundant or just plain inane.

I see you fell down the creek bank. Well spotted.

What are you doing down there? Oh, you know, just enjoying the ambiance.

Are you all right? Sure, never better.

Can you get out? Yeah, just don't feel like doing it yet.

She considered and rejected several openers in what seemed to her a short period of time, but must have been longer than she thought, because the cowboy finally asked,

"Are you just going to stand there and stare at me all day?"

His astringent tone broke the awkwardness.

"I'm trying to figure out what to do," she answered, just as tartly. "How bad are you hurt?"

"What makes you think I'm hurt?"

"Well, the fact that you're still down there is a pretty good indicator."

His scowl deepened. "I tried climbing out, but the bank's too steep here, and a little undercut up top…and my ankle won't hold me anyhow."

He clearly didn't like admitting he was hurt; he said it as if he were confessing something shameful.

"I'd've called my granddad to come get me out," he said, "but I don't seem to have my phone on me. Must've dropped it when that fool dog knocked me down."

"My dog?" Macy asked.

"Is he a big dark brindled fellow with a head like a bowling ball?"

Strange question. She assumed it would have been easy enough for the cowboy to identify her dog, after last night. But she said only, "Yes, that sounds like Gunnar."

"Then yeah," said the cowboy. "His leash and collar got all tangled up in barbed wire, and I cut him loose. I guess he was grateful, because he knocked me over, and down I went."

Compared to all the potential interactions she had been imagining between Gunnar and the cowboy, this was a lot better than it might have been. But it meant that Gunnar was responsible for the man being injured and trapped right now, and therefore she was responsible, too.

"I'm sorry," she said. "I took him out on a leash earlier this morning, but he got away from me."

She didn't like the sound of the excuse. It implied that either Gunnar was impossible to control, or she was too weak to control him.

"That's all right," the cowboy said. "Occupational hazard of having a big, young, energetic dog."

Despite his gruffness, he was being awfully nice about all this. It was as if last night hadn't happened and they were just now meeting for the first time.

"You said you wanted to call your granddad?" Macy asked.

"Yeah. We run our outfit together, the Hager Ranch. You haven't seen him, have you? An older gentleman on a big bay horse?"

"I'm afraid not. But I'm sure the two of us

can manage to get you out of there. You've got a rope on your saddle, haven't you? Why don't I just fasten it to the saddle horn, and lower the lasso down, and your horse can pull you up?"

He shook his head. "It's not that simple." He thought about it a moment longer, then added, "But it might just work. It's not like I'll be dead weight. I'll be climbing. Those mesquite roots look like they'd make good handholds, and once I reach the overhang, I ought to be able to pretty much haul myself out—assuming the top doesn't break off under the strain and crush me like a bug."

"We'll hope for better things," said Macy. "There's a big outcropping of smooth sandstone jutting out over here. It might be easier on the rope to slide over that, rather than all the rough rocks and brambles and such."

"Good. Can you manage my horse?"

"I took riding lessons for eight years, and I know my way around a Western saddle. I'll tie on the horn knot to the saddle horn and lower the business end to you."

He let out a sigh. "Might as well give it a shot."

The horse eyed Macy calmly as she approached. She unfastened the lariat from its strap on the saddle and secured the end to the saddle horn. This was a roping saddle, with a nice high pommel, and plenty of room on the horn to dolly down the rope. The horse was wearing a chest harness—another advantage, as it would distribute the cowboy's weight better than a saddle with a girth only. It stood to reason that the same tack features that helped in roping cattle would also be good for hauling men out of creek beds.

She lowered the lariat over the edge of the bank to the cowboy. He fed some rope through the hondo, forming a loop, then worked the loop around his chest and back, under his arms. He picked up some bits of herbage and stuffed them into the hondo, jamming the space up tight.

"What's that you're doing?" Macy asked.

"Trying to make it so's the slipknot won't keep cinching tighter and tighter around me as you haul me up."

"Oh." That made sense. "I hope it works."

"Yeah, you and me both." He looked around the creek bed. "I wish I had some sort of thick padding to put between me and this rope. My coat's good and heavy, and I've got a lot of layers on, but this rope is thin. Oh, well. Guess it can't be helped."

He gripped the rope and looked up at her.

Even from this distance, she could see that his eyes were a clear, vivid blue.

"Now, I need you to listen to me, and do exactly what I tell you, when I tell you to do it," he said. "When I say go, you go. When I say stop, you stop. No questions, no arguments. Got it?"

"Got it."

She took the horse's reins.

"Ready when you are," she said.

It was a slow process, with lots of starting and stopping. Macy would lead the horse forward a few paces, praising him and urging him on as he pulled the cowboy's weight, and suddenly halt him whenever the cowboy called, "Stop!" She couldn't see what he was doing, but it sounded as if he was readjusting his position and finding new handholds. After a few seconds or minutes, he'd call out, "All right, go ahead," and she'd start again.

Gunnar was delighted with all the unusual activity, and eager to get free and participate, but his leash held him. He kept up a steady stream of his funny muffled *merf* barks.

"What the heck is that sound?" asked the cowboy mildly during one of the halts in progress.

"My dog," said Macy. "I tied him up so he wouldn't interfere."

"Is there something the matter with his voice box? Did you have him debarked?"

"Of course not! I would never do that. That's just the sound he makes when he's excited and a little unsure."

"Huh. Well, you might ought to hitch him up and let him do some hauling. Put that muscle to good use. He got me into this mess, after all."

She smiled. "I'm sure he'd do his best, but I don't happen to have a dog harness with me."

"Too bad. You ready to go again?"

"I'm ready if you are."

"All right. Move him forward another yard or so, and then stop."

They started again. The rope stretched taut as a bowstring between the saddle horn and the edge of the bank. Macy wished she could see what was happening. She could only assume they were making good progress judging from how far the horse had walked and from all the scuffling sounds behind her.

"Okay, stop!" the cowboy called. "Hold him steady."

More scuffling. Then, "I'm almost at the top. From here on out, until I'm out of here, whenever the rope slackens, move up."

She looked over her shoulder and saw the

cowboy crawling and clawing his way onto the bank, hand over hand, in an impressive demonstration of power, his jaw tight, his blue eyes blazing. The rope slackened a bit; she eased the horse forward.

And suddenly it was all over. The cowboy was lying on the bank of the creek, the back of his coat rising and falling with his ragged breath. He'd even managed somehow to bring his hat up. It was lying on the ground beside him.

She started to go to him, but he held up a hand in a clear "give me a minute" gesture, so she stopped. He had his head bowed to the ground. His hair was lighter than she'd realized last night, a hue of bright gold that suggested he must have been a regular towhead as a kid. It was cut short and had a lot of dried leaves and other debris caught in it.

Slowly and painfully, he sat up, holding his right leg at a careful angle, and removed the rope from under his arms. Macy walked over to him and crouched down beside him, unsure of what to do for him now. He looked a good bit more scraped and dinged up than he had before they started.

He straightened his coat and brushed it off. "Well," he said, "we did it."

"We sure did," she agreed.

He picked up the cut lengths of barbed wire that were within his reach and started bending and fastening them into a bundle.

"What are you doing?" she asked.

"Taking care of business," he said. "These old coils of barbed wire should never be left lying around. They're a hazard to man and beast."

Interesting that that was his first thought. He wasn't even on his feet again, and here he was, doing this task.

She started picking up the pieces that were out of his reach, and came across a phone in a tough-looking case.

She handed it to him. "I assume this is yours?"

He took the phone and looked at her with those bright blue eyes. "You assume correctly. Thanks, for all of it. You did a good job back there."

She shrugged. "You're welcome. But the whole thing was my dog's fault, and therefore my fault, so it was the least I could do. And you did the hard part yourself—you and your horse."

"You were the one who came up with the idea. And you had to put up with me yelling at you and telling you what to do."

Macy considered. "I wouldn't call that yelling. Maybe you were a little brusque, but that was what the situation called for—quick and direct speech. There wasn't time for nuance or metaphor."

He chuckled. "A lot of folks wouldn't have seen it that way. A lot of folks would've got their feelings hurt, and talked back, and the whole thing would've turned into a huge fight."

"Yes, well, a lot of folks are way too sensitive."

"Amen to that."

She took the end of the rope off the saddle horn and brought it to him. He wound it into a neat coil.

Then he put on his hat, settling it low on his forehead.

"All right, then," he said. "I'll be on my way."

He got to his feet, favoring his right ankle and using a nearby tree for support. When he tried to put weight on the ankle, he let out a suppressed groan. It was barely more than a hum, but Macy could see the pain and tension in his face.

"What can I do?" she asked.

"If you could bring my horse over to me, and

help me into the saddle, I'd be obliged. Once
I'm up there I'll be all right."

She doubted that, but after all, he was
probably the best judge of what he could and
couldn't manage.

She led the horse over. The cowboy stood
waiting, holding on to the tree, his right knee
bent to keep the foot off the ground.

He fixed her with those bright blue eyes
again.

"Okay, here's what has to happen," he said.
"I'm going to take hold of the saddle horn
and the pommel, and then I've got to pick
up my left foot to put it in the stirrup. That'll
be tricky, because my right ankle won't hold
my weight. What I need from you is…well,
I need you to push from behind. As in, put
your hands on my backside and push me up.
Once I have my left foot in the stirrup, I'll be
okay. Can you handle that?"

Her eyes strayed down to his hips. He was
a very attractive physical specimen, and his
worn jeans showed him to advantage, but she
put that ruthlessly out of her mind.

"Yes," she said. There was nothing else to
say. She would think of the whole operation
as strictly mechanical, and him as a body of
mass, not a living, breathing man.

She positioned herself behind him. He started to reach for the saddle, then turned and told her, "Oh, and try not to get kicked in the head."

"I'll do my best," she said.

He took hold of the saddle horn and pommel. "Ready when you are."

She took a deep breath and dove right in.

It wasn't easy, but she did it. A few awkward moments later, the cowboy had his left foot in the stirrup, and Macy let go and stood back.

As he swung himself up and over, he let out another groan, still suppressed, but louder this time. Why was he so determined not to show weakness? It was as if he were a wounded gazelle and she were a hungry lion.

And then he was in the saddle, breathing hard, head low. Beneath the brim of his hat she could see the muscles working in his jaw and a contained tension in his compressed mouth.

Then he raised his head and took a deep breath. The horse was a tall one, and the cowboy was way up there now. As he looked around, the hardness in his face gave way to a different expression, softer, uncertain.

"Is something wrong?" Macy asked.

"Well, I don't rightly know," he said. "I must've lost my bearings somehow. I'm not real sure where I am right now. I must've ridden a fair bit out of my way." He pointed. "There's an elm mott like that over on the Masterson place, but the cross-fencing's all wrong. Did Granddad change the fencing and not tell me?"

He was talking to himself now more than to her, and looking lost. "The whole lay of the land is wrong," he said. "And this snow isn't helping. Where'd it all come from, anyhow?"

Something clicked in Macy's mind. If the cowboy was confused by the snow, then that meant he didn't remember the Extreme Winter Weather Event whose coming had been foretold for the past several days. And if he didn't recognize his surroundings in their present form—if he was still thinking of it as the Masterson place and not Masterson Acres—then that meant he didn't remember the land being sold, or the new houses being built there.

The cowboy was concussed.

CHAPTER SEVEN

HE LOOKED LUCID ENOUGH, up there on his horse, scanning the horizon with those vivid blue eyes. But something was clearly wrong.

"Did you hit your head when you fell?" she asked.

"Nope. It's about the only thing I didn't hit."

"Well, you still need to get yourself checked out. Your ankle is clearly hurt, and it's possible to get a head injury without a direct blow to the head. A significant jarring can do it, too—and I'm sure you got jarred plenty when you fell down that creek bank. You should have an X-ray and an MRI."

He waved a hand dismissively. "No. I don't need a doctor."

"I really think you should see one. I'd be happy to drive you to the ER."

That was stretching things. She wouldn't be at all happy to have a strange man in her car and her entire day disrupted. But it was her clear duty in this situation.

He looked at her as if she'd sprouted horns. "In this weather? We'd be risking our lives with the car ride, and putting other motorists in danger, too."

"I could call an ambulance, then."

His expression grew more incredulous still. "An ambulance? Do I look like I need an ambulance?"

"Well, you're clearly disoriented," she said. "You don't even know where you are."

"Ma'am, if I called an ambulance every time I took a fall and turned my ankle, I'd be up to my eyeballs in debt. Besides, with all this ice and snow, emergency services are going to be taxed to the limit. They'll have enough going on with people who are really hurt—and driving on frozen roads to get to them. Maybe I got my bell rung a little, but I'll be okay. I just need to get home."

Macy thought fast. Should she press the issue, telling him exactly how bad a memory gap he'd suffered and calling the ambulance for him if he still didn't want her to? Instinct told her that was the wrong thing to do. She was pretty sure that part of the reason he was being as tractable as he was right now was because he couldn't remember their first meeting. He'd made it clear last night just how much he resented his new neighbors in Masterson Acres.

Besides, and perhaps most importantly, this was a strong, proud, stubborn man. Trying to take charge of him would only make him dig in his heels.

She could wish him well and send him on his stoic, macho way. Hadn't he said his grandfather was around here somewhere? The two of them would probably run into each other if they rode around long enough.

But that was a ridiculous argument, and the only reason she was entertaining it was because she didn't want to let a man into her life, however marginally—even a man who obviously needed her help. Not giving him that help would be stingy and selfish and wrong.

She couldn't simply turn an injured and disoriented man loose and hope for the best. He didn't recognize his surroundings, and while he might figure things out enough to find his grandfather, or his house, he might not. He could get lost, or pass out and fall off his horse. He could freeze to death.

The wind was starting to kick up sheets of snow. Desperate, Macy scanned the land around her. If the cowboy's grandfather showed up now, her problem would be solved.

But no older gentleman on a big bay horse appeared.

The bottom line was, she was the one here now, and that made the cowboy her responsibility—at least until she could locate a family member to pass him off to.

She'd have to use the guile of the serpent here.

"I'm sure you'll get your bearings in a minute," she said. "In the meantime, why don't you come over to my place to get sorted out?"

"Where's your place?" he asked.

"Not far. An easy walk." She pointed. The walk hadn't been all that easy, but it would be a lot easier now that she wasn't trying to find Gunnar. Also, the way home would be downhill. And the cowboy, at least, wouldn't be doing it on foot.

He squinted into the distance. From where Macy stood, she could just glimpse the roof of her house, but he could surely see more from his elevation on the horse.

"Oh, yeah," he said. "I think I see your metal roof, with some stovepipe sticking out."

"That's the place."

He frowned. "Seems like I've been there before, but that was a long time ago."

There was a hazy, faraway sound in the

words that was almost eerie. He had a deeply ingrained assurance and competence about him, but everything was a bit off. It was like having a conversation with a sleepwalker.

Now was not the time to remind him how they met, or that it had only happened yesterday afternoon.

"Right," she said. "So how about it? You did save my dog. The least I can do is offer you a cup of coffee."

He considered. "Well, I wouldn't mind setting a spell, resting my ankle. Thank you, ma'am."

He gave a sharp whistle. "Fletch!" he called. "Come on, boy."

He looked around expectantly, but nothing happened. He turned back to Macy. "Have you seen my dog?"

"I don't think so," she said. The cowboy hadn't had a dog with him yesterday. "What breed is he?"

"Aussie–border collie mix. Blue merle coat with copper on his legs and face."

"Sounds striking. I'll bet he's smart, too."

"Oh, yeah. Smarter than me by a long sight."

Macy fervently hoped this Fletch was okay, wherever he was. Anything could have happened to him that the addled cowboy had since forgotten.

What if Fletch and Gunnar had gotten into a fight? Collies weren't built for fighting, physically or temperamentally. Gunnar had always been friendly to other dogs at the dog park, but he certainly had the physiology to do well in a fight if he ever got started on one.

"Maybe he went home," she said.

But she didn't believe it. Any dog belonging to this man would stick right by his side through thick and thin—not merely because he'd been trained to, but because he wanted to.

"Yeah, or maybe he's with Granddad," the cowboy said vaguely. His mental processes were getting fuzzier by the minute. He'd seemed fine before, but maybe that was only because he'd had something tangible to do.

His gaze returned to her. "Ma'am, I'm awful sorry, but I can't seem to recollect your name."

"Actually, we haven't been formally introduced. I'm Macy Reinalda."

"Pleased to meet you. I'm Dirk Hager."

He looked like a Dirk, straight and sharp and strong.

Macy untied Gunnar and brought him over,

keeping him close at her side. She could feel how excited he was, but he behaved himself.

"This is Gunnar," she said.

"Howdy, Gunnar," said Dirk. "And this knucklehead here—" he patted his horse's neck "—is Monte."

Without thinking, Macy said, "Monte! Like in *The Virginian*."

As soon as the words were spoken, she could hear Andrew in her head, sneering at her. *You and your literary references. You think you're so smart, talking about books no one's read, but really you just sound stuck up.*

Dirk's gaze sharpened a bit. "That's right," he said. "That's exactly who he's named for, the Virginian's horse in the book."

"You've read it?" she asked.

"Years ago. My Texas history teacher back in seventh grade gave me a copy. Great lady. Grandmother of my good friend Alex. His place is right over..." He trailed off as he looked around, and suddenly he looked lost again. "Well, it's around here someplace."

He could remember the name of a horse in a book he'd read decades earlier, and the teacher who'd given him the book, and forget things that had happened in the past twenty-four hours, and a matter of months before that.

"Alex Reyes?" Macy asked.

"Yeah. You know him?"

Alex had been one of the general contractors for Macy's house, but that wasn't something to get into right now. Maybe she'd give him a call later and ask for help locating Dirk's relatives.

"We've met."

She led the way toward her house, with Dirk and Monte following alongside. Gunnar was clearly eager to improve his acquaintance with the strange big animal that was carrying a man on his back, but he kept close to Macy's side.

"How's the ankle?" Macy asked Dirk. He was riding with it outside the stirrup and a little apart from the horse's side. It had to hurt, getting jostled with every step Monte took.

"It's all right," Dirk said, by which Macy knew he meant it hurt like blazes, but he could handle it.

A silence fell. Macy felt somehow that she ought to keep him talking—to distract him from the pain, and maybe get his mind sorted out, or at least gather information about him.

"Are you planning anything special for Christmas?" she asked.

"Christmas." He said the word in an odd,

disconnected way, like he was trying to fit it into his memory. He must have come up with something, because he went on, "Yeah, my wife's throwing a big party at our place in town. Catered food, booze, the whole nine yards. Guest list about a mile long."

"Oh." The word had a hollow sound in her own ears. Somehow Macy hadn't pictured Dirk being married—though why she should assume he was single, she didn't know.

Anyway, he was married. That was good. It meant he had a wife to take charge of him and see to it that he got his head checked out.

"We're supposed to have tables set up in the backyard by the pool," Dirk went on. "Fairy lights in the trees, luminarias and I don't know what all. Kyra planned the whole thing. But I guess this weather will put a damper on that." He looked around, his expression dazed. "Good grief. Where'd all this snow come from, anyhow? I've never seen it this deep here before, and I've lived here most of my life. If this keeps up, we won't have to go to Colorado after all. We'll just stay in Limestone Springs, drive out to the ranch and slide down the banks of the stock tank."

"Oh, do you have a trip to Colorado planned?"

"Yeah. Leaving the day after Christmas. Skiing. Aspen."

He sounded underwhelmed by the prospect, maybe because of his ankle. No doubt his injury would put as much of a damper on a skiing vacation as the snow would on the fancy outdoor Christmas party.

Another silence fell. Then Dirk said, "This is some weather we're having, isn't it? Where'd all this snow come from, anyhow?"

She stole a quick look at him. He kept looping back to the weather.

Without waiting for an answer, he went on, "What day is it? I mean, what month?"

"It's December twenty-second," she said. "The first day of winter."

"Huh," said Dirk. "Well, Kyra and I are supposed to go to Aspen the day after Christmas, but if this keeps up, we might as well stay home."

He was definitely talking in circles now, but his speech was clear, and he didn't seem to be having any trouble riding the horse, other than his hurt ankle. His procedural memory was intact, at least.

"What dog is that?" he asked, as if he'd only just noticed the big leashed animal at Macy's side.

"This is Gunnar," Macy said. "He's mine."

Macy tried to keep her tone light and natural. If she could keep him calm long enough to get him to her place, and then get in touch with his wife or grandfather, then she could hand him over to them and everything would be fine. Well, maybe not fine, but out of her hands.

"Where's Fletch?" asked Dirk. He gave another piercing whistle. "Fletch! Here, boy!"

His call died away in the cold, empty air. No Fletch came running to meet him.

"I should get home," said Dirk. "I need to check in with Granddad and make sure the cattle are all where they need to be. I don't know where all this snow came from."

"We'll just go to my house for now," said Macy. "You can call your grandfather when we get there."

She spoke with an easy authority, as if that settled the matter, hoping he'd go along and not argue. Sure enough, he said, "Okay," with a hazy agreeableness that she was pretty sure wasn't the norm for him.

Macy's property had come with several preexisting outbuildings, including an old open-front shed not far from the house. Macy had liked the solid, honest, timeworn look of them, as well as the storage potential.

Now, with Monte temporarily on the place, she was doubly grateful that she hadn't had them knocked down.

"Well, isn't this handy?" said Dirk, looking around inside the plain but serviceable structure. "Monte, old son, you'll be snug as a bug in here."

Helping the cowboy off his horse should have been both easier and less awkward than helping him on, but somehow it was neither. Dirk was gray-faced and breathing heavily by the time he reached the ground, and Macy was agitated from all the close contact with his strong, lean shape.

Balanced on one leg, Dirk tied Monte to a wall support. He left the horse's saddle on.

Now Macy had to get Dirk into the house.

"We've got maybe twenty feet to cover between here and the back door," she told him. "I left it unlocked, so we'll be able to go right in. Just lean on me and keep moving. It won't be a lot of fun, but we can do it."

He nodded. "Ready when you are."

She steeled herself and went to it, wrapping her arm around his waist from his right side, hooking her fingers under his belt on the left. He draped his arm over her shoulders and looked down at her.

"You're just the right height for this," he said. "Strong, too. Nice sturdy shoulders."

"Thanks," she said.

She held Gunnar's leash in her right hand. She gave him a stern look. He had better behave himself and not get tangled up in their legs.

The three of them started lurching toward the house. Gunnar kept close to Macy's side without crossing their path.

"I'm sorry for being so heavy," Dirk said as they stepped up to the deck. His voice sounded tight, as if he had his jaw clenched.

"You're not heavy," said Macy. "I mean, you are, but not disproportionally so. You're tall, but you have a lot of muscle mass."

She felt her face flaming. What was she *talking* about?

"Glad to hear it," Dirk said.

They reached the deck, then the door. Macy opened it.

The towel she'd used earlier to dry melted snow off the floor was still there. Gunnar trotted inside, tail high and wagging, and looked back over his shoulder, as if proud to show off his home to his new friend.

Macy kicked the door shut behind her. Slowly, steadily, they made their way to the sectional sofa. Dirk sat down and leaned into the back cushion with a long sigh that seemed to ease his face and body. Gunnar stood beside him, tail still wagging.

Macy dropped onto the cushion beside Dirk, muscles aching. "We did it," she said.

Dirk smiled at her. He had a nice smile. "Yes, we did."

He shut his eyes for a few seconds, then opened them and scanned the room. She saw him take in the white-lights-only Christmas tree, the floor-to-ceiling bookcases and the doggy ottoman.

His gaze came to rest on the wood-burning stove.

"That there looks like a pretty handy piece of civil engineering," he said.

"Oh, it is. I just started using it this morning. It really puts out the heat."

The flames had died down since she'd last fed the fire, but the logs still had some life in them. She went over to the stove, lifted the griddle, added some small logs and opened the damper.

"There," she said. "That ought to heat things up. How's your ankle?"

He grimaced. "Not too bad."

"Would you like to take your boot off?"

"No. Once I get it off, it won't be easy to get it back on again, and I'll need it on to ride home."

"Well, you can elevate it, at least. Scoot over to the chaise end of the sofa and put it up on the cushion."

Dirk glanced uneasily at the long chaise cushion. "I don't want to mess up your furniture with my dirty boot."

"Oh, please. Look at the size of my dog. All my furniture is covered in heavy-duty, machine-washable slipcovers."

"Well, give me a towel, at least, to keep the mud off."

She got a towel from the hall bathroom and spread it over the end of the chaise. Slowly and carefully, Dirk scooted over and settled both feet on the cushion.

"That does feel good," he said.

He took off his coat, revealing a plaid flannel button-down with a waffle-weave undershirt visible at the neck. His lean but powerful build showed itself admirably through the multiple layers.

"Are you verifying my muscle mass?" he asked.

His eyes were fixed on her with disturbing bright blue clarity, and the corners of his mouth were barely edged up.

"Everything seems to be in order," she said.

Then she got briskly to her feet and went to the kitchen. "I'll go see about that coffee."

The power was back on, so that was good. She filled the electric kettle with water and started it heating. As she was spooning coffee grounds into the French press, he asked, "What is all that stuff in your dining room?"

"I don't have a dining room," she said. "I have a work room."

"Then where do you eat?"

"Right here," she said, pointing to the kitchen bar with its three stools.

"What about the rest of the family?"

"There is no rest of the family. Just me and Gunnar."

"And what if you have more than two guests?"

"I don't."

He thought about it. "All right, then. More power to you."

Steam started hissing out of the spout of the electric kettle. Seconds after the switch flipped up, indicating that the water was ready, the power went out. Another brownout.

Macy poured the water into the French press, placed the lid on the top and set a vintage manual egg timer for five minutes. The timer was shaped like a chicken, and it ticked.

The breakfast dishes were still in the sink, covered with soapy water. Macy had been about to take care of them that morning when Gunnar had whined to go out. She pulled on her latex gloves and went to work. While the power outages lasted, there was no point in using the dishwasher as anything but a glorified drying rack.

Once the dishes were done, she wiped the counters and sink. She loved her kitchen. Everything was so new and pretty and clean, and all hers.

Dirk had been quiet for a while now. Macy could see the top of his blond head above the back cushion of the sectional. Maybe he was texting his wife or grandfather at that very minute. If not, she'd get some coffee in him, then see about getting him home. One thing at a time. She had him in her house and off his feet, anyway.

The egg timer went off with a ding. Macy slowly pressed the plunger down and poured the rich black brew into two generous-sized mugs.

"Coffee's ready," she called. "Do you take anything in yours?"

No response.

She left the coffee on the kitchen island and walked out to the living room.

The cowboy was fast asleep on her sofa.

He'd been semirecumbent to start with, leaning back on the chaise with his feet up. Now his head was tilted back and his eyes were shut. His right arm lay across his chest, and his left dangled down to the corner of the chaise, with the hand resting on Gunnar's head.

Was he *asleep* asleep, or had he passed out from his head injury? Should she call an ambulance? She quailed at the thought. Once ambulances were called, somebody had to pay for them, and Dirk had already said in no uncertain terms that he didn't want one.

She might try to wake him and see what happened.

Or she could take this opportunity to try to get in touch with his family.

She crept over and picked up his coat from the sofa. She hadn't seen what he'd done with his phone after she'd handed it to him. She hoped he'd put it in here, because if it was in his jeans pocket…

The first pocket she tried had a bag of coffee in it. San Antonio Blend, the package said.

What was he doing riding around with a bag of coffee in his pocket? She set it down and tried again.

This time she found the phone.

She clicked it open. It wasn't password-protected.

She quietly crossed the work room, went into the garage and eased the door shut behind her. It was chilly in here, but the garage was farther from Dirk's place on the sofa than any of the bedrooms, and she really didn't want to wake him. The peacock glared at her from its shelf.

It felt underhanded, taking his phone and calling his relatives behind his back, but surely this was the right thing to do. She had to find someone responsible for him so she could turn him over.

What had he said his wife's name was? Kendra? Kayla? Macy scanned the *K*s. Kyra, that was it.

There was only one Kyra in his contacts. Macy placed the call.

After just one ring, a click sounded, and a female voice said, "Hello?"

Macy was all set with her telephone voice and prepared speech. "Hello, Kyra? This is—"

"Hello?" the voice said again.

"Hello?" said Macy. "Can you hear me?"

"I can't hear you," said Kyra. "You know why? *Because I'm not here right now!*"

A burst of uproarious laughter came from the phone. Macy pulled away and stared at it, stunned.

The voice spoke again. "This is Kyra. I'm either shopping or partying, so leave your name and number, and if you're cool, I'll call you back. And if you're not cool…then why are you even calling me?"

More uproarious laughter, followed by a beep.

Macy didn't leave a message. That had to be the tackiest outgoing voice mail greeting she had ever heard in her life. Kyra sounded like a handful, and frankly not what Macy would have guessed to be Dirk's type.

She searched Dirk's contacts again and found Granddad. No first or last name, just Granddad, which was lucky for her. Hoping for better things, she hit Call.

After a moment of dead air, a voice said that the number was no longer in service.

She stood there a moment, staring at the phone, hoping fresh inspiration would strike. It didn't. She went back to Kyra's number, let out a deep sigh of distaste, steeled herself and hit Call.

She was all set to hear the tacky outgoing message again, and had mentally composed her own message to leave at the beep—basically the same one she'd come up with before, but modified for voice mail.

She was thrown completely off her rhythm when a brusque female voice answered, "What?"

Macy didn't know what to say. What kind of greeting was *What*? Had they gotten cut off? Had Kyra been about to say more?

"H-hello?" said Macy. "Is this Kyra?"

"Yeah," said Kyra. "Who is *this*?"

No doubt Macy's voice didn't sound much like Dirk's. She did her best to collect herself. "My name is Macy Reinalda. I'm calling to tell you I have your husband."

Definitely not how she'd have phrased it if she'd had her wits about her, but the best she could do on the spur of the moment.

Kyra gave a caustic laugh. "Well, you're more than welcome to him, honey, but I'd think twice if I were you. I know he's good to look at, but he isn't much fun. All he cares about is that stupid ranch."

"You don't understand," Macy said. "Your husband is—"

"Ex-husband," said Kyra.

Ah, yes, of course. Macy wondered how long it had been since the divorce. How far back did Dirk's amnesia reach?

There was no point in telling Kyra that Dirk was hurt. Even if this woman had been willing to come get him and look after him, which Macy very much doubted, Macy couldn't leave Dirk to her tender mercies. She wouldn't trust Kyra with a house plant.

"Can you tell me how to get in touch with his grandfather?" Macy asked. "The number I have for him is no good."

"The old man is dead," said Kyra, as casually as if she'd said he'd moved to Florida.

"Oh. Does he have any other family?"

"Just his kid sister."

"Is she local?"

"I doubt it. She's probably overseas."

"Do you know how I could get in touch with her?"

Kyra made a scoffing sound. "What am I, Google Person Finder? Ask him yourself."

She hung up.

This was one thing Macy and Dirk had in common—a mean ex. She felt a sudden swell of sympathy for the tough cowboy. Did it sting him to be berated by Kyra, the way Andrew had hurt Macy? Of course there were always at least two sides to every story, but there had been something vindictive in Kyra's voice and words, and Macy's instinct told her that Dirk was more sinned against than sinning.

But that was just a feeling, and she couldn't trust it. And anyway, it didn't matter. What mattered was that there was no one left to call. The cowboy was all alone—just like Macy.

She liked being alone. Solitude was safe, and clean and quiet—as long as things were going well and you had everything you needed. But if you were hurt and confused, with no one to take care of you, solitude might not be so great.

In any event, her own solitude had collided with his. What on earth was she going to do about it?

CHAPTER EIGHT

DIRK AWOKE FROM a confused and uneasy dream to find a full-grown peacock staring him in the face.

He shut his eyes and opened them again. The peacock was still there, standing along the back of a sofa, practically beak to nose with him. The sofa wasn't Dirk's sofa, and the house wasn't his house—and yet there was something familiar about it, as if it had come out of that weird dream he'd just had, or he'd seen it a long time ago, or both.

Was he hung over? Maybe. His head didn't feel great. But it had been years since he'd had enough to drink to feel the effects the next day, and even in his wildest days he'd never blacked out.

He was in what appeared to be the living room of a house. Beyond the peacock, he could see a kitchen, with an open door in the side that led to what looked like a garage.

The wall to his right was one giant bookcase, filled with books. A Christmas tree stood in front of it—artificial, white lights, no ornaments. Straight ahead was an enameled heating stove, flanked by windows, and outside was snow, a lot of it. More than he remembered ever seeing on the ground in this part of the state where he'd lived most of his life.

The sofa he was resting on was a big sectional, proportioned for tall people, and covered in some plain, tough-looking fabric. Dirk thoroughly approved of the sofa. It was attractive, but comfortable and not fussy—unlike the one in his living room, with its hard seat cushions and throw pillows that he wasn't allowed to lean against. Kyra had picked it out, along with everything else in the—

Wait a minute.

A memory came bubbling up. A memory of himself standing outside the front door of his house, trying and failing to insert his key. Of the text he'd sent to Kyra: Really? You changed the locks? Of her reply: I didn't want you coming over and taking things away without me being there.

Indignation flared in him now, just as it had then. He'd typed back, As if I wanted any of that crap, to which Kyra had responded,

Don't be childish, Dirk. All you have to do is arrange a time that's convenient for both of us to be there. Then you can get the stuff that the two of us agree is yours.

Instead, he'd called a locksmith, gotten the door unlocked and gone right in. A neighbor must have alerted Kyra, because she'd showed up, looking furious, just as he was carrying out the last of his few boxes of personal belongings. She'd even threatened to call the cops on him. He'd said, For what? This is my house. My name is on the title. It isn't breaking and entering when it's your own house.

So. He and Kyra were divorced, and had been for…he didn't know how long. How could he have forgotten a thing like that? He remembered it fine now—well, not fine exactly, but he knew it had happened. The whole memory felt kind of detached, like it was just floating around in his head, without being part of any timeline. He didn't know what month it had been when he'd gone to the house to get his stuff, or what month it was now—although judging from the thick layer of accumulated snow outside the window, it was some time in winter.

Maybe he hadn't really woken up. Maybe

this was all a dream. It had to be. Peacocks didn't belong in living rooms.

The peacock was still staring at him. It had its head tilted a little to the side, and its feathery crest was cocked, like a fancy hat from a royal wedding.

Meanwhile, something, or someone, was snoring loudly from the floor beside the sofa. Dirk's left arm was hanging down in that vicinity, and he could feel a furry head beneath his hand. He broke away from the peacock's gaze to peer over the sofa's edge. A big dog was lying there, with a short, brindled black-and-gold coat that reminded him of Alex's Brahma bull.

He knew that dog. He knew this place.

Or maybe he'd imagined them both.

Dirk's movement disturbed the dog. It woke with a sleepy snort, yawned, licked its lips—

And saw the peacock.

The dog did a double take. It jerked clumsily to its feet and gave a single bark.

Instantly the peacock spread its tail feathers in a brilliant humongous multicolored display that must have been ten feet in diameter all told. The dog jumped back and let loose with a whole stream of barks—weird, muffled, hoarse barks that made him sound like he had laryngitis.

Dirk was plenty startled himself. It wasn't that he was scared of peacocks; he just hadn't expected this one to spread its enormous brightly colored tail at that exact moment. He tumbled away from the peacock, off the sofa on the other side—it was the kind with a sticking-out part built into one end—and was in the process of getting to his feet when a sharp pain in his ankle sent him back onto the seat cushion.

From across the living room and kitchen, he heard an exasperated sound like his oma used to make whenever one of the barn cats would dart inside the house when she didn't want it to. A woman now stood in the open doorway to the garage, glaring at the posturing peacock whose spread tail was taking up half the living room.

She picked up a broom and strode over. Dirk had a confused impression of long slender legs and a thick mass of honey-blond hair pulled back in a messy bun. She said to the bird in a no-nonsense tone, "Come on, hurry up. Back to the garage. Go."

Dirk could see right away that she had taken exactly the right approach. The peacock folded his tail feathers back down and half ran, half flew across the rooms and through the door.

The broom-wielding woman followed the bird and closed the door behind him, taking extra care to get it shut all the way. Then she turned back to Dirk with an expression on her face that he couldn't quite define.

It was a face well worth looking at, with high, broad cheekbones, a firm jaw and dark deep-set eyes. There was something very sweet about the mouth, though she wasn't smiling. She had a healthy, wholesome look to her, like a stereotypical milkmaid or farmer's daughter, and at the same time something sharp and shrewd.

And Dirk knew her.

This was the woman who'd hauled him out of the creek after he'd fallen down and hurt his ankle—hauled him with his own rope, which she'd attached to Monte's saddle. Or had that been another dream? It felt like a dream, and it sure sounded like a dream when he arranged it into words in his head, but the pain in his ankle was real enough.

He also had a niggling sense that the creek episode hadn't been their first meeting, that he knew this woman from somewhere else.

But where? Why was his head so swimmy? Was *any* of this real?

She walked back over to him and took a seat on the sofa. "Sorry about that," she said. "I went into the garage to make some calls and must not have shut the door all the way."

As explanations went, that one left a whole lot to be desired.

"You keep a peacock in your garage?" Dirk asked.

"Well, not ordinarily. It showed up last night after the snow started. I didn't want it to freeze to death, so I brought it inside."

The black dog had gone over by the door to the garage and was giving it a thorough sniffing. He seemed a whole lot braver now that the bird was safely out of sight.

Gunnar, Dirk thought suddenly. That dog's name was Gunnar.

"How are you feeling?" the woman asked.

"I, uh, I've been better," said Dirk. "My head hurts, and my memory's a bit fuzzy."

"What do you remember? Do you know who I am?"

"Um… Maisy?"

"Close. Macy. Macy Reinalda. And how do we know each other?"

"You hauled me out of the creek after I fell in."

She smiled. "In a manner of speaking, yes. Though I'd have to say Monte did the heavy lifting on that job. Is that how we met, at the creek bed after you fell in?"

"I want to say no. I feel like I know you from somewhere else, but I don't know how. What's going on? Why can't I remember?"

"I think you got a concussion when you fell. In fact I'm certain you did."

Dirk ran a hand through his hair. "That can't be right. I mean, yeah, my head does hurt a little, but like a headache, not like I hit it against the ground."

"It's possible to get concussed without a direct blow to the head. A hard enough blow to the body can cause the brain to slam against the skull."

Dirk started to shake his head, but stopped when the movement made him queasy. "I don't have a concussion. I just got my bell rung a little, is all."

Macy let out an impatient sigh. "That's what being concussed *is*. You're clearly suffering from mental confusion."

"No, I'm not."

"Prove it. Can you tell me what day it is?"

He opened his mouth and closed it again.

"How about the month?"

"December," he said. *Or maybe January if you're the kind that leaves your tree up 'til then.*

Macy's gaze strayed to the tree and back to Dirk. "What year?" she asked.

Dirk searched his memory and came up blank.

"Quit interrogating me," he said. "I'll be all right in a minute. I'm a little hazy because I just woke up."

"Because you lost consciousness on my sofa."

"I fell asleep on your sofa. It's a comfortable sofa, and I was tired. Probably didn't have enough coffee this morning."

"How much coffee did you have? Do you remember? What did you have for breakfast?"

He searched his memory and came up blank.

It was a deeply unsettling feeling. As far as he knew, he could have had *anything* for breakfast—even one of those green smoothies Kyra was always trying to get him to drink, unlikely as that seemed. Anything could have happened since…since when? What was the last thing he *did* remember? He didn't even know that. He didn't know what order the memories went in.

Macy hadn't finished her interrogation. "Can you tell me your full name?" she asked.

Finally, a question he could answer. "Dirk Elizondo Hager," he said without hesitation.

Her eyes narrowed.

"No, seriously," he said. "My dad was a state trooper. He had a partner named Luis Elizondo and I'm named after him. Look, I'll show you."

He reached over to his coat, took his wallet out of the pocket and handed it to her. She opened it, then glanced back and forth between his face and his driver's license photo like a cashier who suspected fraud.

"Are you married?" she asked.

"Used to be."

"As of when?"

He opened his mouth and closed it again.

She gave back his wallet and said, "All right, Dirk Elizondo Hager. You are clearly suffering cognitive impairment as a result of your tumble down the Serenidad Creek. It's time we got you some medical attention."

"What? No. No, no, no, no, no. I'm not going to any doctor."

"Then maybe I'll call an ambulance."

He gave a derisive laugh. "Go right ahead. I'll refuse treatment."

She let out another impatient sigh. "Then let me drive you to an urgent care facility."

"Drive? In this?" He held out a hand toward the snow-covered landscape outside the window.

"It's just a little snow! Why are you Texans so paranoid about driving in it?"

You Texans. One of his least favorite terms in the language. It was rarely followed by anything complimentary.

"Because it isn't just a little snow, Miss I'm-from-the-north-and-Southerners-are-so-incompetent. It never is. It's a slick sheet of ice covering the roadway. And no one can drive on ice."

"They can once the road is sanded."

"Well, we don't sand our roads down here. We don't have snowplows or sanding trucks or any of that stuff you have up north. And it's not because we're a bunch of ignorant hicks. It's because we get so little snow that it'd be a waste of money to invest in that sort of infrastructure—money that could be better spent on public works that could save lives, like flood control tunnels. On the rare occasions when we do get frozen roads, it makes more sense to shut everything down and wait it out. So if you and I go on the road now, we'll be risking an accident. And if you call an ambulance, you'll *still* be risking an accident, plus taking first responders away from situations where their help is truly needed, which in weather like this is probably a lot."

He leaned back against the sofa cushion, suddenly exhausted.

"I don't need a doctor," he said. "I just need to rest."

"You can't be sure of that. You might have a subdural hematoma, and if so, I won't be able to drill into your skull to relieve the pressure, however much the idea might appeal."

"I'll take my chances. I'll sign a waiver if that'll make you feel better. I, Dirk Elizondo Hager, do hereby absolve Macy Reinalda of any and all liability resulting from not meddling in my affairs while I make my own choices regarding my personal health care."

She scowled. "I suppose that'll have to be good enough."

"Thank you. I appreciate it. And I apologize for inflicting my company on you in the meantime."

"Oh, well, it can't be helped. So how about that coffee?"

"Coffee?"

"That was how I lured you here to begin

with, under the pretext of providing coffee. Or don't you remember?"

He scowled back. "The sarcasm is not necessary. But I wouldn't say no to a cup of coffee, if you really did make some."

"I really did."

She went to the kitchen island, which he now noticed held two steaming mugs. "How do you take it?" she asked.

"Black."

She brought both mugs over and handed him one.

"I poured this up a few minutes ago," she said. "Should be just drinkable now."

He thanked her and took a sip.

"Mmm. Nice and strong, just the way I like it. I commend you on your coffee-making abilities."

"Thanks. I commend you on your taste."

Gunnar ambled back over and laid his muzzle on Dirk's leg. Dirk stroked his head.

"So that was the plan, was it?" Dirk asked. "Lure me to your house with coffee and then try to convince me to go to the doctor?"

"Something like that. We discussed the matter of medical care earlier, before I brought you here. You didn't much care for the idea then, either. I figured if I pressed the issue, you'd just bolt and ride on home."

"That was a good guess."

Macy drank some of her own coffee, then said, "So… I did something that may have created a problem for you. If it did, I'm sorry. I thought I was acting for the best."

"That's quite a preamble," said Dirk. "What did you do?"

She took a deep breath. "I took your phone out of your coat pocket and called your ex-wife."

Dirk's stomach tightened. "You called Kyra? Why?"

"Because you were hurt, and passed out on my sofa, and I wanted to get in contact with someone who could take responsibility for you. I didn't realize she was your ex-wife. I thought you were still married. You mentioned her on the ride over here, and you called her your wife."

"I see. So how'd the call go? Do I even want to know?"

Macy's face took on a carefully neutral expression. "Kyra informed me that the two of you were no longer together. Based on that information and her overall manner, I inferred that she would not be assuming responsibility for your care."

"Oh, I'll bet." Dirk let out a sigh. "Well, it's not your fault. I'd've probably done the same thing in your place."

"Thank you for saying that. But there's more." She squirmed. "I'm afraid she…misunderstood the intent of my call. I told her I had her husband, and she thought I was a new girlfriend, calling to gloat."

"And she gave you to understand that there was nothing to gloat about. Is that right?"

Macy's uncomfortable silence was all the answer he needed.

"Seriously, don't worry about it," Dirk said. "You didn't upset any plans for reconciliation or make our relationship any more strained than it already is."

"Thank you. I'm glad to hear it."

She took his phone out of her back pocket and handed it to him. He remembered putting on this phone case when it was new. He did not remember it getting so scuffed.

"Maybe you should look through your phone," Macy said. "It might help orient you in the present. And if I can help fill in any gaps, I will. You and I don't exactly run in the same circles, but I'll do what I can."

"Thanks," he said.

He took the phone. The date on the screen

stared blankly back at him. It was the twenty-second of December, the first day of winter, in a year that was mostly a bunch of empty spaces for him.

He opened his text messages. Alex's name was at the top. He clicked on the thread and started scrolling. The messages were unremarkable for the most part, the sort of messages that he and Alex could have exchanged at any time, but eerily devoid of any specific memories. It was as if someone was impersonating a conversation between Alex and Dirk.

He continued scrolling up, looking for something distinctive, something for his mind to take hold of, until a brief message from Alex sent a sharp stab of pain through his heart.

Sorry to hear about Fletch. He was a good dog.

It was dated November 16. Over a month earlier.

His own reply to Alex was a simple Thanks, followed by, I miss him. Alex had responded, Yeah.

"What is it?" asked Macy. "Did you remember something?"

He shook his head. He didn't remember,

didn't want to remember, didn't want it to be true.

But if he was going to put together a functioning timeline of the past year, he couldn't shrink away from the truth.

"My dog died," he said.

"Oh. I'm sorry. I thought he might have. You were asking about him earlier, if I'd seen him."

"Yeah, I guess I would. He was always with me, all day every day."

"I'm sure that made him very happy. He must have loved having an active outdoor life with you, doing work he was good at."

He liked the way she said this—sympathetic, but matter-of-fact. He couldn't have taken it if she'd gone all gooey on him.

"Yeah," he said again.

He swallowed through the tightness in his throat and closed the messages app.

"I'm going to take a look at the weather," he said as he tapped the icon. "Maybe something in there will jog my memory. Snow in this part of the state is always an event, especially this much snow."

"So I've learned," said Macy. "They're even calling it an Extreme Winter Weather Event."

"Looks pretty extreme, all right," said Dirk, scrolling through forecasts of snow, sleet and temperatures well below freezing. "This is some serious stuff. I got to check on Grand-dad."

Macy didn't speak or move, but something in her manner changed microscopically, and Dirk knew. For the second time in as many minutes, his heart hurt with actual physical pain.

"Granddad's gone, too, isn't he?" Dirk asked.

"I'm afraid so. I'm sorry."

Dirk rubbed his face with his hand. "Um… how did you know about it?"

"Kyra told me. I don't know how or when, just that he's gone. You're having a rough year, aren't you?"

"Yeah, looks that way."

How much else had he lost that he couldn't remember yet? He wanted to go off by himself and process things, but he couldn't, not yet. If there were any other nasty surprises waiting for him, better to go ahead and find out about them now.

"Did Kyra say anything about my sister?" he asked.

"She did. It sounds like your sister is traveling, possibly out of the country. Hey, maybe you should look at your photos. That might give you some clues."

"Sure, why not? I'm not one for taking a bunch of pictures, but—oh, hold up. Looks like I suddenly developed an interest in landscape photography."

Macy came closer and took a look. She smelled nice—sort of floral but not too sweet.

"These must be recent. The snow only started last night. Check the time stamp."

He did. "Looks like I took 'em all today. I wonder why."

"Maybe you were excited about the snow."

He made a derisive sound. "Yeah, and maybe I'm going to make me a nice little snowman with a carrot nose and a corncob pipe and a top hat. What am I, a child?"

"Well, you did take the pictures. You must have had a reason. Do you recognize the location?"

"No," he said, still scrolling. "There's a creek, obviously. Might be the Serenidad, might not. Oh, wait. This is the old Masterson house."

He clicked on an image of the sixteen-room Victorian mansion and held out the phone to Macy.

"Beautiful house," she said.

"Yeah, it really is. But it's been deserted for sixty some-odd years now, and slowly going to ruin for as long as I can remember. It's a shame."

"Yes, I remember seeing it on the plat."

She watched him as she said it, as if she was probing to see if he remembered something. Dirk had a feeling he was about to hear more unwelcome news. "What plat was that?"

"For Masterson Acres."

"Come again?"

Macy took a deep breath. "It's a subdivision in Limestone Springs. It just went in this past year. There are twelve lots, ranging in size from twenty to two hundred acres. My place is one of the smaller ones. I'm on Lot Eight. That's where we are right now. My twenty acres back up to your place across the creek."

Dirk felt like the ground had been pulled out from under him. So the Mastersons had sold out at last.

"I take it this is bad news," Macy said.

"You bet it's bad news."

"You didn't want them to sell?"

"I wanted them to sell to me. And they said they would, when they were ready. Instead, they went and carved up the place and sold it off piecemeal so they could line their pockets with city dollars."

He knew he sounded like a kid, accusing another kid of not playing fair, but he couldn't help it. This really wasn't fair. It was a travesty.

"I was counting on that land," Dirk said. "I've been leasing it for years, for grazing for my cattle. That's how I was able to grow my herds to the size they are today. Now I'm going to have to sell off my stock, because I won't be able to afford to feed them anymore."

"I understand your disappointment," said Macy. "But to be fair, it was their property to dispose of as they saw fit, and you didn't have a formal agreement. You can't honestly blame them for wanting to get the best price they possibly could."

"Sure I can. What they did affects the whole community. It raises land prices and brings in outsiders. Outsiders who are now cheek by jowl with me, sharing boundaries with my property, sharing fence line."

She stiffened. "As I said, I understand that you're disappointed," she said. "But speaking as one of those outsiders, I have to say that your attitude borders on xenophobic."

"Oh, yeah? Is it xenophobic when folks who've lived their whole lives in the same inner city neighborhood complain about gentrification?"

Macy thought about this. "Okay, fair point. But you have to realize that regardless of your history with the Masterson family, the people who bought the lots didn't do it to stick it to you personally. They did it for themselves, because they wanted some acreage of their own. Space for a big garden, maybe a llama or two."

"Llamas?" Dirk burst out. "That's the best example you can come up with? No, I know how it goes. First it's llamas, then alpacas, then wildebeests and giraffes. Pretty soon the whole place is crawling with exotics, just like the great ratite bust of the nineties."

A vertical crease formed between her eyebrows. "I'm sorry, did you just say ratite bust?"

"Yeah. The rise and fall of ostrich farming in Texas."

The crease deepened. "Ostrich farming? Why would anyone want to farm an ostrich?"

"Hides and meat. See, back in the eighties, the US enacted some trade restrictions with South Africa, so bootmakers couldn't get the hides anymore. And somebody got the bright idea of raising them here. A lot of farmers and ranchers in Texas started ostrich farming in a small way, and others completely lost their heads. Outsiders got in on it, too. Suddenly you had city folks who didn't know the first thing about agriculture buying up land and ostrich eggs left and right. Have you ever seen an ostrich up close and personal? Eight feet tall, aggressive and territorial, and with talons long and sharp enough to kill a man. Emus are smaller and easier to manage, so some folks went that route. People kept buying and buying, driving the prices up to around eighty grand for a breeding pair of ostriches, and about half that for emus. But it didn't last. Slaughterhouses weren't equipped to deal with them, so the hides weren't harvested properly, and trendy restaurants got tired of waiting for the meat and dropped their ostrich dishes from their menus. Pretty soon the bubble burst, and people were left with flocks of giant, dangerous birds that they couldn't afford to feed. Some folks got tired of dealing with theirs and just turned 'em loose and left 'em to fend for themselves. We had feral emus running around for years, spooking horses and cattle and wrecking cars, before they finally died out."

Macy listened to all this with obvious suspicion, then pulled out her phone and did some typing.

"Huh, what do you know," she said. "It's true."

"Course it's true. What possible reason would I have to tell such an outrageous lie?"

"Well, you are concussed."

"Not enough to come up with a fever dream like that out of thin air. I don't have the imagination for it, even if I wanted to."

"My ex did."

She pressed her lips together, as if she hadn't meant to say it, then went on. "He could spin an elaborate nonsense story right off the top of his head, all while looking solemn as a judge."

"Why?"

"Just to mess with me. He loved to put one over on me—the more outrageous, the better."

"He sounds like a Grade-A jerk."

"Thanks," Macy said, laying down her phone. "He was."

She turned to face him. "Anyway, I do see your point about the Masterson land. I'm not sorry I moved here, but I am sorry it had to be at your expense."

"Well, thanks. That's very fair-minded of you." He dug down deep and rose to the occasion. "I see your point, too. Obviously I can respect the desire to own land—though that does come with an obligation to husband it properly, which a lot of folks don't seem to— but never mind. What I mean is, you're right. Your wish to have a little spread of your own is not an affront to me personally. It just feels like it is. I mean—"

He let out a sigh. "I'm not doing a terrific job at this. But I will say this. As neighbors go, I could have fared a lot worse. You're obviously a smart woman, coolheaded in a crisis and good with horses. And you've got a really nice dog."

Gunnar's tail thumped against the floor.

Macy chuckled. "You didn't think he was all that nice when you first saw him last night. Do you remember that?"

Dirk thought a minute. "You had a fire going outside. I saw the smoke from across the creek and came to check it out. We…had words. And Gunnar objected to my tone."

"That's about the size of it. Sounds like your memory's getting clearer."

"Yeah, it's like a dawning awareness slowly breaking through the haze of confusion."

The memory of last night's encounter was getting clearer every second, and making

Dirk more and more uncomfortable. He'd made a lot of wrong assumptions about this woman, and taken out his frustrations over other things on her. He owed her an apology.

But before he could put the words together, Macy beat him to it.

"I'm sorry about last night," she said. "I didn't know about the burn ban, but ignorance of the law is no excuse. I'm the newcomer here, so the onus is on me to learn about what is and isn't allowed."

"Well, that's all right. No harm done. It's not like you were burning any toxic materials, right?"

He said it as a joke, but her mouth twisted in a grimace. "Actually, I kind of was. I was burning some old correspondence."

"From the Grade-A jerk?"

"That's right."

He pointed at the wood-burning stove. "You couldn't just light 'em up in there?"

"I didn't want to pollute the stove with them."

"That bad, huh?"

She nodded glumly. "That bad."

He was getting curious about this ex of hers. But apparently the subject was closed for the moment, because she went on, "And

I'm sorry about not having a fence for Gunnar. I can see why you wouldn't want dogs running loose around your stock. Just because he rolls onto his back for me to scratch his belly and snuggles on the sofa with me doesn't mean he isn't an apex predator."

She had an odd way of putting things, but it was fun to listen to and got her point across.

"Well, thank you," he said. "That's very generous of you to say, especially after the way I went off on you last night. It was uncalled for and not very neighborly of me."

"You were just protecting what's yours."

"And Gunnar was just protecting what's his. I respect that. I'm sorry for being harsh and abrupt."

Dirk rubbed Gunnar's ears. Gunnar's eyes went blank with sleepy delight. Last night's snarling cur was just a dopey dog now, comically friendly.

Then he sat up, turned an earnest face on Dirk and pawed his thigh with an enormous front paw.

"Aw, Gunnar's sorry, too," Dirk said. "That's it, buddy. Shake hands and make up, right? It's okay. We're all good here."

He smiled at Macy. "He doesn't hold a grudge, does he?"

"Well, you did free him from the barbed wire, so I'm sure that went a long way toward establishing your character." Macy reached over and gave Gunnar a pat on the shoulder, then said, "While we're all apologizing, I'm sorry about this morning, too. Letting Gunnar get away from me, I mean. I really did pay attention to what you said last night, but it turns out he has a deep-seated hang-up about going potty while on a leash. Eventually he got a little frantic and managed to get away. So I'm not sure what I'll do in the short term to keep him contained. But as soon as the weather clears, I'll get a fence made for him."

Dirk considered. "Well, maybe I could help with that. If you don't mind something plain, like T-posts and field fencing, I can get the post driver and the come-along out here and get 'er done right quick."

She smiled, and the sweetness of her face came into full bloom. "Plain is fine. Thank you. That would be very helpful."

"It's no trouble at all. You know what they say—good fences make good neighbors."

Her smile faltered just for a second. "Mmm, yes, they do say that."

"What's wrong?" Dirk asked. "Did I put my foot in my mouth?"

"No, no. I'm just thinking of Robert Frost."

Dirk waited, then said, "I'm going to need more information."

She sighed. "Well, Robert Frost wrote a poem about that saying, called 'Mending Wall.' But the way the whole thing is framed, the poet isn't agreeing with the expression, he's questioning it, and the thinking behind it."

"He doesn't like fences?"

"It isn't that he dislikes them. He just questions their usefulness in a particular case. It's really a very beautiful and thought-provoking poem."

"Huh. Well, I wouldn't know about all that. I like reading, but I've never been one for poetry."

"I think you'd like Frost. He wrote a lot about rural life, using the idioms of everyday speech."

Dirk's phone went off. He looked at the screen.

"Uh-oh," he said. "It's Alex, and he's calling, not texting, which means it must be important."

Dirk felt funny about talking to Alex before having his memory back 100 percent, but he answered anyway.

"Hey there, neighbor," Dirk answered. "What's up?"

"Hey, Dirk. Just checking in to see how you're holding out."

"So far, so good. How're things at your place?"

"Well, we're staying warm and fed, and the cattle are fine, but our pipes froze."

Dirk frowned. "What? How? Aren't they insulated? Didn't you flow them, hot and cold?"

"They are, and I did, but the brownouts have been lasting a lot longer than predicted, and coming a lot closer together. Long enough and close enough that our well tank to the house emptied and couldn't refill, and our pipes froze with the water that was left in them."

Dirk dropped his head back against the sofa cushion with a groan. "Son of a gun. How big is your pressure tank?"

"Twenty gallons."

"Same as mine."

"But yours is still okay?"

"Well, I don't actually know. I'm not exactly at home right now."

"Oh, really? Where exactly are you?"

Dirk felt shy about telling Alex he was reclining on a chaise in the living room of his attractive new neighbor, especially after the hints Alex had dropped this morning. "I rode Monte down Petty and up the Serenidad. I'm still on the far side of the creek."

"How long have you been gone?"

"Not sure. Few hours, maybe."

"Well, you might have an unpleasant surprise waiting for you when you get home."

"Sounds that way. Guess I'd better head on back."

"You should probably go cross-country. The roads are impassable. A water main broke and some electric lines came down."

"Seriously? Boy, it's just one dang thing after another, isn't it?"

"Yep. We are officially snowbound."

CHAPTER NINE

DIRK ENDED HIS call and stared down at his phone, ice-blue eyes scowling, mouth flattened in a frown. Whatever he'd just found out clearly hadn't made him happy.

"Problem?" Macy asked.

"Oh, yeah. Alex's pipes froze, which means mine probably did, too."

"You didn't drip your faucets?"

He gave her a look. "Course I did. But Alex and I are both on well water, and pressure tanks run on electricity. These dang brownouts have been lasting a lot longer than what we were told, so Alex's tank emptied and couldn't fill up again, leaving whatever water was left in the pipes to freeze."

"My water is still running fine," said Macy.

"Because you don't have a well. You and the rest of Masterson Acres are all on city water." He shook his head in disgust. "What a mess. I'd have been better off draining my pipes altogether and shutting off the water to the house."

"I don't understand," Macy said. "It isn't that cold. Why are the pipes freezing to begin with? Where I come from, this wouldn't be an issue."

"That's because building codes are different up north. The pipes have to be placed in such a way that they don't easily freeze, like indoors, or inside the insulation. They can still freeze, but not at the same temps as down here."

He said it in a bored, impatient way, with a slight edge of hostility. He was awfully defensive about his state, getting testy whenever anyone even hinted that Texas might not be the absolute best in every way.

"It was a question, not an accusation," she said.

"Sorry. It's a sore subject. My grandfather's second wife was from New Jersey, and she loved giving us grief about things like this. It got tiresome real fast."

"Your grandfather married a northern woman? How did that happen? How did they even meet?"

"On a Mediterranean cruise. Got married there, too. A wedding at sea. He went away for seven days of fun and sun and came home with a brand-new wife."

"Wow! That must have been a shock."

"Yep. My dad was mostly concerned about the property aspect of the thing. The new wife had kids and grandkids of her own, which might muddy the waters, inheritance-wise. He said Granddad ought to know better at his age than to risk his legacy to his own descendants by taking up with a northern gold digger. Granddad said he'd worked hard all his life, and now he was going to enjoy the years he had left with the woman he loved, without being guilted and harassed by his only son, who ought to want his old father to be happy instead of worrying that he was going to use up all the inheritance money. He also said that my dad was a fine one to preach about taking care of his own when he'd practically abandoned my sister and me to be raised by our grandparents. It was not a happy time in the Hager family."

"What about you? What did you say about your grandfather's second marriage?"

He shrugged. "I didn't say much of anything out loud. But I didn't like it. The new wife was loud and abrasive and always making fun. To hear her talk, you'd think she was living in a frontier town in the 1800s. Everything that was different in Texas was countrified and backward, and had to be gone over and laughed at six ways to Sunday. And she was always bringing her obnoxious grandson Roque to visit the ranch, and expecting me to look after him. It was like I suddenly got relegated to being a hired hand, only without the pay."

He let out a long sigh. "But none of that is your fault. I'm sorry I snapped. And now I'd best get back home and do some damage control."

"I hope it isn't too bad."

"Yeah, you and me both. I really don't have the time or money right now to be doing major plumbing repairs and putting up new drywall. The ranch house is old, and…"

He trailed off, stared into space a second, then said, "And I'm living there. I'm living in the ranch house. I moved in there after Kyra and I split."

"That's good!" said Macy. "Good that you remember, I mean."

"Oh, it's good all around, believe me. I'm having a fine bachelor time of it, eating what I want, when I want—"

He stopped again, then slapped the arm of the sofa and said, "Bacon."

"I beg your pardon?"

"Bacon. It's what I had for breakfast."

"Just bacon?"

"Bacon and coffee. All the nutrients a man needs for a morning of ranch work."

That didn't seem right, but she couldn't fault his results. That lean, powerful body of his must be metabolizing bacon into pure energy and muscle.

He gave her a smug smile. "See? I told you I'd be all right. It's all coming back to me now. I remember cooking it, and eating it, and..."

He trailed off again. His blue eyes widened, then snapped to attention as he turned back to Macy. "I have a cat. A kitten. Taffy."

He didn't look smug anymore. He looked close to panic.

"I have a cat!" he said again. "I forgot all about her. How could I do that?"

"In fairness, you forgot a lot of things," Macy said. "And you have a good excuse."

She understood the anxiety, though. Gunnar was the first animal she'd ever owned, but before adopting him, she used to have a recurring anxiety dream where she suddenly remembered she had a pet that she'd completely forgotten to take care of. Right now, Dirk was living that dream.

"Okay," Macy said. "Let's think this through. Is she an indoor or an outdoor cat?"

"Indoor. She's way too tiny to be outside all by herself."

Macy suppressed a smile. "Does she have access to food and water?"

Dirk's face was taut with the strain of trying to remember. "I think so. I'm not sure."

"I'm going to go out on a limb and say you probably left food and water out for her. And you've been away, what? A few hours? She's probably fine."

Dirk was still thinking hard. "You're probably right. But I need to go home right now. I'm sure she's cold. I didn't start a fire before I left because I wouldn't be around to see to it, and that old furnace doesn't work worth a flip."

"All right," said Macy. "I'll drive you home."

Dirk gave her an incredulous look. "Oh, no, you won't. I'll ride."

"Are you sure you can manage? Things got pretty dicey the last time you rode with your hurt ankle."

"This isn't about what I can manage. It's about what I have to do. I've got my horse here. You couldn't put him in your car, and I'm not leaving him behind. Anyhow, Alex says the roads are downright impassable now. I'll ride Monte back to my place. My ankle's all right. I've been resting it. It feels a lot better now."

He eased his hurt foot to the floor, then carefully got up, balancing on his good leg. His face went gray. In a tight, strained voice he said, "There. See?"

"Oh, yeah, you're looking real strong there, cowboy."

He sat back down with a groan. "I just need a crutch, is all. Or one of my granddad's old canes with a rubber tip."

"And how are you going to get off your horse and into the house to find it? You'll slip on the ice and stay down, and who'll look after your horse and your cows and your kitten then?"

"Well, I don't have much choice. I'll figure it out. I have to."

Macy thought a moment, then said, "Look, I'll go with you back to your place. Just long enough to get you situated. And in the morning, if your ankle isn't better, I'll come back and help you with your chores."

"I can't let you do that," Dirk said.

"Why not?"

"Because you've done so much for me already."

"That's because it's my fault you're hurt. It was my dog you were rescuing, remember?"

"That doesn't mean you owe me."

"Well then, how about this? I'll help you because we're neighbors, and neighbors help each other, or they should."

She couldn't believe she'd just said that. She'd come to this place with the intent of getting away from neighbors, of insulating herself against people. And now, here she was, preaching the value of community and mutual support to a man who was perfectly willing to go away and leave her in the solitude she craved.

But the simple truth of the matter was that he wasn't ready to be on his own. And she couldn't in good conscience let him try.

"No," said Dirk. "It's too much. You'd have to be out in all this foul weather, and—"

"Oh, please. I'm from New York, remember? Your Extreme Winter Weather Event can't scare me."

"You can't drive."

"Then I'll walk. I'm a good walker."

"No. It's too far, and the snow is too deep."

"Well, what about your horse? Could he carry both of us?"

Dirk thought a moment. "That could work," he said. "He isn't trained to carry double, but he could do it for a short distance. Can you ride well?"

"I took lessons for eight years."

"Okay, but can you ride well? A good rider will ride lighter than one that just sits there like a sack of potatoes."

"I'm a good rider," she said. This was no time for false modesty, even if she'd been inclined that way.

He gave her a searching glance, as if he could read the truth in her face, then gave the rest of her a once-over.

"You're tall, but on the slender side," he said. "Horses shouldn't carry more than twenty percent of their weight, tack included, for very long at a time, but it's possible for them to carry more when needed. I'm a buck seventy-five. Add the saddle to that, and… well, we're going to be over twenty percent. But for this short a distance, it ought to be okay. So Monte'll get us there. But how will you get back?"

That stumped both of them. Then Dirk said, "You might could take the four-wheeler."

"Four-wheeler?"

"It's an all-terrain vehicle. Pretty light and maneuverable. You can cross the creek in it if you do it in the right place. Then once you make it home, you can keep it here, and use it to get back to my place in the morning if I do need help then. Have you ever driven a utility vehicle before?"

"No, but I'm a quick study. I'm sure I can figure it out."

Dirk gave her another assessing look, then reached for his coat. "All right, then. Let's get to it."

Macy got up. "I'd better put out some more dog food for the peacock before we go."

"They eat dog food, do they?" asked Dirk.

"This one does. The internet says cat food would be better, but beggars can't be choosers."

"I have a good supply of kitty chow laid in at my place. I'll give you a bag to bring home to your bird."

"He isn't my bird. But thanks."

"No problem. Hey, while you're in the garage, see if you can find something to use as a mounting block to help you get on Monte. You won't be able to use the stirrup."

"I've got a fold-up step stool that's pretty sturdy."

"How high is the top step?"

"About four feet."

"Sounds perfect."

She took a small scoop of kibble to the garage. By the time she got back with the step stool looped through her arm, Dirk had his coat on. She helped him hobble over to the work room. He leaned his right hip against the harvest table with his right ankle off the floor while she put on her own outdoor gear.

"How's our fine feathered friend?" he asked.

"Oh, he's having a great time befouling my garage. I'm going to have to pressure-wash the floor when he goes home."

Dirk chuckled. He had a nice chuckle, throaty and warm. "You've got all kinds of strays to look after right now, don't you?" he asked. "And in your nice, clean, brand-new house, too."

As soon as Macy pulled on her snow boots, Gunnar began to cavort around in his usual way, no doubt expecting a nice romp in the show.

"Sorry, boy," she told him. "You can't go. This trip is going to be complicated enough without you along."

Dirk didn't have to put his boots on, because he'd never taken them off.

"I wouldn't wonder if I ended up having to cut that boot off you eventually," Macy said.

Dirk looked at her as if she'd suggested cutting off the entire foot. "The heck you will," he said. "I'll take it off when I'm good and ready."

"How? It's not as if you can unlace it. Isn't it awfully tight on your ankle?"

"It's containing the swelling, like a compression bandage. I'll finagle it off with the bootjack when I'm done outside for the day."

Macy took the step stool outside and set it up, then came back for Dirk. She had to get him out the French door on his bad ankle without letting Gunnar out as well. Gunnar was sitting now, his body taut with contained energy, and staring hard at Macy, as if to show what an extra good boy he was.

"Stay," she told him sternly. "Stay."

He stayed, and went on watching them through the glass after she'd shut the door. Macy felt like a heel, leaving him behind, but it couldn't be helped.

"You ready?" Dirk asked.

"Ready," said Macy, slipping her arm around his waist and taking hold of his belt like before.

He packed a lot of muscle on his lean frame. His chest and abs were rock-hard against her.

"This would be easier if I could put you in a fireman's carry," she said.

Dirk draped his arm over her shoulders. "Getting tired of lugging me around, huh?"

Actually, she wasn't. She was enjoying the

close contact way too much. They were getting good at it, too. They fit together well.

She walked him to the Adirondack chair, and he leaned against it while she led Monte out of his shed to the step stool and tightened his girth. Monte bore Macy's attentions with haughty tolerance.

"He sure is a good-looking horse," Macy said. "Nicely built, and so striking, with that blond mane against the sorrel coat. And the light area around his muzzle makes him look like a big hinny!"

"Yeah, it does. That's the Belgian Draft in him."

"I wondered if he had some draft ancestry. He's such a big, solid guy, but a bit finer-boned than a pure draft. I guess that's where his calm temperament comes from, too."

"He's more spirited than a pure draft, but still pretty steady. He can be kind of a knucklehead, though. He knows his horse feed comes in big bags, so any time he sees a bag of something, he rips it open with his teeth. Doesn't matter what it is—dog food, wood chips, charcoal briquettes. No matter how often he's disappointed, he won't quit trying."

Macy chuckled. "Well, you can't fault his

reasoning skills. He's just starting with faulty assumptions."

It was time to mount. Dirk turned to Macy with a serious face.

"Just a couple things before we set out," he said. "Like I told you, Monte isn't trained to carry double—most horses aren't—so I want to make this as easy on him as possible. It isn't just the extra weight that's the issue, it's how it's distributed. That means you have to sit close to me. And when I say close, I mean *close*. Right up against me, like we're one person. Hold on tight and don't let go—and don't fall off, or you'll take me with you. Keep your legs as forward as you can, right next to mine, otherwise they'll tickle his flanks. He's going to crow-hop some at first, because he won't like it, and things might get a little Western for a minute or two. But he's a good horse and he'll soon settle down—if you do what I say. Got it?"

"Got it," Macy said, sounding more confident than she felt. It had been years since she'd actually ridden a horse, but she wasn't worried that she couldn't do it; she remembered the principles and trusted her muscle memory. It was the prolonged physical contact with Dirk that had her agitated. They'd already had their arms around each other several times today. Now she was about to be hip to hip and thigh to thigh with the man for a considerable time.

Get a grip, she told herself. *This is the only way. It has to be done, so do it.*

Dirk got on first, mounting from the left with Macy supporting him, as before. This time wasn't as difficult as the last time, but it was difficult enough. Dirk's ankle was still clearly hurting him, but he powered through. Once in the saddle, he sat a second with his face tight and his eyes shut. Then he let out his breath, looked at Macy and said, "All right. Your turn."

She positioned the step stool close to Monte's left side, climbed to the top step and took a second to assess things. The saddle had a low cantle, which would make it easier for her to get in there. Dirk already had his hips forward in the saddle to make room for her.

"Tell me when you're ready so I can lean to the right," Dirk said.

Macy took hold of the cantle. "Ready."

Moving quickly, she swung her leg over Monte's back and slid on in, pressed her body close against Dirk's and wrapped her arms around him.

Monte didn't hesitate to react to the unac-
customed weight on his back. With a snort,
he kicked up his back legs, forcing Macy forward against Dirk. She fought to keep her balance as Dirk spoke soothingly to him. Monte
crow-hopped once more, then settled down,
with a loud whooshing sound to register his
disapproval.

"Well," Dirk said. "That could have gone
a lot worse."

From behind the French door, Macy could
hear Gunnar doing his muffled bark. This
might be the strangest and most exciting thing
he had ever seen.

Dirk clicked to Monte, and the horse started
walking.

"You don't have to hold your legs out that
way," Dirk said. "Pull them in and slide them
forward, right next to mine, away from his
flanks."

She did, fitting their knees together, her
thighs snug against his.

"Doing all right?" he asked.

"I'm good," she said.

She felt better than good. She felt fantastic. Being on a horse again, so high above the
ground with his movements rippling through
her, was exhilarating. Dirk's back was strong

and solid against her. She laid her face against his coat. It seemed like a strangely intimate gesture, but there was really no place else for her face, and they were already in such close physical contact that a little more hardly seemed significant. His coat was rough, but not scratchy, and smelled like the outdoors—of oats and hay, and clean, healthy animals, and earth and rain.

"How's the ankle?" she asked, speaking into his shoulder.

"Better," he said. "But I'll be glad to put it up for a spell when I get home. I'm sure it'll be fine in a few days. Just needs rest and time."

"I'm guessing you don't go to the doctor very often," Macy said.

"No, I do not. It's a good thing you didn't try to strong-arm me about that ambulance deal, because it would not have been pretty."

"Oh, I know. That's why I didn't do it. I once made the mistake of calling an ambulance for my father when he didn't want one. Believe me, I had no desire to repeat the episode with a stranger."

"I take it he refused treatment?"

"And how. He had a major meltdown, and said I was never to do such a foolish, wasteful thing again."

"How old were you?"

"Twenty-eight."

"Oh! I figured you were just a kid. You were his caregiver, then."

"That's one way of putting it. He had COPD, probably because he worked his whole life in a manufacturing environment, making machinery. The day I called the ambulance, he'd had an exacerbation—that means his baseline symptoms got worse. He was drowsy and wheezing and disoriented. But by the time the EMTs got there, he was feeling better, and absolutely refused treatment. Unfortunately, while it's true that emergency workers can't force you to accept treatment, or take you to a hospital against your will, they will certainly try their best to convince you to go, and they might just bill you even if you refuse their services."

"Ooh, did they send you a bill?"

"Yes, they did. It took months for me to straighten it out, and my father fretted and groused about it the whole time."

"How long did you have to look after him?"

"Almost eleven years."

"Eleven years! How old were you when you started?"

"Eighteen."

Dirk let out a low whistle. "How did that come about?"

"Well, he and my mom married late. He was fifty-one and she was forty when I was born, and I was their only child. Then in the spring of my senior year of high school, my mom got sick. It was ovarian cancer. Once she was diagnosed, things progressed fast. There wasn't much they could do besides try to make her comfortable. I spent graduation day in the hospice center with her, and the next morning, she was gone."

"Wow. That's rough."

"Yeah. So as you can imagine, everything was at loose ends. I put off college for a year, but by the time that year was up, my dad's health had started to go, and he had to retire, and in the end…"

"You didn't go at all."

"No. I stayed home to take care of him."

"You couldn't make other arrangements? Hire someone?"

"He said we didn't have the money—and I believed him."

"Was it true?"

"He thought it was. You have to understand, my father had always been a difficult person. Conscientious and hardworking, but kind of a bully. Everything that happened in the house, every penny that was spent, had to be justified. It was exhausting. After my mother died, he got worse, and it was just the two of us with no buffer anymore. He'd always been fixated on money, and once he couldn't work anymore, it became an obsession. He always talked like we were one unpaid electric bill away from financial ruin. I think it was his way of maintaining control in a situation that was growing increasingly beyond his control."

"That sounds like a very charitable assessment," Dirk said.

"Well, like I said, he did have his good qualities, and I try to be fair to him."

They reached the cover of trees around the creek.

"You see this trail we're following?" Dirk asked. "It leads right to a shallow part of the bank where it's easy to cross. You can come this way on the four-wheeler, too. It's broad enough. I've done it plenty of times. See that cedar tree with the twisted trunk? Just keep to the right of it, and you'll do fine."

"Okay."

They crossed the creek and continued following the trail up another shallow slope to the top of the bank.

"How's Monte doing with all this, you think?" Macy asked. "Is he okay?"

"He's fine. We don't have much farther to go, and you're doing a good job."

"Thanks. It's nice to be riding again. I used to ride in Central Park when my mother was alive."

She began to get a scope of the ranch, the depth and breadth of it. She understood why Dirk was protective of it.

Not much farther to the ranch house now, and that was a good thing. In spite of the rocky beginning to their relationship, she had on the balance enjoyed being with him—enjoyed it far too much for comfort. Things had escalated so quickly. She couldn't possibly have imagined at their first meeting that less than a full day later, she'd have her arms around him this way and be telling him about her childhood. She hadn't shared that much since Andrew, and while part of her felt uneasy at the revelation, another part wanted to go on, and find out more about him, too. In spite of his rough-hewn country boy thing, he had a clear way of expressing himself and an excellent vocabulary. She enjoyed talking to him.

But that was only an emotion, and it would pass. Once she didn't have to be around him anymore, all this would fade into distant memory. Other things would take the ascendancy again—security, tranquility, solitude. The things that remained.

Yes, it was high time that Dirk went back to his house, and she went back to hers, so she could get her equanimity back. She needed to rediscover the luxury of being alone.

CHAPTER TEN

THE LANDSCAPE STRETCHING before Dirk was familiar and strange at the same time. The snowfall had transformed everything, covering all the different-colored grasses in a white blanket, softening all the little ridges and rivulets into broad, sweeping contours. Here and there the top of a shrub stuck out, its bare branches or clinging foliage looking darker than usual against the white glare.

The land wasn't the only thing changed. That presence at his back, those arms tight around his middle, was making an entirely new thing out of horseback travel. Macy was doing well, riding light, her motions perfectly matching his. Her face was just behind his shoulder, almost level with his own. When she spoke, her breath fogged the air and warmed his cheek.

All this made it hard to keep his mind on what he was doing, but that was just fine, because the whole thing was so easy and natural that he didn't have to think about it. His body did what it was supposed to, leaving his mind free to wander.

And wander it did. His ankle and head hurt, but the pain felt separate from him, as if it didn't really matter. Something had come to life in him that had been sleeping quietly for a long time.

He kept pointing out landmarks as they passed them—the blackened old oak tree that had been struck by lightning, the little hollow where Granddad had once showed him a nest full of baby rabbits, the high-water mark from the last big flood two decades ago.

"It's a beautiful place," Macy said. "And it's wonderful that there's so much personal and family history attached to it—and that you can remember it all."

"Yeah," Dirk said.

Speaking of memory…

Keeping his gaze fixed straight ahead, Dirk asked, "So, uh, what exactly did I say before, about Kyra? You know, when I was so addled and…thought I was still married to her."

"Nothing much," said Macy. "Nothing cringe-inducing. Just that the two of you were planning a big Christmas party, and a ski trip to Aspen afterward."

"Oh, yeah," said Dirk. "We did plan all that.

So, what, I thought the party and the trip were yet to come?"

"That's right."

It was weird to think his mind could do that to him, just delete a whole chunk of time from his memory, taking him back to when he and Kyra were...well, not happy, exactly. They were never really happy; he could admit that now. Their whole relationship had been built on falsehood from the start.

"So how was the party?" Macy asked.

Dirk let out a *humph*. "Judging from the pictures and the caterers' bills, I'd say it was a rousing success."

"You didn't go?"

"No, I did not."

A long silence passed. Then Macy said, "You don't have to tell me about it if you don't want to, but I'm game if you are, and we do have plenty of time."

"Well, it was like this. Kyra wanted to throw a Christmas party at our place in Limestone Springs. She said she wanted to show her Austin friends and clients an authentic ranch Christmas, which apparently was something you couldn't have without caterers, and rented party equipment and kale-and-salmon tacos on vegan tortillas. I wasn't too sold on the idea, but I said it was all right by me as long as we spent Christmas Day at the ranch with Granddad. She agreed to that at first, but as the time drew near, she changed her tune and said why should we waste Christmas Day at the ranch when Granddad could just come out to our place for the party? I said Granddad wouldn't be comfortable at a big fancy party like that, and she said he didn't have to dress up or anything, he could just wear his boots and jeans and a snap shirt and a Stetson and maybe a bolo tie. Like he was some sort of *prop*. He didn't even *own* a bolo tie or a snap shirt. Long and short of it is, Granddad did not go to the party, and neither did I. The two of us spent that evening together, looking after a sick cow."

"How about the Aspen trip?"

"That was dicey from the start. Theoretically, we might have been able to be away that long, if Granddad had been in good shape, and if he'd had a reliable hired man to help him. But what we had in reality was a guy named Two Dollar Bill, who left without giving notice to pursue his destiny as a bronc rider. And Granddad had a bad cold. Well, I couldn't go off and leave him all alone on the ranch. So I stayed home, and Kyra went to Aspen with-out me."

"I'm sorry," Macy said.

"Don't be. I didn't want to go anyhow. Kyra consoled herself in the resort bar and gift shop. No doubt she had a much better time on her own."

They were drawing near to the house. Dirk wanted Macy to like it. He thought she would. It was a small house, only two bedrooms, but well proportioned, with high ceilings giv-ing the place a spacious feel. Native lime-stone masonry, gorgeous millwork. Two huge old pecan trees grew, one on each side, with branches almost meeting overhead at the peak of the roof. Yes, it was a beautiful old place.

Of course, as he remembered with a sudden qualm, the inside of the house was not exactly looking its very best right now. For a moment he wished he had cleaned up that morning, or not been such a slob to begin with.

They rounded a coppice of live oaks, and the house came into view. Dirk raised his hand to point, saying, "My place is just over…"

The words died in his throat. Something was wrong, very wrong, in the shape of his house, and of the trees. Specifically, one of the trees wasn't just arching protectively over the roof anymore. It was *on* the roof.

Make that *through* the roof.

Dirk didn't speak. He couldn't have put together a coherent sentence to save his life. Macy didn't say anything either, though she must have seen what he saw, and he was grateful for that. Talk was no use to him then. He wanted to hurry over, but kept Monte to a walk. He was already demanding a lot of his horse, and it wasn't as if getting there faster was going to help matters.

Slowly, and yet all too quickly, the distance closed. Every step made the damage clearer, and drew the knot in Dirk's belly tighter.

Finally, they reached the back corner of the house where the dining room was—or had been. Now the old metal roof was smashed under the crushing weight of a massive snow-covered tree limb.

From what Dirk could make out, it looked as if the stone walls hadn't been damaged. But he couldn't tell for sure, and even if he was right, the damage to the roof was plenty to be going on with.

"Welp," he said at last. "I guess I should have trimmed the trees."

Macy didn't answer. Dirk kept walking

Monte around toward the front. The L-shaped covered porch that went around two walls of the living room had its roof bent, and most of its posts were either splintered or off-kilter, but the stone chimney on the side wall was still standing. Past the front of the house, they rounded the corner of the front-facing gable of one of the bedrooms, and continued beyond it to the smaller covered porch outside the laundry room door. This side of the house looked all right.

Dirk stopped Monte at the laundry room porch. It stuck out a bit from the rest of the house and had a stoop that was a good height for Macy to dismount. She did, then held out her arms to help Dirk down. He waved her off. He didn't want her help. He wanted to hurt. He was angry at himself. He could feel six generations of German ancestors looking at him, demanding to know how he could have let this happen.

"Dirk, let me help you."

Macy's quiet, calm, reasonable voice cut through the noise in his head. He accepted her help without further protest.

It seemed sad and funny at the same time for Dirk to have to unlock the door when there was a giant hole through his roof, but he did.

He and Macy went in through the laundry room, a late addition to the house, along with the hall bath it shared a wall with. They'd been built in the early 1930s in what used to be an open space between the bedrooms where the horse-drawn carriage was kept. Dirk's great-grandfather had closed in the space and built one of the first modern bathrooms in this area. Dirk had been looking forward to telling Macy that; she'd have appreciated it, he thought. But it seemed a little anticlimactic now.

With Macy supporting him, they went through the short hallway into the living room. He scanned the wreckage for Taffy and called out to her.

The fireplace was straight ahead, empty and black; ash had blown out of it, coating the floor. The pictures that used to hang on the walls—old lithographs, mostly, done by an artistic Hager early in the twentieth century—lay on the floor, their frames and glass splintered. Where the ceiling should have been, there was only open sky and tree limbs. Granddad's grubby old club chair leaned drunkenly, its back broken beneath a branch.

The dining room was toward the back of

the house, catty-corner to the living room, with a diagonal wall separating it from the kitchen. Along that wall was a built-in china hutch that Granddad had made as an anniversary gift to Oma. It was shattered now, and the china with it. The old harvest table that had crossed the Atlantic from Dresden was split clear down the middle.

Snow had fallen through the roof and drifted into corners, against walls, against every vertical surface, and piled in mounds on every horizontal one. In the kitchen, Dirk's bacon pan was filled with snow, dried leaves, sticks and dirt. Baby-sized kitty kibble was scattered across the snow-covered floor.

The sight of that kibble just about undid him. Had Taffy been crushed by falling limbs or broken furniture? Maybe she'd been so scared that she'd lost her head and climbed up the pecan limb and out into the cold. There was no telling how many hours had passed since this had happened, how long she'd been all alone without shelter or care.

"Taffy!" he called. He could hear the fright in his voice. "Taffy, kitty!"

Then came a beautiful sound: a tiny, frantic, high-pitched mew, mingled with the tinkling of a small bell. Taffy crept out from beneath the remains of an end table, her fur damp and spiky. Dirk let go of Macy and bent awkwardly to pick her up and hold her to him. She stopped mewing and began to purr. He could feel her trembling through his coat.

Straightening, he leaned his hip against the arm of the living room sofa. He could see Macy looking around, taking in the sight, and was ashamed of his slovenliness. Of course no house looked its best with a tree through the roof, but anyone could tell that this place had been a wreck to begin with. He should have looked after it better.

He was angry at the snow and the cold; at the Mastersons, for selling out and leaving him in the lurch; at Granddad, for marrying an outsider and sowing division in the family; and even at Macy, for her quiet sympathy and for being part of the wave of newcomers overrunning the community. But mostly at himself, because he'd known all along that that old pecan tree needed to be trimmed, but there was never enough time or money or energy to deal with all the demands of keeping the ranch together.

What an idiot he'd been, wanting to show off the house to Macy. Where had that come from? All he wanted now was to be alone with his misery.

Macy wished she knew what to say. For the most part she'd been stupidly silent ever since they'd first seen the silhouette of the wreckage up ahead—the wreckage of Dirk's ancestral home. She'd been frantically searching her mind for comforting words but hadn't come up with anything that wasn't a cliché. Now Dirk was standing there with that glazed look in his eyes, silently taking it all in, hugging his kitten to his chest like a child.

Dirk was the one who broke the silence. With quiet dignity he said, "Thank you for your help getting me here. I'll go rustle up one of my grandfather's canes from the back bedroom to help me get around, and then I'll take you to the four-wheeler so you can go home."

It took a moment for his meaning to sink in. "You don't mean…you don't actually think you're going to stay here, do you?"

"Why wouldn't I?"

She looked around, sputtering, gesturing. "Because you… Dirk, you can't live like this."

"Sure I can."

"No, you can't! You're hurt, you're concussed, you don't have water or utilities, and there's a giant hole in your roof. And we aren't even halfway through the Extreme Winter Weather Event."

"It's only the living room roof that's caved in. The bedrooms look fine. And the cold snap won't last forever. A week from now this'll all be over, and folks around here will be wearing shorts and running their air conditioners."

"A week is a long time to live in subfreezing temperatures."

"One of the bedrooms has a fireplace. I'll stay in there with Taffy."

"With the power cutting off the way it has been?"

"Why not? People can live without electricity. The first Hager that came to Texas survived a heck of a lot worse than this. He didn't have electricity. He got snakebit and sunstroked and shot, all in one summer, and when winter came his cabin burned down and he ended up living in the barn 'til spring, bedding down with the hogs."

If it hadn't been for the jut of his chin, she'd have suspected he was making a bizarre joke. But he was serious. Was this the concussion talking, or was he always this stubborn? She'd already had qualms about leaving him alone with his head injury, and that was when she'd thought he was probably past the worst of it. But the way he was acting now, she was starting to doubt that.

"You can't stay in a house that's suffered this kind of damage," she said. "The walls could fall down around you. You can't assess how structurally unsound it is until the snow goes away."

"I'll get the chainsaw in here, cut this tree into firewood and get a tarp over the roof," he said. "If anything needs to be shored up, I'll rig some bracing with two-by-fours. Then once the weather warms up, I'll get the roof fixed."

"You think you're going to do all that on your bad leg? Stack wood? Operate a *chainsaw*?"

The look in his eyes was more than just pigheadedness. It was desperation.

"Do you have a better idea?" he demanded.

Macy didn't answer right away. She had an idea, but she wouldn't call it a better one. In fact, it was a terrible idea. But it was the only way.

"You'll come back with me," she said. "You and Taffy. You'll stay at my place, and the two of us will come back here as needed to feed cattle. We'll keep it up until the storm is over and you can make other arrangements."

Dirk shook his head. "I can't do that."

"Of course you can. You have to. It's the only way."

He started to speak again, but Macy cut him

off before he could get going. "Just stop. You know as well as I do that you can't stay here. I get that you have a lot of ideas about independence and proving how tough you are. But it's cold, and I'd like to get home before it starts snowing again. So let's pretend we argued about it another twenty minutes and I finally convinced you."

He glowered at her. "I don't like being in your debt, taking your charity."

"It isn't charity. These are exigent circumstances. The truth is, we're both better off if we pool our resources, especially with electricity being in short supply. It doesn't make sense to keep two households running when one can support the both of us."

It was quite a speech for someone who prized her solitude and self-sufficiency. She was amazed to hear herself extolling the virtues of community cooperation for the second time that day, and using phrases like *the both of us*. But it had to be done. These *were* exigent circumstances. She couldn't leave Dirk here like this—or his cat, for that matter.

"You know I'm right," Macy said. "Accept it and let's get on with this."

Dirk glowered a moment longer, then bowed

his head. Taffy lifted her face and touched the tip of her nose to his.

"All right," Dirk said. "Thank you."

"You're welcome. Now, what do we need to do?"

He considered. "First thing I need to do is hunt up one of Granddad's canes so I can stop using you as a human crutch. Then I'll get Monte unsaddled and in his pasture. The four-wheeler's parked in a lean-to outside the barn. I'll bring it to the house and load it up. That won't take long. I just need cat supplies and some clothes for me, and maybe some stuff from the kitchen."

"Let me take care of Monte," Macy said. "It'll save time. Is the tack room in the big barn?"

"Yeah. I'll walk you over there. I'm heading that way anyhow for the four-wheeler."

The barn had that hushed, hay-scented calm that Macy associated with her horse-riding days. She took off Monte's bridle, slipped on a halter and tied him up. Once all his gear was off and put away in the tack room, she led him to his pasture and gave him some hay.

By the time she got back to the house, Dirk had parked the four-wheeler outside the small porch on the undamaged side of the house. He'd already loaded an army-green duffel bag onto the cargo area, along with a small litter box, a bag of litter and a bag of kitten food. As she came in, he was headed out with a bottle of wine, a vintage cookie tin with a Christmas scene on the lid and two packages of bacon.

The temperature was dropping, and it smelled like more snow was on the way.

"Where's Taffy?" Macy asked.

Dirk patted his side. "Zipped up in an interior pocket of my coat. I figured that's the safest way to transport her. The lining's soft and warm, and she seems content."

He took a last look around the forlorn house and laid his hand on the back of a broken club chair like it was a deceased friend. The chair was ripped, sodden and dirty, with gouges through the fabric and padding. It had clearly been in rough shape to begin with—the upholstery was worn, and the arms were shiny with grime and wear—but the piece had good bones.

Then he said, "Oh, hold on. There's one more thing I need to pack."

He went to the kitchen and came back holding a stick with a wad of paper tied to the end.

"What is that?" Macy asked.

"Taffy's toy," Dirk said. "I thought she might like to have something from home."

Macy held back a smile. It was funny and sweet to see how unashamedly affectionate this big tough man was with his little scrap of a kitten. That pink collar with its jaunty bell was no wider than a strand of linguine. Had Dirk picked it out himself? Macy tried to picture him standing in the pet aisle, his face fixed in serious concentration as he made his selections. It wasn't a hard thing to imagine.

The four-wheeler was smaller than Macy expected. Sitting behind Dirk, with his hands spread on the handlebars and her arms around him, she felt like she was on a motorcycle. The engine noise ruled out conversation, leaving Macy free to think. Her thoughts were far from comfortable.

Barely a week after moving into the house that was supposed to fulfill a lifetime's worth of dreams about solitude and independence, she had invited a guest to stay with her for an undetermined period of time—an attractive male guest. Since moving in, she had been profoundly thankful for stillness and silence, for being alone in her space, free from the fear of intrusions of any kind. Now she was voluntarily giving up that luxury. Dirk was about to stay overnight in her home, and all of the next day and night, for as long as the storm lasted. What would that lead to? He would know things about her. The pristine shell around her home, her life, would have a crack in it. More than a crack—a chasm.

It would be one thing to invite a houseguest for a set period of time under normal circumstances, with a plan for meals and sleeping arrangements. And she didn't even want that. It was not for nothing that her second and third bedrooms had no beds in them. She'd made no accommodation in her house for guests, because there wasn't anyone in her life whom she wanted to invite to stay with her.

But the point was that if she had, she'd have handled it differently. This situation was something else entirely. The two of them would be largely housebound, except for walks and chores—forced together for hours on end, without reliable electricity. When she came out of her room in the morning to make her coffee, Dirk would be there. When she sat down to do some hand-quilting, Dirk would be there. When she woke in the night, troubled by bad dreams or regrets, and unable to go back to sleep again, Dirk would be there—not right there in the room, but somewhere in the house, having to be accounted for. She couldn't just stroll out to the living room in her robe to stare at the Christmas tree in the middle of the night, or reorganize her fabric scraps on impulse, or go through an entire P. G. Wodehouse book in a single afternoon. She couldn't soothe her anxiety by filling a parfait glass with Reddi-wip and eating it with a spoon. Everything she did would have to be thought through and explained. She would have to be "on" all the time.

When would she read?

When would she *think*?

A normal person wouldn't feel this way. A normal person—like her aunt Lindy—would cheerfully roll with the situation and be glad she was able to help a neighbor. She'd toss some sleeping bags on the floor and say, *Make yourself at home!*

But Macy wasn't like that. She never had been. And she'd carefully structured her environment to keep her away from situations like the one she was in right now.

Dirk parked the four-wheeler close to the back deck and cut the engine.

Gunnar had noticed their return and was giving his weird muffled bark. Macy suspected he'd been waiting by the French door the entire time they'd been gone.

"Your dog is merfing again," Dirk said as he dismounted the four-wheeler.

She smiled. She'd always thought of it as merfing herself, and Dirk had chosen the same word.

"I know," she said. "He's had plenty to merf about today."

"Yeah, I reckon he's had a pretty wild time of it. A peacock, a horse, a strange man and now an ATV. That's a lot to take in."

He rubbed a hand over his face. "Speaking of which… I want to make it clear that I won't be, uh, putting any undue pressure on you regarding our temporary living situation. I know it's got to be weird, having me stay in your house. It's a sacrifice on your part, and I want you to know right from the start that I'm going to respect your privacy and your boundaries and whatnot."

He looked so awkward and earnest and decent that Macy instantly felt better.

"Okay," she said. "Thank you for saying that."

He gave a quick nod.

"We're not the only ones that are going to be sharing space," she said. "I don't know that

Gunnar's ever even seen a cat, and there's no telling how he'll react. We need to make a plan before we go inside. I have an empty bedroom where we can put Taffy and her litter box, and—"

"You want to keep her shut away all by herself?" Dirk sounded shocked and hurt.

"No, not permanently. Just whenever we aren't around to supervise. I know she'll need to be out by the fire most of the time to keep warm. She and Gunnar can take turns. I'll go shut him in my room now to give her a chance to run around and get warm and play in the living room. I'll stay in there with him so he's not alone. Then later Taffy can go into the corner room while Gunnar gets to be in the living room."

"That sounds good to start with. But we could try introducing them, you know. They might get along fine."

"And they might not. Remember how he barked and growled at you last night, when we first met?"

"That was a defensive reaction, not prey drive. You said you take him on a lot of walks, right? How does he do with squirrels and little dogs and such?"

"He notices squirrels, but he doesn't try to

get away and chase them. And he likes little dogs—all dogs, really. I never had a problem with him at dog parks."

"Will he chase a tennis ball and bring it back? Or chase it and not bring it back?"

"He doesn't chase it at all. Just watches it go by and gives me a confused look. I never could interest him in fetching anything."

"It sounds like he might not have a strong prey drive. It's your choice, but I think we could safely give it a try."

Macy thought about it. "Okay. For now, I'm going to go ahead and put him in my room so he'll be out of the way while you get Taffy inside and situated. Then when things settle down, we'll see."

She carried Taffy's bag of food to the house while Dirk carried the litter and litter box. On the other side of the French door, Gunnar was nearly wagging his backside off in excitement.

"I'll go in first," Macy said. "Then after I shut Gunnar in my room, you can bring Taffy inside."

"Don't you think you're being a little over-cautious?" Dirk asked. "What's he going to do, tackle me to the ground and unzip my coat to get to her?"

"I don't want to leave anything to chance," Macy said. "We can't afford to make a mistake here."

"Okay," said Dirk. "Your house, your rules."

Macy went in the house, set down the cat food bag and knelt in front of Gunnar. He whined and licked her on the face.

"I know," she said, rubbing his neck and ears. "I missed you, too."

When he'd worked out most of his wriggles, she said, "Come on, boy," and started down the hall. Gunnar frisked joyfully alongside, never suspecting a thing. Inside her bedroom, she knelt again and petted him.

"Good boy," she said. "I'm sorry I was gone so long. I know things are weird, but it's going to be okay. You're going to stay in here by yourself for a little while, but I'll be back soon."

Quickly, she slipped out the door and shut it behind her, feeling like a terrible person.

Dirk was waiting at the French door. Macy let him in, picked up the cat food bag and led the way to the empty room.

"This is it," she said. "You can set up her food and water and litter box in here. The floors are all hard-surface, so cleanup will be easy."

Dirk took a look around. "Wow. When you said empty room, you really meant an empty room. What are you planning to do with it?"

"Nothing."

"Really? Nothing? Then why have it at all?"

"Because it's good to have a little more than you need, in case of exigent circumstances."

"Exigent circumstances," he repeated. "Right."

She had never anticipated circumstances as exigent as these.

Within a few minutes, the filled litter box stood ready in one corner, two small dishes for food and water in another, and a snug nest of soft fabric scraps in between. Then Dirk unzipped his coat, pulled Taffy out of the inner pocket and set her on the floor.

Taffy stood a moment, looking around with wide eyes, then stepped daintily around the perimeter of the room, her short tail held high.

"Why do you call her Taffy?" Macy asked.

"Because she's yellow and sticky and sweet."

She glanced at him. "Sticky?"

"Her claws."

He looked defensive, as if he'd been caught in a weakness.

Before she could stop herself, Macy asked, "Do you know the difference between a cat and a semicolon?"

Dirk blinked. "A cat and a…? No, I do not."

"One is a pause at the end of a clause. The other has claws at the end of its paws."

He stared blankly at her for a moment, then rolled his eyes and grinned.

When Taffy came back around to where she'd started, Macy picked her up in one hand, flipped her over and took a look.

"Huh," Macy said. "She really is female."

Dirk made an indignant sound. "You had to check? You don't think I know a girl cat when I see one?"

"Well, it can be hard to tell at this age. And it's unusual, a female orange cat. Not incredibly rare, like a male calico, but unusual."

"You're just full of information, aren't you?" Dirk asked.

For a moment Macy felt stung. Her last few months with Andrew, she'd learned to think carefully before speaking, asking herself whether her words could be construed as showing off, or twisted into some kind of affront to him, or used against her in any capacity later. It had gotten to where it was easier just to keep quiet—until he'd accused her of being sullen.

And now here she was, making that semi-colon joke, and talking about sex-linked traits in felines. Opening herself up to criticism.

But Dirk was smiling.

"Do you know anything about the genetics of equine coat colors?" he asked.

"No," she said.

"Oh, boy. That's a hole with no bottom. Dozens of possible color and pattern configurations, all deriving from two base colors, some dilution genes and some patterning genes. Black, bay, chestnut, sorrel, buckskin, grullo, palomino—every one of them comes from a red or black base coat."

Macy thought about that. "What about white?"

"Most whites are really light grays, with a black base coat and black skin. The true white is different. It has a patterning gene that causes spotting, only in this case the spotting covers the entire coat. It can occur with any base coat color."

He went on, explaining about bays and roans, pintos and dapples. It was clearly a complex and fascinating subject. Macy liked listening.

When he started talking about the genetic profile of brindle horse coats, she came back to herself with a start.

"Speaking of brindles, I forgot about Gunnar," she said. "I left him in my bedroom all alone. We need to get the four-wheeler unloaded so I can be with him."

"I'll handle the four-wheeler," Dirk said. "You go love on your dog. Oh, and take my jacket with you, for him to sniff. That way he can get used to Taffy's scent before he meets her."

He took it off. Her eyes traveled down his strong, lean frame, then back up to his face.

"Good idea," she said, taking the jacket in her arms. It was still warm.

Gunnar was waiting just inside the door of her bedroom. She shut it behind her, dropped to the floor and sat with her back against the wall. Gunnar put his paw on her shoulder, then climbed onto her lap.

"Hey there, buddy," she whispered. "What a good patient boy you are, waiting so nicely for me to come back. I know you're tired of being cooped up all alone. But I'm home now, and I'm not going anywhere the rest of the day."

She was still holding Dirk's coat. Gunnar

sniffed it, casually at first, then with increasing interest, burrowing his snout deep inside.

"Are you getting a hit of kitten?" she asked. "That's Taffy. She's going to be staying here awhile."

She laid the coat on the floor, then got to her feet and locked the door. She liked locked doors, even when she was alone in the house. They made her feel secure. And now...

She sighed. In less than twenty-four hours, her life taken on a lot of unforeseen complications. She'd taken custody of a peacock and gone on a cross-country horseback adventure. And just across the hallway, behind another closed door, were a man and a kitten. Her clean, pristine, empty room was now a cat hotel.

"It's only temporary, Gunnar," she said softly. "As soon as this storm ends, they'll go back home, and it'll be just the two of us again."

She wasn't sure which of them she was trying to reassure.

CHAPTER ELEVEN

WHILE TAFFY PROWLED around her new temporary home, Dirk finished unloading the ATV. His ankle throbbed, but the pain was manageable, and he was getting used to the cane.

He took his duffel bag to the closet in Taffy's room and put his toiletries bag in the hall bathroom. He stowed the bacon in Macy's fridge, set the wine bottle on her counter and put Miss Ida's cookie tin on the kitchen island. It looked festive there, he thought.

Everything in this house was clean and bright. The counters didn't have a bunch of stuff on them, only things like ceramic soap dispensers and glass salt and pepper mills—functional, but pretty. You couldn't just strew your belongings wherever in a place like this. This was a neatness that demanded respect.

He opened the pantry to store some cans of chili he'd brought from home and stood a moment staring. The space was filled with rows and rows of home-canned soups and vegetables. Hand-lettered labels clipped to the shelf edges told the jars' contents—beef stew, chicken soup, vegetable soup, chicken stock, beef stock, carrots, green beans, fruit preserves. The few rows that did not contain home-canned goods held empty canning jars, ready to be filled the next time around. Above all this, resting at the pantry's top just beneath the ceiling, loomed a big pressure canner, next to a gleaming stainless steel stock pot.

He squeezed his cans of chili next to some jars of seasoned ground beef and closed the door.

When he'd first come in, he'd set his cowboy hat on the big table in what Macy had called the work room. He picked it up now and took it to the small closet near the front door, where he'd seen Macy put her coat. As small as it was, the closet was pretty bare, holding only two heavy coats and one jacket, all on nice wooden hangers. Gunnar's leash hung from a hook on the wall. A basket up on the shelf had a label tied on with a ribbon, with Hats and Gloves written by hand.

Dirk thought of all the junk crammed into his own closets at home. He set his hat on the top shelf.

Back in the living room, Taffy was giving

a thorough sniffing to a big, low ottoman that looked to be the right size for Gunnar.

Dirk hobbled back over to the work room. He wasn't sure what sort of work she did, but evidently she made or repaired stuff. Judging from the materials he could see in the clear plastic bins under the table, she might be a seamstress, though he didn't see a sewing machine. Maybe she kept it in its own special cabinet somewhere. A small red air compressor in one corner roused his curiosity. Her tidy workspace and well-maintained tools would have made his grandfather weep with joy.

There were books here, as well as in the living room, resting on some sort of invisible shelf that made them look like they were floating against the wall. Dirk scanned their spines. Upholstery, slipcovers, window treatments, tailoring, quilting, knitting, crocheting, weaving, spinning—yep, definitely a common theme.

A big wooden frame held an in-process patchwork quilt. Taffy came over with her sassy kitten walk and started to sink her claws into one of the legs of the frame.

"Oh, no, no, no, baby," Dirk said, scooping her up with his free hand. It was tricky to do with the cane and the bad leg, but he managed it.

Still clutching the kitten, he went over to the wood-burning stove. He'd never seen one as spiffy as this one, with its shiny beige enamel and divided glass doors.

Macy hadn't come out of her bedroom yet. Dirk wasn't sure how long she was going to stay in there with Gunnar while giving Taffy the run of the place; they hadn't specified a time.

Dirk went down the hall and knocked on Macy's bedroom door.

He heard a sleepy woof, followed by a stirring sound, like someone getting out of bed. The knob clicked, the door opened a crack and a sliver of Macy's face appeared, looking at him with a guarded expression.

"Yes?" Macy asked.

Her cool, clipped tone took him by surprise.

"Hey," he said. "I don't want to bother you, but it looks like your stove needs more firewood. I'd be happy to do it for you, but I figured I'd better check with you first. I don't want to mess anything up."

"Oh, right. I should have added more wood as soon as we got home. I'll take care of it."

By now, Gunnar had managed to wedge

his nose in the opening between the door and the jamb. Dirk stuck Taffy behind his back before Gunnar could see her.

"Gunnar, get back," Macy told him.

"You can let him out if you want," Dirk said. "I don't want to run you out of your own living room. We can go ahead and introduce him and Taffy and see how it goes."

She thought about it. "All right. I'll come out by myself first and take care of the stove. Then you can get situated with Taffy and I'll bring Gunnar out."

She slipped through the doorway and started to shut the door behind her, but Gunnar was still blocking the space with his nose.

"Gunnar," she told him sternly. "Move your nose."

Reluctantly, he drew back, and she closed the door.

"Uses his nose as a doorstop, does he?" Dirk asked.

"He does," said Macy. "You would think it would hurt to have your nose caught in a door, but it doesn't seem to bother him, and he clearly does it on purpose."

When they reached the stove, Dirk said, "I'd like to make myself as useful as possible while I'm here. I'm not working at full capacity right now, obviously, but I can get around okay and do some things. I'd be happy to help look after the fire, if that's all right."

"Fine by me," said Macy. "I'm sure you can handle it."

She touched a lever behind the upper corner of the stove. "This controls the air vent," she said. She slid it away from her, and a little flap near the bottom, attached to the lever by a chain, opened wide. "Move it the other direction, and it closes. I'm opening it now to get more oxygen in there. If the fire starts to get too warm, I'll move it back the other way. We don't want the stove to burn too hot, or get so cool that it produces a lot of creosote. Just keep an eye on the indicator."

She opened the lid on top of the stove, stuck the poker inside and broke the log into big coals. Then she took two midsize logs from the green tub and put them in the firebox.

"Seems simple enough," said Dirk. "Sure is a nice stove."

"Thanks. My aunt and uncle had one like it at their place in Upstate New York. I used to visit them a lot as a kid, and I learned how to work it."

"That's a handy skill to have. You know, if you don't mind my saying so, you don't seem like much of a city person, in spite of being from New York."

She smiled, a closed, secretive smile that made him want to know what went on inside her head. "You might be surprised," she said. "Most of New York is actually rural. Once you get upstate, past Westchester County or so, it's a whole other world. Lots of beautiful farms—places that look a lot like that Currier & Ives print on that cookie tin you brought from your house. Upstate New York was settled largely by New Englanders, and culturally speaking, it has more in common with New England than with New York City."

"I did not know that. Is that where you grew up? In the rural part?"

"Well, no. I grew up in Brooklyn, in Crown Heights. But I always loved the country, and learned as much about it as I could. And I guess I always had a mindset of wanting to know how to do things for myself."

"I surmised as much. I saw your canning supplies in the kitchen. That's a pretty impressive stash."

"Thanks. I processed most of that while I was waiting for the house to be built. I know it seems silly, filling dozens of breakable glass jars with food only to move them to a new house, but I wanted to be able to stock my new kitchen with things I'd made myself, for my own personal satisfaction. Sometimes I open the pantry door and just stand there and gloat."

"I get that. I do the same thing whenever I reload a bunch of ammo. I stand there at the reloading press, looking at those shiny filled brass casings, and feel all cozy and secure."

She looked down at his feet. "Speaking of standing, isn't it about time for you to put up that hurt ankle and rest?"

"I guess. I didn't want to get started until I knew I could stay down for a while. I brought the bootjack over from my house to help, but taking that right boot off is not going to be any fun at all."

"Maybe you should elevate the foot for a while first. See if you can get some of the swelling to go down before you try to pull it out of the boot."

"Good thinking," he said. He was happy for any excuse to put it off.

They were already close to the chaise where Dirk had rested earlier. He maneuvered his way into the corner where the sticking-out part met the front of the sofa.

"Here, give me the kitten," Macy said.

He handed Taffy over and was glad to see Macy cuddle her. He didn't know what he'd've done if she'd been a cat-hater.

Slowly and carefully, he settled himself onto the chaise and put both feet on the towel spread over the end.

"Better?" Macy asked.

"Yeah," he said, laying his cane on the floor.

He suddenly felt worn out, with his sore ankle and sore head. He was glad he hadn't stayed on his own, glad to be here in this tidy, comfortable house with this intelligent, interesting, capable woman, instead of all by himself in his shabby, cluttered house with the giant hole in the roof.

He held out his hands. "All right. I'll take Taffy, and you can bring Gunnar out so they can get acquainted."

That vertical crease showed up between her eyebrows again. "You're sure this'll be okay? He's a big, strong dog, you know."

"I know. I've seen him. But he's a good dog, and you handle him well. He respects you. Bring him out on his leash and let's see how it goes. And don't be nervous. Dogs can sense that. Be confident."

She handed Taffy to him, and he settled

the kitten onto his chest while she went down the hall.

She came back with Gunnar, on his leash, panting happily, probably expecting to go on a walk. When Macy led him into the living room instead of outside, he gave her a questioning look, but followed. And when he saw the little orange fluffball resting on Dirk's chest, his mouth closed and his eyes became intent.

"Make him sit and stay, right over here by me," Dirk said.

Macy did. Gunnar studied the kitten with his head cocked to the side, his eyes round with amazement. Taffy was watching him with her own wide-open, alert golden eyes.

"Don't let him hyperfocus on her," Dirk said. "Make him look at you."

"Gunnar," Macy said. "Look here."

Gunnar looked at Macy, then back at the kitten. Macy said his name again, and again he turned his attention to her. Then, on his own, he looked back and forth between the kitten and Macy, as if to ask, *Can you believe this nifty little thing?*

"So far so good," said Dirk. "See how soft his eyes are?"

"Yes. And look at Taffy. She isn't the least bit afraid."

"Yeah, she's probably never even seen a dog before. Now you take a seat at the other end of the sofa and make Gunnar lie down by you."

Macy did what Dirk said. Gunnar clearly wanted to stay where he was and go on observing the kitten at close quarters, but he obeyed. With his head resting on his paws, he kept right on watching Taffy.

"Alrighty, then," said Dirk. "We'll just stay here awhile so they can get used to each other."

He nodded toward the work room and asked, "What is it that you do over there, anyhow? Are you a seamstress?"

"Kind of. What I'm focusing currently is on furniture reupholstery."

"Oh, I see. So I guess that platform is for raising the furniture to a comfortable level for working on?"

"That's right."

"What about that little air compressor?"

She smiled. "It powers my pneumatic staple gun."

"No kidding! That must be fun to use."

"Oh, it is. A whole lot more fun than removing the old staples."

"I'll bet. Have you been in business long?"

"Well, I haven't exactly started. I've been

waiting to get settled in the house first. But I found a gorgeous old wing chair at an estate sale a few months ago. It's in the other bedroom now, along with the new fabric and all the supplies I'll need—batting, foam, tacking strips. When I'm ready to start, I'll bring the chair out here, strip it down and go to work. Once it's finished, I'll put it on eBay."

"eBay, huh? Local pick-up only, I guess?"

She shrugged. "I'd rather ship by freight."

"Sounds expensive."

"Yes, but not unreasonable given the quality of my work. Other sellers have done it successfully, and I expect I can, too."

He liked her quiet confidence. There was no false modesty about her, and no grandiosity either. She knew what she could do and didn't pretend otherwise.

"I guess if they like it well enough and they've got the money, they'll be willing to pay," he said. "And you wouldn't have the overhead of a storefront. But why not find local customers and take commissions? It would simplify transportation, and you'd be sure you were making exactly what the buyer wanted. It'd be a lot more efficient."

"True. But it would also defeat the whole purpose of my business model."

"Which is?"

"Working alone, without meeting the public or engaging in any in-person encounters with customers."

"Oh." He was a little taken aback. "You don't like people?"

She considered the question. "I don't dislike people on principle. I just find it tiring to deal with them. I like working alone, and living alone. I realize that by reupholstering furniture on spec and selling it on the internet, I probably won't move merchandise as fast as if I did what you suggested, but I don't mind a lag time between sales. It's fine by me if business is slow or sporadic, as long as I get to work the way I want."

She must not be hurting for money, if she could afford to make choices like that.

"Sounds like you have the right idea, then," Dirk said.

So she didn't dislike people on principle. That was…nice, he guessed. But they did tire her out. Maybe his feelings should be hurt right now, but no, it was impossible to take offense when she was so matter-of-fact about it. She hadn't said it to be mean; she was just honest and direct.

"I guess I shouldn't be trying to make small

talk with you, then," he said. "You've probably used up your word quota for the day or whatever."

"No, that's all right," she replied. "Under the circumstances, with the two of us staying under one roof for the next several days, it would be strange for us not to talk, and ultimately more stressful for both of us. Small talk is a useful convention. It lubricates the machinery of interaction by affirming our common humanity."

He wanted to laugh at this, but he could tell she wasn't saying it to be funny.

"I admire people who can do it well," she went on. "They put other people at ease. That isn't something that comes naturally to me."

"I don't know about that," Dirk said. "You and I talked all the way back from the creek after you hauled me out. I thought you kept up your end of the conversation just fine."

"Well, I had to, didn't I? You were hurt and disoriented and didn't know what year it was. I had to keep you talking, to get information from you and to keep you focused."

Dirk thought about that. "Yeah, I guess you did."

"Anyway, while we're on the subject, I will need to spend some time alone each day while you're here, to stay in a good headspace. As long as you respect that, we'll be fine."

"I can do that."

He remembered what Ava had said on the phone earlier that day, about how Dirk wasn't a genuine introvert himself, just a grumpy extrovert who was down on his luck relationshipwise. Maybe she was right.

"So…are we still on for small talk right now?" he asked.

"Might as well," said Macy.

"Well then, suppose you tell me how you got so good at sewing and reupholstery and whatnot."

She tucked her long legs under her. "I learned how when I was little. My mother sewed, and she taught me. She used to make all my doll clothes and costumes for school plays and things, and mend and tailor clothes for the family, and make dresses sometimes. In her day, sewing was simply a skill that women were expected to have. They didn't worry about whether they were creative or *crafty* types." She rolled her eyes on the word *crafty*. "They just did the work."

"Yeah," said Dirk, thinking of his oma. "They did it because they had to. But nowadays, with ready-made stuff so cheap and easy to come by, it takes an unusual mindset to go to the trouble."

"That's one thing I've always had," Macy said drily. "An unusual mindset."

"I can see that. You're driven and disciplined, and you don't do things a certain way just because that's how everyone around you is doing them. And unlike those who learned because they had to, I think you are a creative person, and a very focused one as well. It's one thing to learn to hem a pair of pants or mend a torn seam, but it's another thing altogether to go out and buy a pneumatic staple gun and start ripping up old furniture and making it new again."

She shrugged. "That was largely a product of necessity. I told you how tight my father was with money. Once his COPD got bad enough to keep him housebound, he wouldn't let me buy much of anything new. So when our old sofa and chairs started to fall apart, I recovered them. Actually, I made slipcovers to start with, which are harder in some ways than upholstery, because you have to make a way to take them off again. I bought a how-to book—Dad never minded if I bought books, because he considered them an investment purchase—and went to it."

"So you learned by doing," Dirk said.

"Well, by first reading and then doing, then reading some more," said Macy. "I've always been a reader."

"I gathered," said Dirk, with a glance at the bookshelves. "So you finished that first set of slipcovers and took off from there, huh?"

"Yes. Eventually I recovered every piece of upholstered furniture in the house, and made new window treatments. I also started salvaging secondhand stuff. It kept me busy."

Taffy had gone to sleep, curled up in a tight doughnut on Dirk's chest. Idly, Dirk ran a finger back and forth along her fuzzy forehead.

"It must be very solitary work," he said. "Do you watch TV? Listen to music?"

"I listen to audiobooks, mostly." A dreamy look came into Macy's eyes. "There was this one rolled-arm sofa with a tufted back and a T-shaped deck that I reupholstered in velvet, years ago—a beautiful piece. I did the work while listening to an audiobook of John Locke's *An Essay Concerning Human Understanding*." She smiled as if remembering some very pleasant time. "Locke was so foundational to the Enlightenment, and to the American founding. For months afterward, whenever I looked at that sofa, I'd think of Locke."

"Where's the sofa now?" Dirk asked.

Her smile faded, and a shadow passed over her face. "I left it in New York."

Then, before Dirk could follow up, Macy said, "You've had your foot elevated for a while now. Maybe you should go ahead and take that boot off."

"I can't do it *now*." He pointed at Taffy. "I have a sleeping kitten on me."

"Ah, yes. That is a valid excuse."

He looked around the room. "So did you upholster the furniture in here? This sofa, the chair? That Gunnar-sized ottoman?"

"Reupholstered them, and made slipcovers for them."

"That's quite an achievement."

"Thanks."

She was quiet a moment, then said, "Do you know why most people don't try to learn new things? It's because they mistake talent for skill. If they aren't good at something right off the bat, they say they just don't have the talent for that thing, and they give it up. But unless you're some sort of prodigy, then with every new thing you learn, you have to go through a time when you're doing the work, but not getting the results you want."

"An apprenticeship period," said Dirk.

"Yes. It's uncomfortable and frustrating, and it takes patience. Those first slipcovers I made were not professional quality, and they didn't come easy. I had to rip out a lot of seams and sew them over again. But I didn't give up. And I got better, and built on that skill to learn more new things."

"I reckon that's true," said Dirk. "Once you're really good at something, like riding a horse, you make it look easy. But you have to put in a whole lot of hours of practice to get to that point."

"Exactly."

Introverted though she may be, Macy sure wasn't shy about expressing her opinions. Dirk liked that. She thought about things, and had convictions, and acted on them. Granddad would have said she was a real go-getter.

"Are you hungry?" she asked. "I just realized it's probably been a long time since your bacon and coffee breakfast."

"I could eat," said Dirk.

Macy got to her feet. "How about if I heat up some home-canned beef stew?"

"Sounds perfect."

She was still holding Gunnar's leash. "Come on, boy," she said. "Come to the kitchen with me."

Gunnar looked from Macy to Taffy and back again, then followed Macy to the kitchen. She fastened his leash to one of the turned legs supporting the island bar.

Dirk scanned the titles of the books closest to him. From what he could see, Macy's library was pretty diverse, with old, impressive-looking leather-bound volumes alternating with modern hardbacks and worn paperbacks. A lot of history and biography, and a good bit of poetry, but a lot of popular fiction, too. Dirk saw what looked like a complete set of Louis L'Amour along with other books, fiction and nonfiction, about the American West.

"That's an impressive library you've got there," he said.

"Thank you. My books have been my education. That's one thing I'm grateful to my father for, that he never tried to stop me from getting books. He interrupted my reading a lot, especially in his later years, with his constant demands, but he still let me buy books."

"Good for you for taking advantage of it. I enjoy reading, but I don't often get lost in a book anymore like when I was a kid. I wasn't a half-bad student, though I never distinguished myself academically. I was content to do well enough. Looking back, I kind of wish I'd applied myself better, but more for my own satisfaction than anything. I don't regret not going to college."

He pointed at one of the books in the Western section. "I see you have a copy of *The Virginian*."

"Oh, yes. The prototypical Western novel. I have most of Wister's novels, some of his story collections and his book about his friendship with Theodore Roosevelt."

"He was friends with Teddy Roosevelt?"

"They met at Harvard. Wister dedicated *The Virginian* to him."

"Huh, I didn't know that. Or if I did, I forgot."

Dirk craned his neck around to look at Macy. She was emptying a big jar into a pan at the kitchen island.

"So the father of Western fiction was a Harvard boy," he said.

Macy set the pan on the stovetop and turned on the burner. "Maybe it took an outsider to see it romantically enough to mythologize it," she said. "Besides, most of the characters in *The Virginian* are from somewhere else. Molly is from Vermont. The narrator of the book is a New Yorker. Even the Virginian is from Virginia. That's kind of the point. They all go West, and the West shows them what they're made of."

"I'd forgotten about that New Yorker narrator," said Dirk. "I probably forgot a lot of things in that book. I ought to give it another read."

She smiled at him. "Well, you couldn't pick a better time. You can borrow my copy."

She walked over to the bookcase, took down *The Virginian* and handed it to Dirk.

"Thanks," he said.

He held the book cradled in his hands. It was a modern paperback with worn covers and cracks along the spine. It felt like a big gesture, Macy entrusting him with one of her beloved books. He felt as if he'd just been admitted to a secret club—a very exclusive club, with a membership of one.

He had known Macy for only a day. At their first meeting, he never would have dreamed that he'd be sitting here now, with his boots up on her sofa, discussing literature with her while she made him a meal. But here he was.

He opened the book. Sure enough, there was the dedication to Theodore Roosevelt.

"I sure picked a good place to be snowed in, between the library and the canning pantry," he said.

He almost added *and the company*, but something stopped him, maybe because there was too much truth in it.

CHAPTER TWELVE

MACY BROUGHT THE bowls of hot stew to the living room and set them on the coffee table. Dirk maneuvered into a more upright sitting position, waking Taffy, who lifted her head and started sniffing.

"I'll take Taffy to her room so we can eat in peace," Macy said.

She picked up the kitten in one hand and carried her away. The kitten's plaintive mews followed her back down the hall. She went back to the kitchen and unclipped Gunnar's leash from his collar. He immediately headed down the hall to sniff at Taffy's doorway.

Dirk had his long lean legs stretched out on the chaise, the hems of his worn, faded jeans giving way to the scarred brown leather of his boots. What was it about the shape of cowboy boots that was so attractive? Those thick, sturdy heels, that honest stitching along the welt, that gracefully pointed toe…

She came to herself with a start, suddenly realizing that she was spending way too long staring at his legs. He knew it, too. He was smiling at her, just a little.

Inspiration came to her rescue with a good excuse.

"How about taking off that boot now?" she asked. "You've had time for the swelling to go down a little."

His smile went away. "Yeah, I guess I've put it off long enough. Might as well get it out of the way before we eat."

He'd already set the bootjack beside the sofa. Now he pivoted on his hips and set his feet down on the floor, then fit the heel of his right boot into the notch and set his left foot on the flat part. He took a moment to steady himself before slowly drawing his right foot out of the boot.

His face went gray, and his jaw flexed so tight she could see the tendons standing out in his neck. He let out a low groan that was almost a growl as the foot came free.

He was gripping the edges of the seat cushion now, and breathing heavily with his head hanging low. When at last he lifted his head, he looked worn out.

"Well, that's done," he said. "Not an experience I want to repeat anytime soon...although

I will have to put the boot back on to feed cattle tomorrow. But one thing at a time."

Then he frowned. "How am I going to get the other one off?"

Macy saw what he meant. He couldn't very well push his bad foot against the bootjack.

"Should I just pull it off for you?" she asked.

"No, I have another idea. Come sit here by me."

He lifted his right leg onto the chaise and scooted backward and to his right, making room for her in the corner where the chaise met the rest of the sofa. Macy steeled herself, then took a seat in front of him.

"Closer," he said.

She shifted back until she was right against him, with her left leg touching his. He put his hand on her shoulder. She could feel the warmth of him behind her. It made her heart race. After everything they'd been through today, she ought to be inured to close physical contact with this man, but she wasn't, not by a long shot.

"Okay," he said, his voice calm and quiet in her right ear. "Now put your left foot on the bootjack, and get ready to push."

She did. He set his own left heel into the notch. "You ready?" he asked.

"Ready."

Macy pressed against the bootjack as Dirk drew his foot out.

"There!" he said. "That was a much pleasanter experience."

She thought so, too. She was enveloped—nestled, almost—with his right leg stretched out on one side of her, his chest at her back, and his head just above her shoulder. She had only to lift her own head a little to bring her face to within inches of his. She could brush her lips against that squared-off jaw if she...

He gave her a brisk, unromantic pat on the shoulder. "Thanks for your help," he said. "I'm glad that's over with."

Jumping to her feet, she said, "Sure, no problem."

Her face felt hot. She didn't meet his eyes, but she could feel him watching her.

"I'll put another log on the fire," she said.

She was glad for the excuse to put her back to him for a minute. By the time she had the griddle to the stove closed again, she was back in control, and Dirk had peeled the sock off his right foot.

The ankle was an appalling sight: hugely swollen and discolored.

"That looks awful!" Macy said. "Do you think it's broken?"

"No, it's just a sprain," said Dirk. "It'll be fine in a few days."

He reclined on the chaise again and put both feet up. Macy picked up some down-filled throw pillows and brought them over to him.

She gently picked up his right leg, cupping the calf with her hand, and slid the pillow beneath his ankle.

"Ooh, that's good," he said with a sigh.

The bowls of stew were still steaming. She handed Dirk's to him and took her own to the far end of the sofa.

Gunnar came ambling back into the room and settled down on the floor between them.

"He sure is a good-looking dog," said Dirk. "I'll bet he was a cute puppy—all head, like a black rubber ball."

"I'm sure he was, but I wouldn't know. He was nearly grown when I got him from the shelter."

"He came from a shelter, huh? I guess you wouldn't know anything about his lineage, then. That brindled coat is so striking. And he's a big guy, but not huge. Maybe he's part mastiff."

"I thought the same thing when I first saw him. I figured maybe mastiff and lab.

I wanted a dog that would be good for companionship and protection, and a mastiff mix seemed about right for both. After I adopted him, I did some DNA testing to find out just what he had going on genetically."

"Yeah? What'd you find out?"

She smiled. "Part Rottweiler, part golden retriever."

Dirk let out a sudden shout of laughter, startling Gunnar into jerking his head up. "What a combination! Now that you say it, I can see some Rottweiler in the shape of the head and body, and he's not as jowly looking as a mastiff. Well, the Rottweiler part ought to be good for security, all right. And as for the rest—" He looked at Gunnar. "Aw, I guess you're just a big, goofy, fluffy yellow dog at heart, aren't you, boy?"

Encouraged, Gunnar got up and came over to him, and Dirk rubbed him on the ears and throat.

"How about Taffy?" asked Macy. "Did she come from a shelter, or did you know someone with a litter of kittens?"

Dirk looked gravely at her. "No, when you live in the country, you don't have to go looking for a new dog or cat. City people drop 'em off for you for free. Little Bit just showed up one day about a month ago. I was splitting firewood out back when I heard this weird squawking sound, like a bird, but no bird that I'd ever heard before. It kept squawking and squawking, and finally I realized it was coming from my yard, behind a shrub near the house. I went over to it and there was this tiny scrap of a kitten, meowing and meowing. She'd been alone and scared and crying for her mother so long that she didn't even sound like a cat anymore. At first I thought there was something wrong with her voice box. But I took her in and gave her some canned tuna, and once she settled down and relaxed and realized she had nothing to be scared of anymore, she went back to meowing like a regular cat."

"Poor little traumatized kitty," said Macy. "She's lucky she found you."

"I was the lucky one. I'd just lost Fletch a few days earlier and…well, I needed a friend."

Macy could understand that.

"Why did you call him Fletch?"

"Because he was fast like an arrow, and because he had feathering on his legs." He thought a moment.

"You know, I've had a lot of dogs in my life—hounds, collies, retrievers, mutts. They were all good dogs in their own way, with totally distinctive personalities. Same with cats."

"I know what you mean. I didn't have pets growing up, but my upstate cousins did, and I always made friends with all the dogs and cats in my neighborhood. They were about the only friends I ever did make."

Dirk gave her a curious look. "Why was that?" he asked.

She shrugged. "Well, I'm sure you can imagine that I was kind of a strange kid. Introspective, always reading and…just different. Other kids thought I was weird, and rather than be hurt by that, I decided to own it, to embrace being different. For the most part, dogs and cats were easier to be with than people."

"What about dating?"

"What about it?"

"Oh, come on. You're not asking me to believe that you went all through high school without attracting any romantic attention."

"That's exactly what I did. I didn't go on my first date until I was twenty-nine."

Dirk set his spoon down in his bowl. "Twenty-nine! You're kidding me."

"I'm not."

"How is that possible? A smart, beautiful woman like you."

Macy looked down at her stew and gave it a stir. "You'd be in the minority with that perspective."

"No. Something else had to be going on. Your father was scaring the guys off, or something."

"Well, the men weren't exactly beating down my door, but my dad did make it almost impossible to get to know anyone, once I started taking care of him. I couldn't have gone on dates even if I'd been asked, and I wasn't asked because I never went anywhere to meet anyone."

"That doesn't seem fair," Dirk said.

"No. But he was my father, and he had no one else, no other family. And I had nowhere to go—no money in my name, no property, and no source of income."

"What about hiring someone to look after him? There wasn't money for that?"

"Not as far as I knew. Dad always made it sound like we were on the verge of bankruptcy, and I had no reason to doubt him. It wasn't until after he died that I learned that he was a wealthy man, with a robust investment portfolio, US Treasury bonds, and several very large bank accounts."

"Whoa! Seriously?"

"Yes. The house was paid for and had been for decades, and it had appreciated a lot in value over the years. There was plenty of money. As his only heir, I got everything, and instead of being on the verge of homelessness, like I'd feared, I was very well-off. But it was infuriating. My father could have had such an easier time if he'd allowed himself to. He could have afforded good in-home care. I could have gone to school. We could have lived so differently. And now it was too late."

Dirk took a bite of stew and chewed thoughtfully for a while.

"Well, I guess now you're the one who can choose," he said at last. "You can travel the world, or do whatever it is people do when they have plenty of money. You can follow your dreams."

She smiled. "I did. I moved to Texas and bought a place in the country." She spread her arms. "You're looking at my dream home—a three-bedroom, two-bath house on twenty acres."

"If that's what you truly want, then more power to you."

"It is. I guess all the money-saving habits—all the skills I learned for making do or doing without—are deeply ingrained in me, and I'm frugal by nature anyway. It wouldn't make me happy to spend money on things that weren't important to me just because the money was there to spend. I like the security of having my house and land paid for, of living comfortably beneath my means, and the freedom to do work I like and build my business in a way that makes me happy rather than the way that's going to generate the most income in the shortest amount of time."

"Do you even have to work at all?"

"Not really. But I'll do it anyway. Work is healthy. And it's good to have marketable skills, and more than one revenue stream, because things happen. Stock markets crash. Economies tank. It's smart to be prepared."

He gave that low, throaty chuckle again.

"What is it?" she asked.

"Just that you're a remarkable woman."

He made it sound like a statement of fact rather than flattery—which was more flattering than flattery would have been.

"How did your father die?" he asked.

"Massive stroke. I went in one morning to give him his coffee and he was gone. No hospital, no medical bills. He'd have liked that. He was eighty-one."

"That's only two years younger than my granddad. It was a massive stroke with him, too. He kept working 'til the day he died."

"Your parents must have been young when you were born."

"They were. So were my grandparents. It's good to have your kids right away when you have a family business like a ranch. Get them trained up to work alongside you, when you're still young and energetic enough to show them how."

"Is that a regret?"

"Kind of. I'm thirty-six now. By the time my dad was my age, I was thirteen."

"Well, you're not exactly a spent force," she said. "And there's something to be said for waiting, too. Young parents have more energy, and more years to spend with their kids overall, but older parents bring more wisdom and experience to the table, and are usually better off financially."

"Well, I don't feel very wise, and my finances are not what they ought to be. But I see what you mean. I might not know much, but I know enough not to fall for someone like Kyra again. And the fact that she and I never had kids together did simplify things."

"How did you and Kyra get together, anyway? I didn't talk to her for long, but…well, she didn't seem like what I would imagine would be your type."

"You're not wrong. We weren't well suited."

"So…why did you marry her?"

Dirk let out a long sigh. "For the life of me, I don't know. I guess it was just that she was beautiful and sophisticated, and made me feel admired and appreciated at a time when I wasn't sure who I was anymore. I was rougher around the edges than the men she was used to, and she liked that at first. She said she was tired of city lights and glitz, and I thought she meant it."

"She didn't?"

He shook his head. "She thought being married to a rancher was going to be a lot more glamorous than it turned out to be. She was a city girl at heart, born and raised in Dallas, and living in Austin when I met her. She liked the idea of Western things more than the reality. You're more of a real country girl than she ever was."

The words warmed her through. She knew he wouldn't say them if he didn't mean them.

"She was all about the ranch at first, the wide open spaces and the starry skies," he went on. "But after a while, she started spending more and more time with her friends in Austin. I didn't like her friends, so I stayed home. It got to where I was glad when she went away, and sorry when she came back."

Macy nodded, remembering the relief she used to feel whenever Andrew would go to one of his baseball games or out drinking with his friends.

"I don't mean to make it sound like things were perfectly awful all the time, or that she was an awful person," Dirk said. "She could be really sweet and sympathetic at times. And I could have been a better husband. But after Granddad died…" He sighed. "By then, we knew about the Masterson place being sold, and that I could kiss my plans for expansion goodbye. Kyra thought I ought to revamp the whole property. Turn it into a venue for weddings and such. Put up expensive fencing and landscaping, build some high-end horse barns, buy some horses with fancy pedigrees and prance around like the lord of a manor."

Macy had to choke back a laugh at the mental image of Dirk in jodhpurs and English boots, carrying a riding crop.

"She brought up the idea before the will went into probate—before the funeral, even. It was barely decent. I said so, and she got nasty about it, and we got into a big fight, and the upshot of the matter was that she requested that I move out."

"Wow," said Macy. That was pretty cold.

"Yeah. I planned the funeral all by my lonesome—my sister was overseas, though she did make it back home in time for the ceremony. And once we learned the contents of the will…"

"There were some surprises?" Macy guessed.

"And how. Remember Roque? My step-grandmother's grandson from New Jersey? He stopped coming to the ranch after his grandmother died, but apparently he kept in touch with Granddad over the years. Granddad left him a horse, a trailer and some cash. Two weeks after he was notified, he showed up out of the blue, in person, to claim it all. Guess he never got over his dream of being a cowboy."

"Did he take the horse back to New Jersey?"

"No, he did not. He stayed in Limestone Springs. He's become a local celebrity, swaggering around town with his chaps and spurs and New Jersey accent. I think he was hoping I'd offer him a job on the ranch, but I didn't."

Macy thought about that. In a way, hiring Roque would make sense. Dirk needed the help, and Roque seemed to like the work. But she could understand Dirk's desire to keep free from entanglements, especially with anyone he regarded as an outsider.

"So there was that," Dirk went on. "And as for the rest of the property, it turned out that Granddad had created a trust, to keep the ranch and his bank accounts from becoming community property. To protect me, in other words, from being taken to the cleaners by my wife, in the event of our marriage coming to an end."

"Oh," said Macy. "That's…good."

"Yeah, but it sure was humiliating that he saw it coming. All those years, the family was worried Granddad's second wife would make off with the family property, when I was the one who needed to be protected from myself."

Gunnar came over to Dirk, laid his muzzle on the chaise cushion and gazed up at Dirk in silent sympathy. Dirk stroked his head, then glanced at Macy and asked, "How about you? Ever been married?"

"No, but I had a narrow escape once."

"The Grade-A jerk?"

"The very same. Eventually I realized I had to get away from him, so I did."

"Bad guy, huh?"

"Not bad as in abusive, at least not physically."

It was tempting to tell him the whole sorry tale. He'd confided in her, after all, and she thought he'd understand. But she'd already shared more than she'd intended to about her father. She liked Dirk, but there were boundaries to preserve here.

"Let's just say the whole thing was an excellent object lesson in how there are worse things than being alone," she said.

And don't you forget it, she told herself.

CHAPTER THIRTEEN

THERE ARE WORSE things than being alone.

Macy's face closed off after she said those words, and she concentrated on her stew. Clearly, the exchange of confidences had come to an end, at least for now.

They finished eating. Macy carried the empty stew bowls to the kitchen and set them in the sink.

"I'll go get Taffy," she said, and headed down the hall.

She came back with the little yellow kitten snuggled against her shoulder, her expression softer now. She brought Taffy to Dirk and handed her over.

"What do you say we let Gunnar and Taffy get a closer look at each other?" Dirk asked.

"If you really think it'll be okay," said Macy.

"I really do."

He set Taffy on the sofa cushion beside him. Gunnar crept close and gave her a good sniffing, even lifting her off her feet with his muzzle at one point. She didn't hiss or fluff up.

Then he placed his huge mouth gently around the kitten's body. Macy sucked in a quick gasp of breath, but Dirk held up a hand.

"It's all right," he said. "He's not biting down. See?"

Gunnar was licking Taffy now, and doing a fine job of it. She rolled onto her back and lightly bapped at his nose.

"I think these two are going to be friends," Dirk said softly.

For the next half hour or so, the big dog and the tiny kitten played together. It was wonderful to see how gentle Gunnar was with Taffy, and how unafraid Taffy was of him. Macy and Dirk watched quietly, laughing and commenting.

At last, Taffy got up and ambled off. Gunnar started to follow her, but Macy called him back.

He lay down at Macy's feet and rested his head on his paws, tracking Taffy with his eyes. Taffy wandered around the living room awhile and came to the Christmas tree just as the power came back on. Suddenly the tree sparkled with tiny white lights. Taffy gave a startled little chirrup, then padded across the pale velvet tree skirt and started to claw her way up the trunk.

Dirk stole an anxious look at Macy. Macy shrugged. "It's not as if she can really hurt anything," she said. "She isn't big enough to knock it over."

Taffy climbed higher and higher up the trunk, then ventured out onto a branch. Her pupils were huge and dark in her little face. Gunnar was still lying down but had his head raised now and his eyes on Taffy.

"Are you ever going to decorate that tree?" Dirk asked.

"Already have," Macy said.

"No, you haven't. Those lights are built-in."

"I put the tree skirt on, didn't I?"

"Oh, come on. You don't think white lights and no ornaments is kind of cold?"

"I think it's restful."

"Hmm. I see you are of the minimalist school of thought. My family always believed that when it came to Christmas decorations, more was more. My oma had the most beautiful old glass ornaments from Germany. I wish you could see them."

"I'm sure they're gorgeous. But if I had something like that on my tree, I could hardly let Taffy climb the branches."

"Good point. So what kind of Christmas trees did you have growing up? Real or artificial?"

"We had an ancient artificial that shed its razor-sharp needles all over the floor and pricked my hands whenever I put it up or took it down or hung ornaments on it. The holes in the trunk that the branches fit into eventually got so worn that the branches couldn't stand up at an angle anymore. They just stuck out perpendicular to the trunk. Then they started dropping off altogether. My dad wouldn't hear of getting a new one, so I had to jam stuff into the holes to try to tighten them up. It didn't work very well. I'd be sitting in the living room and a branch would suddenly drop off the tree, dragging the lights down and upsetting all the ornaments. We'd have been better off without *any* tree, but Dad wouldn't hear of that either."

"That's too bad," Dirk said.

Macy shrugged. "I had a nice stocking, anyway. My mom made it. It had these little appliquéd mice with a bag full of presents and a little textured Christmas tree made of chenille sticks. I used to pretend that the tree on the stocking was my real Christmas tree."

"It sounds like you escaped through imagination a lot."

"I did. That and books. How about you? Were your childhood trees real or artificial?"

"Oh, we always had real trees. We have lots of mountain cedars on the ranch, and every year Granddad and I would go out and find one the right size, cut it down and haul it back. But there was one big tree that we never cut down, in the pasture in front of the house. Dad and Granddad strung lights on it. I could see it from my bedroom window at night when I'd sleep over at the ranch. Whenever the wind blew, it looked like the lights were twinkling."

"Is it still there?"

"Yeah, but the lights are gone. They quit working years ago, and I think they eventually fell off. Granddad didn't bother replacing them when it was just him in the house. It's a shame. Plugging in those lights used to be my job when I was a kid. I'd run outside and do it, right after I finished setting up the Nativity set."

"I loved setting up our Nativity set! My mother had a lovely old crèche with porcelain figurines. We always put the wise men in a different part of the house, away from the manger, because they weren't actually present at the birth of Christ. They came later."

"We did the same thing! Every day we'd move them a little closer."

"So did we."

They smiled at each other. Then Dirk looked around the room. "Where is your mother's crèche now?"

Macy's smile faded. "I left it in New York."

She'd said the same thing about that sofa she'd reupholstered while listening to the audiobook of that philosopher guy.

"I'm starting to get the idea that your escape from New York was of a precipitous nature," Dirk said.

Right away he knew he'd made a mistake. He'd meant to be funny, with his eighties action movie reference, but this wasn't funny, this was her life, and he'd apparently hit closer to the mark than he'd intended. That crease between her eyebrows made another appearance, and she said, "I wouldn't call it precipitous. It was abrupt, but not without careful planning and forethought."

Dirk didn't know what to say. He felt like a clumsy, ham-handed jerk. Here they'd been having such a nice time together, reminiscing about their childhood Christmases, and he'd gone and made a joke about something in her past that was clearly painful. Should he apologize? Or would that only call more attention to something she clearly didn't want to talk about?

"You ought to get a compression bandage on that ankle," Macy said.

"Yeah, I should," said Dirk. "But unless you happen to have a spare one lying around, I guess I'm out of luck until the weather clears."

"Oh, I have one," said Macy, as if surprised that there could be any question. "I have several. I also have a suture kit, butterfly bandages, trauma shears, a burn kit, large gauze pads, nonstick bandages…"

"You have all that stuff, just lying around?"

"I have all that stuff, neatly packed and easily accessible. I'll go get an ankle bandage for you."

She went down the hall and was back within a minute with a package in one hand and a pair of scissors in the other.

Dirk chuckled. "I said it once and I'll say it again. I sure picked the right place to get snowed in."

Macy gave him a quick smile. She walked around to the front of the sofa, drew the coffee table close to the chaise, and sat down on the corner. "All right," she said. "Let's do this."

"Oh, um, okay," said Dirk. He hitched up the right leg of his jeans, suddenly uncomfortably aware of how grimy his clothes were and how ugly his bruised, misshapen ankle looked. Somehow he hadn't thought it through to this point, hadn't imagined that his beautiful neighbor was going to wrap his dirty, stinky foot with her smooth, pretty hands.

"Scoot forward," Macy said as she opened the packaging of the bandage. "Get your ankle to hang off the edge."

He did. She laid the end of the bandage over the top of his ankle.

A shiver ran through him. He couldn't help it. Her touch was whisper soft, but the ankle was tender, and his senses felt all dialed up, somehow.

She met his eyes. "Did I hurt you?"

"No," he said. "Just tickles a little."

She made two passes around the ankle, not very tight, before crossing down over the instep to the arch. A long lock of honey-blond hair came free and fell over her shoulder, almost all the way to Dirk's ankle. He watched, mesmerized. His nerve endings were screaming in a confused mixture of pleasure and pain.

Back and forth she went, making the figure eight formation, until the ankle and foot were securely wrapped.

She raised her head, flipping the stray lock of hair back. "How does it feel? Tight enough? Too tight?"

"Feels good," Dirk managed to say.

She clipped off the end of the bandage and secured it with the hook-and-loop closure.

"Thank you," said Dirk. "You did that very expertly."

"I've never actually done it before," Macy replied. "But I've read about it. It's the kind of thing that you want to already know how to do before you need to do it."

"I think you may be the most prepared person I've ever known," he said.

She smiled. "Considering the kind of people you probably know, that's quite a compliment. How's your head?"

"It's all right. Headache's better than it was."

She got to her feet. "You're probably tired, after the day you've had. Do you think you could sleep for a while? An afternoon nap would probably do you a lot of good."

Dirk could recognize a hint when one hit him upside the head.

"That's a good idea," he said. "I didn't sleep great last night. And speaking of the… sleeping situation… I guess I'll just camp out here, on the sofa? I'll be able to add wood to the fire whenever it gets low."

"Sounds good. I'll go get some bedding."

She went back down the hall and came back with an armload of blankets and patchwork quilts.

"Did you make these?" he asked, running his hand over one intricately pieced quilt crowded with hundreds of tiny, even stitches.

"I did."

"Is there anything you aren't good at?"

She appeared to take the question seriously, following it with the thoughtful silence that Dirk was coming to recognize as her usual response to a question before giving a measured, reasoned answer.

"Sports," she said. "The kind you do with other people, especially if it involves catching and throwing things. Small talk, as aforesaid. Human interaction in general."

"I suspect you're better at that than you think," said Dirk.

She smiled briefly. "Thanks."

She added a log to the woodstove. "It should be good for a while," she said. "I'll take Gunnar to my room and leave the door to Taffy's room open so she can get to her litter box. If you need anything, just call. I won't be far."

"Okay."

After she'd gone, he stared into the dancing flames behind the woodstove's glass doors, thinking. In a way, Macy had lived a very narrow life, hemmed in by that controlling father of hers. But she seemed to have a much broader range of experience, because she'd read so much, and thought about things.

His eyes scanned the room restlessly. His body was tired, but his mind was too full for sleep.

The green tub beside the stove held big and midsize logs and a few kindling pieces. One stick had a knot in one end that reminded him of a horse head.

Hmm.

Moving carefully, he eased himself to the end of the chaise and picked up the piece of wood. He studied it awhile, turning it over and over in his hands. Yes, there was the horse's head, and the curve of his neck. Here were his haunches, his legs, his tail.

Dirk had never considered himself artistic,

but he was good with his hands, and he'd been around animals all his life. His dad had taught him to carve wood as a kid, when he'd been laid up with a bad cold. He'd gotten pretty good at it by the time he'd recovered. It was one of the few memories he had of his father really spending time with him.

Maybe there was something Dirk could do to give back a little to this woman who'd had such a rough time in life and come through it with such a fine and generous character.

He took his knife out of his pocket and started to carve.

CHAPTER FOURTEEN

IT WAS AN entirely new experience for Macy, coming out of her bedroom in the morning and seeing Dirk in her living room, folding up the quilts and afghans he'd slept under, and stacking them neatly at the end of the chaise.

He met Macy's eyes across the room. "Morning," he said.

"Good morning," she replied. "Did you sleep well?"

"Like a log."

The fire was burning brightly in the stove, and the room felt warm but not too warm. Taffy was perched on top of the sofa's back, licking herself. Gunnar went straight over and put his muzzle up by her, and she touched her nose to his.

Dirk chuckled. "Little Bit, there, stayed cuddled up under my neck all night long."

"Aw, that's sweet. I'll make us some coffee."

"And I'll fry us some bacon...if that's okay."

"Sure, I'd love some bacon."

It was another entirely new experience to share space with Dirk in the kitchen. She kept stealing glances at him as he stood at the stove, carefully turning bacon with tongs. His back was to her, but she still felt shy about checking him out. He was wearing yesterday's waffle-weave undershirt with plaid flannel pajama pants. His short blond hair made the back of his neck look strangely vulnerable.

"How's your head today?" Macy asked.

"Much better, thanks. My memory seems to be back in order, too. See? I didn't need an MRI. I was right."

"You were lucky," said Macy.

Dirk made a scoffing sound. "Luck had nothing to do with it. I've got a hard head and an iron constitution."

They ate breakfast side by side at the kitchen island. Macy usually had a book in front of her while eating; she felt a little lost without one. And she couldn't remember the last time she'd eaten a meal with another person.

But the meal was over too quickly for things to get awkward. Clearly Dirk was accustomed to making quick work of breakfast.

Since Gunnar wouldn't go potty while on the leash, Macy had decided to let him out unleashed, and then bring him in right after.

She'd told Dirk last night before bedtime, and he'd agreed that this was the best thing to do until she had a fenced yard.

Once the dog, cat and peacock were all fed, Dirk and Macy climbed into the four-wheeler and headed to the ranch.

More snow had fallen in the night, clean and pristine once they got past the small area Gunnar had tramped around in. They crossed the smooth whiteness to the tree line, forded the creek and emerged on the Hager property.

It felt good to lay her head against his back and breathe in the scent of his jacket and feel its texture against her skin. The ride was fairly rough, with the four-wheeler following every little ridge and dip. She had to hold on tight and keep close to him; otherwise she could come unseated.

Dirk drove to the lean-to and parked the four-wheeler beside the tractor. Macy let go and climbed off. Then Dirk hobbled over to the truck and backed it up to the barn.

"We'll load the feed sacks into the bed of the truck," he said as he opened the barn door. "Then I'll climb back there and we'll head out to the pasture. You'll drive and I'll pour."

The feed sacks were heavy, and awkward to carry, and there were a lot of them to load.

Even with a hurt ankle, Dirk worked fast, hefting bags onto one shoulder with ease. Macy tried to keep up. She kept expecting him to say they'd loaded enough, but they kept going until the truck bed was full.

"We're pouring out *all* of that?" she asked.

"I am. You just have to drive. Keep it real slow, about fifteen miles per hour. Go on out past that big live oak tree and then head straight for the windmill. There's a good road bed underneath the snow, and it's a straight shot from the live oak to the windmill, so if you head that way you won't go wrong. Once you reach the windmill, park the truck so we can break ice on the water."

He tucked his cane into the corner of the truck bed, then hobbled over to the tailgate, holding on to the edge to support himself, and hefted himself up and onto the mound of feed bags. Macy shut the tailgate for him and got into the cab. With the back window opened so they could communicate as needed, she started the truck and drove into the pasture.

When she reached the live oak tree, Dirk called through the opening, "Honk the horn so they'll know to come."

She let out a blast on the horn.

It was quite an experience to see the herd

of black cows and calves come running over the horizon in a huge mass, with snow flying behind them. For a second Macy thought they would run into the truck, but they stopped just shy of it and dropped their muzzles into the snow for the feed that Dirk was pouring over the side of the bed. Up ahead, more cows were forming a row, waiting their turn.

On and on they went. Macy was staggered by the sheer number of animals, and the size of the property. From what Dirk had said, she'd surmised that the Hager Ranch wasn't all that big, but it sure seemed big to her.

She parked the truck in front of the windmill. Dirk got out of the bed of the truck with his cane, opened the passenger door and took a sledgehammer out of the cab. Macy followed him to the big circular concrete water tank.

The top layer was frozen solid. Dirk slammed the sledgehammer into it, breaking it into chunks. He started picking up chunks and tossing them away. Macy did, too.

"All right," Dirk said once all the big chunks had been removed. "Turn around and head back to the live oak tree. Then we'll go through the gate into the other pasture and do it all again."

"We're not finished?" Macy asked.

"Nope. We've got a whole other herd to feed."

The gate was held shut by a looped chain. Macy parked the truck and got out to open it.

"I'll get it," Dirk said.

"No, I will. It'll take you too long to get in and out of the truck."

She drove through, parked again and closed the gate behind them. As she walked back to the truck, Dirk said, "The pasture road on this side runs right alongside the barn, and the fence for the home pasture after that. We're not going inside the home pasture today. Follow the fence to the corner, then turn right. You'll see the windmill for the other water tank up ahead. Just head straight for it like you did before and park so we can break ice again."

Once she'd turned the corner of the home pasture, Macy could see another fence, about half a mile to her left, roughly parallel to the pasture road. That must mark the end of Dirk's property.

While they were tossing ice chunks out of the second water tank, Macy saw another truck across that fence heading their way. It drove all the way up and parked in front of a gate.

"Is that Alex Reyes in that other truck?" Macy asked. She knew Alex's ranch was around here somewhere.

"Yeah," Dirk said without looking up.

"It looks like he's waiting for you."

Dirk hurled one last ice chunk. "He is. We'll go over and say hello."

By now he'd poured out all the feed, so he rode in the passenger seat while Macy drove to the gate. On the other side of the fence, Alex's cows were slowly dispersing from the long row they'd stood in to eat. They looked different from Dirk's—lighter in color, with humps on their backs.

By the time she'd parked the truck, Alex was standing at the fence, grinning. Several yards back, his helper was still breaking ice at their water tank.

"I see you got yourself a hired hand there today, Dirk," Alex called as Dirk was getting out of the truck.

"Something like that," said Dirk. He eased himself out of the cab and started making his way over with his cane.

"Whoa, you got a bum leg?" Alex asked. "What happened to you?"

"Had a little accident yesterday," Dirk said gruffly. "Macy, here, is helping me feed cattle until my busted ankle gets better."

"Why, that's very neighborly of you, Macy," Alex said. He sounded pleased, almost smug.

"Well, it was my fault he got hurt, so it's the least I can do," said Macy.

"Ooh, that sounds like a good story," said Alex.

"It is, but it's way too long to get into on a cold day," said Dirk.

"All right, I can wait. Hey, what ever happened with your pipes at the house? I never heard back from you yesterday."

"Oh, yeah, well…" Dirk trailed off. "That's another long story. I'll fill you in later. Everything all right with you folks?"

"We're hanging in there. Have you checked in with Miss Ida?"

"I did yesterday. Told her to stop being chintzy with the firewood. I can go over again today on the four-wheeler."

"Nah, you've got enough going on with your hurt leg. The Henrys said they'd be looking in on her, too. I'll text Matt Henry and make sure."

"Sounds good," said Dirk. "Well, we'd better get back."

"Okay," said Alex. "I guess we'll see you two tomorrow."

"Yeah, see you," said Dirk.

As Macy was turning the truck around, she said, "I sensed an undertone of something back there, with Alex. Is it anything I should be aware of?"

Dirk stared straight ahead. "Alex has this idea that I've been alone too long, and he thinks that you and I...well, he dropped some hints yesterday. I didn't want to encourage him in any matchmaking schemes he might be putting together."

"Oh." Macy didn't know what to say. Alex had dropped hints about her and Dirk yesterday? After their unfriendly encounter the night before? What could have given him such an idea?

Dirk darted an anxious glance at her. "I didn't mean...it's not that I don't find you... you know, attractive. It's just...well, we're both of us alone by choice. And I know it's weird, me staying at your place and all. I didn't want to make things awkward."

"All right," said Macy, but it sounded to her like things were already awkward. Time to talk about something else.

"So, how many cows do you actually have?" she asked.

"Right now, eighty-four. And two bulls."

"And you have to feed them all every day?"

"Not every day. Depends on the time of year and how much grass is available. But they certainly need to eat every day, and be doctored when they're sick or hurt, and kept from getting parasites and such."

"So everything we did today, you did yesterday, by yourself?"

"Yep. Pouring and driving at the same time."

"That sounds like way too much work for one man to do all by himself."

"Oh, it is. Unfortunately, good help is hard to find and harder to keep."

"Why is that?"

He shrugged. "Part of it has to do with the type of guy who's willing to do this sort of work to begin with. You may find this hard to believe, but cowboying tends not to attract the steadiest of men. A lot of them are rodeo guys, and they take off to ride the circuit. Sometimes they get in trouble, fighting or public intoxication or drunk driving or like that. Sometimes they get hurt. And if they're good, reliable, hardworking guys, sometimes they buy places of their own."

"Has it always been that way?"

"I don't think so. Seems like when I was a kid, there were a lot more cowboys around. Granddad used to have a hired man on the place, and bring in extras when he needed to.

I used to ride with them sometimes. But those days are long gone. Even back when I was a kid, it was nothing like in *The Virginian*, with a whole bunkhouse full of men and a foreman and all that. I don't know why. I don't know where all the cowboys have gone."

The words had a forlorn sound.

"Did you actually live on the ranch as a kid?" Macy asked.

"Not officially, but I had a room that was mine, and I stayed there more than half the time, at least after my mother died. My dad was a state trooper, and I guess you could say he threw himself into his work after he lost her. He always said he'd go back to ranching full-time one day, after retirement, but he didn't make it that far. He was killed in a line-of-duty shooting while I was in Iraq. I couldn't get bereavement leave—not unusual for soldiers with overseas deployments. He was buried while I was away."

"That's awful," Macy said. "It must have added to the sense of disorientation when you did come home."

"Yeah, it did. And it wasn't the only thing that changed. By that time, Granddad's Yankee wife had died. She wasn't my favorite person, but she was good to him, and losing her really took the stuffing out of him. It used to seem to me like he'd been about fifty years old my whole life, and I guess I thought he'd stay that way forever, but when I got home, he suddenly looked like an old man."

Macy slowed to a stop at the gate. Before she could put the truck in Park, Dirk had hustled out the passenger door and started hobbling over to open it. She drove through, and he shut it behind her and got back in the truck.

"I thought you might be ex-military," Macy said. "You have that way about you."

His gaze focused on her again. "Oh? What way is that?"

There was a soft challenge in the question, and a hint of a smile in the usually grim mouth.

"Well," she said, "you have a very upright posture. You're attentive to your surroundings and direct in your communication. And there's something very...commanding...in your overall presence, so I'm guessing you were an officer, but you don't have that management vibe, so probably noncommissioned."

He let out a short bark of laughter. "Staff sergeant," he said. "Good eye. You have ties to the military?"

"My uncle was in the Army, the one who

lived upstate. I heard a lot of stories. Do you miss it?"

"Parts of it. I miss some of the guys I served with, the camaraderie, the routine. I don't miss having to take orders from captains who were all theory and didn't have the slightest idea how things were actually done in the field, or being lectured by some wet-behind-the-ears lieutenant on a subject I knew ten times more about than he did. They weren't all like that, of course. I served with plenty of commissioned officers I liked and respected—the ones who led from behind. But I never knew what I was going to get. Here, on the ranch, I'm my own boss. I stand or fall by my own efforts."

"I understand," said Macy. "I work better alone, too. It would be one thing to have a partner you could really trust. But if you take a chance and it doesn't work out, then there you are, stuck."

"Exactly."

"How many years did you serve?"

"Eight. I joined right out of high school, partly to get away from the drama at home. Got out when I was twenty-six."

"Was that when you met Kyra?"

"Yeah, at the wedding of an Army buddy. I

was dressier than usual that day—had on my suit with my good boots and cowboy hat—and I guess I gave a false impression."

An image burst into Macy's mind of Dirk in a well-cut suit, maybe charcoal gray, with polished black boots and a cowboy hat low on his forehead. No wonder he'd caught Kyra's eye. He certainly would have caught hers.

DIRK PUT A fresh log on the fire and settled it into place with the poker. His ankle was aching after a morning spent on his feet. It was going to feel good to have his boots off and his feet up again.

Getting that right boot off, though, wasn't going to be fun at all.

He sat down on the chaise, fitted his right heel into the notch on the bootjack, steeled himself and pulled.

His ligaments were on fire, screaming in protest. He gritted his teeth and kept pulling.

Finally his foot came free. His ankle felt ready to burst with angry throbbing. He sat there a few seconds, catching his breath and waiting for his stomach to settle.

Macy was watching him, her face tight with sympathy, as if she'd felt it all with him.

He lifted his right leg onto the chaise and

held his arm out to her. "Help me with the other one?"

She sat in front of him on the chaise cushion. He scooted forward, nestling against her back, like yesterday, inhaling the floral scent of her thick honey-colored hair.

He put his hand on her shoulder as she set her right foot on the bootjack. Her leg was stretched out full-length alongside of his. She'd shed her outerwear layers to reveal a cowl-neck sweater and skinny jeans. Her jeans were darker than his and less weathered looking.

He rested his left heel in the notch and drew out his foot.

"That was a whole lot more fun than the other one," he said.

He'd said pretty much the same thing the day before, but it was true. It felt good, having her so near him, almost cradled in his arms, the curve of her cheek inches from his mouth. Almost worth the pain of a sprained ankle.

She didn't move or speak, just sat there, her back to his chest, her hair tickling his face.

"Thanks for your help feeding cattle today," he said. "You did good."

"You're welcome," Macy said without turning around. "I had a good time."

Her voice was low and soft. He rubbed his thumb along the soft fluff of her sweater. She sat there for one lovely, frozen moment before getting to her feet. She stood there, as if not sure where to go, then picked up a cushion.

"Here, let's get your ankle elevated."

He scooted back in the chaise and raised his foot. She plumped the cushion and set it carefully under his ankle.

"How's that?" she asked.

"Good," he said.

That was an understatement. It felt wonderful to be taken care of. Luxurious.

"It's supposed to get colder tonight and tomorrow," she said.

"Yeah, I saw that," he replied. "Tomorrow's Christmas Eve."

"Oh, yeah, that's right. I'd better hang Gunnar's stocking."

She went to the work room and opened a drawer. Gunnar ambled after her. She took out a red-and-white-striped stocking and held it out for Gunnar.

"See, buddy? This is for you."

Gunnar gave it a polite sniff.

Macy took the stocking to the bookcase and secured it to a high shelf by pulling a heavy book over the tab. Gunnar's name was stitched across the white cuff in some sort of yarn or thick thread.

"You made that?" Dirk asked.

"Yes, back in July. I was living in San Antonio at the time, buying the land and finalizing plans for the house. It was so hot and dry, and I was longing for cold weather. So I turned my thermostat way down, put on a sweater, made hot chocolate, played Christmas music and dug up some scrap fabric for Gunnar's stocking."

"You had yourself a little Christmas in July celebration," said Dirk.

"Yes, I did. And there was no one to complain or mock me for it—no one there at all except Gunnar, who thinks everything I do is brilliant."

"Did you make a stocking for yourself?"

"No. Why would I? It's not like Gunnar's going to put anything in it."

"Well, you've got me to reckon with now, so I suggest you make yourself a stocking. If you don't, I'll have to hang up one of my own socks for you, and I might not be too particular about it being a clean one."

"What are you going to do? Drive to town for some last-minute Christmas shopping?"

"You don't know what I'm capable of. I'm a resourceful man."

She chuckled. "Okay. I'll have to hand sew it, though, because I don't have my machine."

"A clever, capable woman like you? I'm sure you'll manage."

She opened a drawer and started looking through pieces of fabric. "Thank you for not saying *crafty*," she said. "I can't stand it when people say, *Oh, you're so crafty*, or, *I wish I were crafty like you are.* It always makes me envision myself looking slyly out of the corner of my eye while rubbing my hands together over a basket of yarn and sewing supplies."

She brought some of the fabrics to the living room, along with a sewing basket, and sat cross-legged on the sofa. Her head tilted as she spread out the fabrics.

She darted a glance at Dirk. "There's a movie I've been planning to watch on Christmas Day. It's really a BBC television series— it's five and a half hours long. With the power outages lasting as long as they have, I think we should get started on it today—assuming the power comes back on at some point."

"I'm game," said Dirk. "What's it called?"

"Pride and Prejudice."

"Ooh, Jane Austen."

She blinked. "You've read it? Or seen it?"

"No and no. But my little sister has, and

she's got good taste. Which reminds me, I need to get those pictures of the Masterson Place edited and send them to her."

They worked in companionable silence. Macy chose a fabric—a sedate print in cream and gray and white—and cut out a front and back for her stocking. Dirk had just finished sending the last batch of photos when the lights came on in the living room and the appliances in the kitchen clicked and whirred their way back to life.

It didn't take long for Dirk to get sucked into the movie. It didn't feel like a stuffy period piece; everyone was constantly moving around, saying and doing interesting or funny or outrageous things. There were horses and dogs and coaches. He was truly sorry when the screen went dead about half an hour in.

"I'll make us some lunch while the power's off," Macy said.

"I'll put a log on the fire," said Dirk.

They quickly fell into a rhythm. While the power was off, they handled chores and took bathroom breaks, and Macy cooked things on the propane stove for them to eat. When the power came back on, they plugged in their phones to charge, and Macy heated water in the electric kettle for coffee or tea. Then they settled in on the sofa and started the movie again.

Taffy alternated between climbing the Christmas tree and scaling the books in the bottom shelves, toppling them and falling over into the space behind them. Gunnar watched her from his ottoman, or ambled over to sniff her. Sometimes he gave her a thorough licking, making her fur stand up in yellow spikes.

While the movie played, Macy stitched her stocking, whipping around the edges with thick thread. Once it was finished, she made another from blue-and-green plaid, with *Dirk* stitched along the cuff.

"Who's going Christmas shopping now?" Dirk asked.

"Maybe you'll get a lump of coal," Macy replied.

By the time the sun went down, she'd completed all the stockings, including a tiny knitted one for Taffy.

"That was fast," Dirk said as she spread the stockings out on the coffee table. "I like how you free-handed those letters. That is so *crafty* of you."

She scowled and smiled at the same time, got to her feet and stretched. "Come on, Gunnar. Let's go for a walk before it gets really dark."

Gunnar skipped and pranced around while Macy got her boots and coat on, then sat to get his leash clipped on. "I'll walk him first and get him all tired out before letting him off the leash to potty," she said. "See you in a bit."

After she'd gone, Dirk hobbled over to the firewood tub and selected a stick. He'd been studying this one for a while from across the room and planning what he was going to do with it. Now he'd have to work fast. He sat down on Gunnar's ottoman, took his knife out of his pocket and went right to it, cutting quickly and confidently through the seasoned wood. The room was growing dark, but there was light enough close to the glass doors of the stove, and when he saw Macy and Gunnar coming back from their walk, he had just finished one figure and roughed in another. He shut his knife and pocketed it, then swept the wood shavings into his hand and dropped them into the woodstove. By the time Macy opened the French door, he was back in his spot on the chaise, with today's carved figures safely hidden inside his duffel bag, along with the one from last night.

"Have a nice walk?" he asked.

"Lovely," she said. "How about baked potatoes with chili for dinner?"

"Sounds good to me."

She toweled Gunnar off in the work room, took off her coat and boots and put them away, along with Gunnar's leash. By then Gunnar was back in the living room, busy with his new cat-watching hobby, and Taffy was climbing the Christmas tree again.

The power wasn't back on yet, but the room was warm. Dirk went over to the stove, stirred things up with the poker and added another log. Then he hobbled over to the kitchen, where Macy was rinsing potatoes at the sink.

"Can I do anything to help?" he asked.

"Well, I could use some light. There are some candles in that farthest kitchen drawer, right next to the garage door. Would you take a few of them out and light them? You'd better take one to the hall bathroom, too, since there's no window in there."

The lit candles made the house look like a romantic dinner was in the works. Dirk spread them around to where he thought they'd do the most good, placing them high enough that Taffy wouldn't be able to reach them, then sat at the kitchen island to watch Macy work.

She was pricking the potatoes with a fork now. She met his eyes across the island. The crease appeared between her eyebrows again as her gaze traveled down his chest.

Dirk looked down at himself. "What is it? Do I have something on me?"

"It's your shirt," Macy said. "It has a three-cornered tear. I can mend it for you."

"Oh, you don't have to do that," he said.

"It's no trouble. Also, I noticed your jeans from yesterday are a little worse for wear after your trip down the creek bank. Bring them and the shirt to the coffee table, and I'll work on them during our next *Pride and Prejudice* session."

"Those jeans are dirty. Shouldn't I wash them first?"

"No, that'll make the rips fray. Better to mend them first. We can do a load of laundry before you go back home, though. Help tide you over until you get your plumbing fixed."

The thought of going back home wasn't a pleasant one. Even without the busted pipes and the hole in his roof, home would feel cheerless and cold after Macy's neat, clean, comfortable house.

"I'll take my shower now and get dressed for bed," said Dirk. "Then I'll set the jeans and the shirt on the coffee table for you."

"Okay. These potatoes are small enough

to cook fast, so we'll be ready to eat pretty soon."

It was pleasant, talking with her this way, making their little household plans together, helping each other. If it had been Kyra that he'd been snowbound with...

He shuddered.

"What's wrong?" Macy asked.

"Just thinking it'd be a good idea for people to get snowbound together, with limited resources and at least one injury to deal with, before they get married. I don't mean you and me," he added quickly.

She held up a hand. "No need to explain. I understand completely, and I agree."

CHAPTER FIFTEEN

CHRISTMAS EVE DAWNED with a blast of fresh ice and howling winds. The power had been off all night, and stayed off for most of the morning. Macy had to heat water for coffee on the propane stove.

She watched from the kitchen as Dirk stirred up the coals in the woodstove and added kindling. He had grown very proprietary about that stove. It was cute. He was doing a good job with it, too. He was a great houseguest, quick to spot what needed to be done and do it.

And that wasn't all she liked about him. Dirk was smart. A man of action, and not one to spend much time pondering abstractions, but not because he wasn't capable of it. He could hold his own in conversation and challenge her with fresh perspectives.

Macy checked the weather on her phone, hoping to see that the wind would die down in the next half hour or so, but no such luck.

"I guess we'd better get going right after

breakfast," she said. "The wind and sleet are only supposed to get worse, and the temperature isn't expected to rise all day."

"You don't have to come today," he replied. "My ankle's a lot better this morning. I can handle the feeding by myself."

She placed the lid on the French press and set the egg timer for five minutes. "Nice try. I saw your ankle last night. You're in no condition to do all that work alone."

"I can still drive the truck with my left ankle."

"And load it? And open the gates? And break ice? Stop arguing. You're not going alone and that's final."

He scowled, then smiled. "Thank you. I know it's rough, going out in all this—especially to feed cattle that aren't even yours. I appreciate it."

"You're welcome. But seriously, I've dealt with a lot worse, weather-wise, every winter of my life. I can take it."

The ride to the ranch in the ATV left them both covered with sleet. It was a relief to get under cover in the feed barn for loading, and then into the cab of the truck, but Macy felt sorry for Dirk, exposed to the cutting wind and stinging ice in the truck bed. They didn't stop to talk with Alex today, but went straight home after breaking the ice in the second water tank.

"Boy, I am chilled to the bone," Dirk said as he took off his coat. "I'll build up the fire, and then I think some hot showers are in order. I'm sure glad you're on city water and have a propane water heater."

"So am I," said Macy.

The LED displays on the kitchen appliances were blank. If the power had come on since they'd left, it had gone off again.

Macy started the hot water running in her shower and stripped off her wet, cold, clinging clothes, shivering in the chilly room. It was an exquisite luxury to step into the clouds of steam and let the pounding water warm her through.

She dressed in snug layers—fleecy snowflake-print pajama pants over leggings, a thick hoodie over two long-sleeved T-shirts and long fur-lined socks. This was her home, and she wanted to be comfortable for as long as she could until she had to go back out into the cold. And it wasn't as if she needed to dress to impress her houseguest.

Apparently Dirk had had the same idea. He'd put on flannel pajama pants and one of his waffle-weave shirts with a T-shirt showing at the collar.

The power stayed out for most of the afternoon. Dirk and Macy ate their lunch, drank coffee and read their books. Macy made popcorn with her old-fashioned stovetop popper, and they ate it by handfuls out of one big bowl, occasionally tossing a piece to Gunnar, who caught it in midair. Taffy gnawed hers and batted it around on the floor.

When the power finally came back on, Dirk jumped up as if he'd personally received a fresh boost of electricity. "Where's the remote?" he asked. "Hurry up. Let's start the movie!"

Watching Dirk watch *Pride and Prejudice* was almost as much fun as watching the movie itself. He'd gotten deeply invested in the story right away and was visibly stressed every time Mrs. Bennet, Mr. Collins or Miss Bingley appeared. Macy kept stealing glances at him, staring wide-eyed at the screen, slowly putting popcorn in his mouth. The tough cowboy had clearly become a Jane Austen fan.

She was looking forward to seeing his reaction to the proposal scene. But no sooner had Darcy said how ardently he admired and loved Elizabeth than the screen went black.

"What?" said Dirk. "Noooooo! That ain't right! That couldn't have been more than twenty minutes, and after we went without power all day long!"

Macy was disappointed, too, but she at least had seen the movie ten or twelve times already. "It's too bad, but there's nothing we can do about it," she said.

She went back to her book, but Dirk couldn't settle down to his. For a while, he entertained Taffy with her stick-and-wadded-paper toy. Finally he set the toy down and said, "Didn't you say you had a wing chair that you needed to do some demo work on? How's about if we bring it out and I get started on that for you? I'm tired of reading. I need to do something real."

"Fine with me," Macy said.

She dragged the chair out of its room by herself—it wasn't heavy, and Dirk would have been in the way with his cane. Then she set a chair in front of it for him and gave him the special staple-removing tool, along with a pair of pliers for stubborn prongs.

"Start here, with the dustcover on the underside," she said. "Then move on to the back, then the sides. Basically, you take pieces off in reverse order from how they were put on. You'll be able to figure it out."

He went right to work, pulling out staples and tack strips. Macy was growing tired of reading, too. She'd already mended Dirk's shirt and jeans, and made a little stuffed felt mouse to put in Taffy's stocking. Now she found herself mindlessly browsing on her phone, looking up things like *Texas snowstorm power outages*.

"Huh," she said after a while. "Did you know that Texas has its very own power grid?"

"That's right," Dirk said without turning around. "We didn't want to be subject to federal and interstate regulations, so we decided to opt out and go it on our own. Other states wanted to do the same thing, but we were the only one with the size to pull it off."

"Well, it doesn't seem to be doing a very good job," said Macy.

Dirk made an indignant sound.

"Don't get testy," Macy said. "I'm not picking on your state, just making an observation. The grid isn't keeping up with demands."

"That's because it was never meant to support half the state of California."

"What do you mean? Are you talking about the energy that gets exported?"

"Partly, but mainly I'm talking about all the Californians who've moved here. We're leading the nation in raw population growth, and over the last decade we've resettled more refugees than any other state. So the grid was strained to begin with, before we got this hundred-year storm."

"It sounds like the grid ought to be expanded, then."

Dirk grumbled something she couldn't make out.

"Well, it's true," she said. "I know you don't want newcomers overrunning your state, but like it or not, we're here, and there's nothing you can do to change that. Griping won't help. You've got to deal with reality."

He ripped the back panel off the chair. "I know. I just don't like change, especially with something I love. With everything that's gained, there's something lost."

Macy thought about that. "It doesn't have to be a zero-sum game," she said. "Who knows? Maybe some good will come of all the change."

He turned around. "It already did, when I met you."

She felt her face heating up. "That got you hurt, though," she said.

"It was worth it. Being here with you now, it's the happiest I've been in a long time."

THE AFTERNOON WORE ON. It felt to Dirk as if the day would never end. The semidarkness in the room had a weird quality to it, between the blue-white glow from the snow outside and the flickering gold of firelight and candle flames. The wind howled, scouring the outside of the house with sleet, like coarse-grit sandpaper. Dirk wondered what kind of damage that wind and sleet were doing inside his own house, with no roof overhead to protect it.

It seemed like yesterday and the day before had just been warm-ups for today. He felt raw inside, worn out from the worry, and the sound of the wind and the darkness.

"The WiFi's getting glitchy," Macy said. "I wouldn't be surprised if we lost it altogether soon."

Dirk laid down his upholstery tools and picked up his phone. "I'd better go ahead and send a merry Christmas text to my sister. It's already Christmas where she is anyhow."

He typed his message and hit Send. It didn't go through. He tried again. Still no luck.

"Looks like we've officially lost internet," he said. "We're having ourselves a regular snowpocalypse, aren't we?"

"Mmm-hmm," Macy said, but not before Dirk saw the crease form between her eyebrows.

"What?" said Dirk.

"What do you mean, what?" asked Macy.

"You're doing that thing again, with your face."

"What thing with my face?"

"The eyebrow thing. It means you're deep in thought about something. Half the time it's because I said something wrong and you don't want to tell me."

She shook her head. "It's not important."

"Oh, go ahead and tell me. How else will I ever learn?"

She smiled. "It's just…we're all using that word wrong."

"What word?"

"*Apocalypse.* When we say snowpocalypse or zombie apocalypse or postapocalyptic… that's wrong. We're using *apocalypse* as a synonym for disaster, and it doesn't mean that. It means revelation."

Dirk frowned. "Revelation? You sure about that?"

"I'm sure."

"Huh," Dirk said. "I guess I've been using the word wrong my whole life. You're a regular human encyclopedia, aren't you?"

Macy didn't reply, just picked up her book again and hid behind it. He could feel her irritation.

"I just said something wrong again, didn't I?" he asked.

"No."

"Yeah, I did. What was it?"

"You didn't say anything wrong. It's my problem, not yours."

"What is?"

"I don't want to talk about it."

He'd hurt her. He hadn't meant to, but he'd done it.

"That Grade-A jerk did a real number on you, didn't he?" he asked softly.

Macy lowered her book enough to peek at him over the top, then laid it on her lap. "I guess he did," she said quietly.

"Want to talk about it?"

"No."

"Oh, come on. You've heard horror stories about my ex. It's only fair that you tell me yours. The mood is right, with the darkness and the howling wind and whatnot."

He could see her thinking about it. He went to the kitchen and picked up the bottle of wine. "Come on. Let's open this and sit down by the fire, and we'll have a regular gabfest."

She turned to face him, the ghost of a smile barely curving her lips. "Why do you even have that bottle of wine?" she asked. "You look like a beer and whisky guy to me."

"You're not wrong. But a friend of mine opened a vineyard in Fredericksburg, and Kyra and I went to visit and brought back a case of this stuff. I could have left it with her, but he was my friend, and I thought it was only fair that I get custody of the wine. It's pretty good."

He opened the bottle with the corkscrew on his multitool. "Where are your wineglasses?" he asked.

"I don't have any. I don't really drink alcohol."

He took down two mugs. "Well, I'm going to have some wine. You're welcome to join me, or you can have cocoa if you'd like."

A minute later, they were seated at opposite ends of the sofa, with the wine bottle on the coffee table.

Macy took a sip. "Mmm, it's good."

"I'm glad you like it."

She had her back against the arm of the sofa, her knees pulled up to her chest and one of her bright patchwork quilts over her legs.

"My oma had a quilt like that, with those squares and triangles and things arranged just that way," Dirk said.

Macy ran her fingers over one of the blocks. "This pattern is called churn dash. It's the first quilt I ever finished. I made tops for years out of scraps from my other sewing. Had a whole stack of them in the linen closet, waiting to be put together with batting and backing. I used them as packing material when I mailed my books to myself."

He wasn't sure he'd heard right. "Mailed your books to yourself?"

She nodded. "I had to get them out of the house without making Andrew suspicious. I had so many of them, it wasn't like I could toss them all into a single box and put them in the trunk of my car. So I packed them up, little by little, box by box, and mailed them to myself, book rate, at my new address in my rental in San Antonio."

Her face turned hard. "Andrew never liked my books. He was jealous of them, like they were his rivals for my affection. But he couldn't come right out and say that, so he told me it was stupid of me to have so many, that I was wasting space and showing off and that there was no good reason for anyone to keep a book they'd already read. When he saw me boxing them up, he demanded to know what I was doing and why. I told him I was decluttering."

She smiled. "He believed me. The whole thing was deliciously ironic. All those times when he'd accused me of hiding things from him, of going behind his back, of being *up* to something—and then when I finally did have something to hide, he never suspected a thing."

She took what looked like a large swallow of wine, and her smile turned inward. "To be fair, I didn't lie. I just didn't tell him that what I was decluttering was him."

Gunnar came over to her, laid his head on the cushion where she was sitting and looked up at her with adoring golden-brown eyes, as if he sensed that she needed moral support. She stroked his face and ears, and without looking at Dirk, she said, "Andrew was… overpowering, like a force of nature. He used to make these pronouncements about what we were going to do, where we were going to go, with no discussion, like there was no way I could possibly resist him. And I couldn't, in the beginning. He was the first man who ever pursued me. It was exhilarating, to be wanted. I was on my own for the first time in my life, making my own decisions, and it seemed to me that something wonderful was happening."

She laid her head against the back cushion. "I don't mean that our whole relationship was him constantly bossing me around. He could be sweet sometimes. He seemed so compassionate about what I'd been through with my father. And he used to write me these letters every week or so and put them through the letter slot in my front door on his way to work. I thought it was the most romantic thing. Actual physical letters, written on beautiful thick creamy paper and put into envelopes with my name written in black ink with flourishes. I treasured those letters. I penciled numbers into the corners of the envelopes to keep track of their sequence, and tied them up with a silk ribbon."

A flush rose across her cheekbones—embarrassment, or wine.

"Why, Macy," Dirk said gently, "you're a romantic."

"I was an idiot," she said.

"You were young."

She shot him a hard glance. "I was twenty-nine."

He shrugged. "Young in experience."

"That's true enough. Still, I should have known better."

"Those were the letters you burned, the night we met?"

"Yes. It was so humiliating, Dirk, opening them up and reading them with fresh eyes after a year away from him. I used to think they were so beautiful with their emotional intensity, but they were just manipulative and creepy. I don't know how I ever fell for him in the first place."

"What opened your eyes?"

"It wasn't any one thing. Sometimes he was so *mean*, out of nowhere, and the next day he'd be sweet and loving again. One day I realized I was in a relationship with a self-centered, demanding, domineering man, just like my father."

Dirk had been thinking the same thing.

"I never knew what would set him off. Everything I did or said was a potential minefield. He'd get upset over some tiny thing and ascribe all sorts of evil motives to me. I was constantly thinking ahead, trying to predict whether the thing I was about to say could come back to bite me. I'd had plenty of practice keeping my thoughts to myself with my father, and it served me well when I started planning my escape from Andrew."

She emptied her mug and reached for the wine bottle.

"Yes, I know how overdramatic that sounds. Why didn't I just leave? Tell him I didn't want to see him anymore? What was stopping me? It wasn't like he was keeping me prisoner. But I felt so beaten down inside that I couldn't think straight. I knew that if I told him how I felt, he'd talk me down, and I'd end up staying. I had to make a clean break, and get away for good."

"I think you're exactly right," said Dirk. "I'm glad you realized it, and did something about it."

Her expression relaxed. "The money helped. I don't like to think how I would have managed without having any resources. There were just so many things to consider, and I couldn't take care of everything overnight. I didn't dare write anything down, or leave anything in my internet search history that he could find. I had to keep the knowledge of what I was doing to get away in a separate part of my mind, like a file folder. I couldn't afford to give anything away."

It explained a lot about her. She was a private person by nature, but experience had taught her to play things close to the vest for her own protection.

"What did you do?" he asked.

"I found a Realtor, walked into his office and explained the situation. I chose him partly because he reminded me of Denzel Washington, and that seemed like a good sign, because I wanted someone who wouldn't be easily intimidated if Andrew ever tried to hunt me down. I told him I wanted to sell my house without putting a for sale sign out front or having a lockbox on the door or doing anything that would let Andrew know I was selling it. I didn't know if that was even possible, but it was. The Realtor said he'd make it a pocket listing—tell other realtors about it privately without listing it on MLS. Showings could be held at times approved by me. The only thing was, we needed a hook, something to get buyers interested and make it worth the trouble. I wasn't desperate for money, so I set my asking price well below market value."

"I'll bet that moved things right along."

"Sure did. The very first people that looked at the house offered more than my asking price. They knew it was a good property in a good neighborhood and wouldn't last long at the price I was asking. They wanted every-thing—furniture, appliances, window treat-ments. I accepted their offer, and the house was sold without Andrew ever knowing it had been on the market."

"That worked out well. But it's too bad you had to give up all your pretty furniture that you'd fixed up."

"Yes, but it was for the best, because it made it possible for me to move fast. I loved making and fixing all those things, but the best part of them was what I took with me—the ability to do it all again."

"True. So then what'd you do?"

"Well, my Realtor got me set up with a rental in San Antonio. I knew I wanted to go to Texas and figured San Antonio was as good a place as any to start. I mailed my books to myself, wrote Andrew a farewell letter, put my engagement ring inside and stuck it through his letter slot, while he was at work. Then I loaded up my car with my sewing stuff and a suitcase full of clothes, and started driving west."

"Must have felt good," Dirk said.

"It felt fantastic. I had a full bank account and a full tank of gas, freedom ahead of me and nothing behind me that I couldn't do without."

"And Andrew never tracked you down?"

"No. I'm sure he made up some version of the story to tell his friends, where I was the villain and he was the victim, but I didn't care. I'd outsmarted him, and that was all that mattered."

Dirk had his right leg stretched out on the chaise and his left foot on the floor, but he had to keep turning his head to look at Macy. Now he shifted his hips into the corner and turned to face her, resting both legs on the long main part of the sofa.

"I'm impressed," he said. "Not just by how you outsmarted him, but by how you came through the whole thing with your character intact."

Macy made a scoffing sound. "I don't know that I did. Personally, I think my character's a little wonky."

"No. Your character is outstanding. After everything you went through with a mean, controlling father and a mean, controlling fiancé, after you'd finally made your way to the security and solitude you'd been craving all your life, you took in a man who was hurt and alone, and looked after him, because it was the right thing to do—even though he'd given you good reason to steer clear of him. I'm sorry you went through all that with Andrew. You're a smart, strong, beautiful woman, and he wasn't man enough for you. He put you down because that was the only way he could keep you, by making you feel less than. I'm glad he didn't succeed. Glad you got away. And... I'm glad you're my neighbor."

Her gaze softened. "I'm glad of that, too."

She downed the last of her wine, poured another mugful and stretched out her legs. Her toes almost reached his.

"You know what I like about you, Dirk?" she asked.

She was smiling at him, and sounding downright mellow.

Dirk swallowed hard. "No idea," he said.

"You're not charming."

"Oh! And that's...good?"

"Mmm-hmm. See, the word *charm* comes from Latin by way of Old French. It means an incantation or a magic spell. Charm enchants people, clouds their reason. You can never be sure what's behind it. But you don't have any of that. You say what you mean, even when it isn't what people want to hear. So when you say something nice, I can believe you."

She looked so soft and open and sweet, snuggled under her patchwork quilt with that pink flush spreading over her cheekbones. In an instant, all Dirk's resistance was gone. Macy had pushed through the wall he'd built around himself as if it was nothing more than tissue paper. He'd been so concerned with keeping his heart safe, and now he didn't care. She was worth the risk.

But he was pretty sure that a lot of how she was acting now was due to the wine, and maybe relief at finally telling someone about Andrew. This was a deeply private woman. She'd just confided in him a lot, and he was thankful for that. He wanted to get past the last of her reserve, but he didn't want to use alcohol to do it.

Gunnar had gone back to his ottoman. Taffy was up there with him, curled up at his side, asleep. He nuzzled her gently, and she batted her paw at him without opening her eyes.

"Look at them," Dirk said quietly.

"I know," said Macy. "I never get tired of seeing them together. It's so sweet and un-expected, a big tough dog so besotted with a little scrap of kitten."

Besotted. Dirk never would have thought

to use that word, but now that he heard it, he knew it was exactly how he felt about Macy. But he would keep that to himself until the time was right.

"I want some popcorn," Macy said. "Do you want some popcorn? Let's make some popcorn."

She hurried to the kitchen and got her old basket popcorn popper.

"Make extra," Dirk called. "We can make popcorn strands and drape them on this plain Christmas tree of yours."

The power didn't come back on for the rest of the night. Dirk kept the fire burning; Macy made popcorn and heated some more stew for their dinner. They made the popcorn strand together, one length of stout thread with a needle on each end. The near darkness didn't matter; they only had to poke the needles through the thickest parts of the popped kernels and slide them through. For some reason Macy thought the sight of Dirk doing this was hilarious—again, it was probably the wine.

The strand reached about four feet in length before Taffy noticed it and started biting the popcorn and attacking the thread. Macy tied it off then. It wasn't long enough for the tree, so she looped it up with the stockings on the bookcase shelf.

"That looks nice, doesn't it?" Macy asked.

They were standing side by side, staring up at the four stockings in all their different sizes and colors, with *Macy*, *Gunnar*, *Taffy* and *Dirk* spelled across their cuffs. When Gunnar saw them, he came over, sat down at their feet, and stared, too.

"They sure do," said Dirk. "And now we'd all better get to bed so Santy Claus can come."

This sent Macy into a fit of giggles. Dirk had never heard her giggle. He liked the sound of it.

After she'd gone to bed, Dirk threw the empty wine bottle away and went to work, selecting another seasoned stick from the kindling in the firewood tub. He was going to have to carve fast and well to get done in time, but he knew he could do it.

Somewhere around midnight, the scouring sleet gave way to snow.

CHAPTER SIXTEEN

CHRISTMAS MORNING DAWNED bright and clear. Macy opened her eyes to see a fluffy white world, tinged faintly pink by the rising sun, just outside her bedroom window. The power still hadn't come back on, and as far as she knew it hadn't come on all night, though she couldn't be sure. After all that wine, she'd slept soundly.

She shut her eyes again. She felt…not hung over, at least she didn't think this was what a hangover felt like, but definitely a little fuzzy in the head, as if she'd taken some extra strength cold medicine and then gone into a nine-hour hibernation.

Memories stole softly into her mind. Memories of Taffy, pouncing on the popcorn strand. Of Gunnar, walking over and putting his head on her lap while she'd been telling Dirk about Andrew. Mostly of Dirk himself, listening to the whole Andrew story, his hard, serious face set and intent, the eyes soft with sympathy. It had felt good, telling him all that, like releasing a tightly clenched muscle. Just looking at him felt good. As they'd sat together on her sofa, exchanging confidences within their circle of firelight, almost touching but not quite, it had felt as if they were the only two people in the world. He'd looked so strong and safe and good. She'd wanted to crawl over to his side of the sofa and rest her head against his chest.

It must have been the wine, loosening her tongue, stirring up those emotions, making her giggly. But no real harm was done. She'd just dial it back today.

She got dressed and went out to the living room, Gunnar following her. The rich, meaty aroma of bacon came to meet her, mingled with the scent of strong coffee.

Dirk stood behind the stove, already dressed in a fresh button-down and jeans, turning bacon with tongs. His bright blue eyes met hers across the stovetop.

"Merry Christmas," he said.

"Merry Christmas," she said back.

Gunnar walked into the kitchen for morning pets. Dirk bent down to him, rubbed his head and said, "And a merry Christmas to you, too, Gunnar."

It melted her heart to see this big, tough man so sweet and tender with her dog, only a few days after he'd doused her fire and warned her to put up a fence. A lot had changed in a short time.

She put Gunnar outside for his morning constitutional and went to the kitchen just as Dirk was pushing the plunger down in the French press. He sure knew his way around her kitchen.

"Do you want to do stockings before feeding cattle, or after?" he asked.

"After."

"That's what I thought, too. Then we can relax and enjoy the day. We've got Miss Ida's cookies to munch on, and if the power grid ever comes back online, we can finish *Pride and Prejudice*."

"Sounds perfect. So, listen, I think I might have had a bit too much wine last night."

He chuckled. "If that's your idea of a bender, I don't think you have much to worry about. We'll stick with cocoa today if you'd rather."

It would be next to impossible to dial things back while sitting around a Christmas tree drinking cocoa together. Maybe she shouldn't worry about it today. There'd be time enough after the holiday was over. In fact, the situation would take care of itself. Once the storm passed, he would go home, and their relationship would settle into something cordial and bland—when they saw each other at all, which probably wouldn't be that often.

THEY ATE THEIR BREAKFAST.

"I'll do the dishes," Macy said, gathering their plates.

"And I'll feed Hoss," said Dirk.

"Hoss?"

"The peacock."

As soon as the garage door shut behind him, Macy slipped his gift into his stocking. Her own stocking already had something inside it. What could it be? What could Dirk have possibly come up with as a Christmas present for her? She started to reach for it, then pulled her hand back. Honestly. She was a grown woman, not a child.

She tucked Taffy's and Gunnar's gifts into their stockings, leaving the tops sticking out a bit. The uneven loops of the popcorn strand gave them a harmonious, connected look.

Feeding cattle was a lot more fun today than it had been yesterday. The snow gleamed a brilliant white under the sun, and even the cattle seemed more cheerful.

When they reached the end of the road bed,

Alex and his helper were waiting for them on the other side of the fence—not the man he'd had with him the first day, but a woman, in a turquoise coat, purple paisley scarf and stocking cap the color of a tangerine. Alex introduced her as his wife, Lauren. She was pretty, with a heart-shaped face and big brown eyes.

"Nice to meet you, Macy," Lauren said. "I hear you're from New York. What borough did you live in?"

"Brooklyn. Crown Heights neighborhood."

"I love Crown Heights! I did some of my best urban photography there."

"Oh, are you a photographer?" Macy asked. Lauren definitely looked like an artist, with that diamond stud in her nose and the bold colors of her clothing.

Lauren chuckled. "Among other things. How about you?"

"I'm in the upholstery business."

"Oh, how fun. I did some minor upholstery work when I customized my live-in van, but I didn't really know what I was doing."

"You lived in a van?" asked Macy.

"Mmm-hmm. For six years."

"Wow, that's…"

Macy wasn't sure what adjective to use.

The idea of living in a van, no matter how customized, sounded awful to her.

Lauren laughed. "It isn't for everyone. I loved it while I was doing it, and I wouldn't trade those years for anything, but the ranch is home now, and I love it, too."

Dirk broke in on their conversation. "So what are you doing out here today, Lauren? You taking over from your cousin as Alex's hired hand?"

"No, I just thought I'd give him the morning off as a Christmas present," she said. "Besides, after three days of being snowed in, I was getting a little cabin fever. Nathaniel's back home, taking care of Peri."

"How's that busted ankle of yours?" Alex asked Dirk.

"Better," said Dirk. "Swelling's gone down a lot. I ought to be back to full speed in a few days. Once the storm lets up, I'll be calling you about clearing the pecan tree out of my living room."

"Clearing the what out of where?" asked Alex.

"Oh, didn't I tell you? One of those big pecan branches came down through my roof."

Alex looked stunned. "What? When was this?"

"Same day the pipes froze."

"That was three days ago! I can't believe you didn't tell me."

"Yeah, well, I had a lot going on, between falling down the creek bank, getting concussed and spraining my ankle."

"You were *concussed*? I thought it was just your ankle that got hurt. Sounds like you left a lot out of this story."

Dirk shrugged. "I was forgetful. I did have a brain injury, after all."

"Huh. Well, you can fill me in later. We'd better get back and open presents."

"Yeah, we need to do the same thing," said Dirk. "Merry Christmas, y'all."

"Merry Christmas," they all said.

As they were walking away from each other, Lauren called out, "Hey, Macy, we've got an old Spanish colonial trunk up at the house. The wood's in great shape, but the upholstered top really needs to be replaced. I'd love to have you do the work, if you're interested."

"Okay," Macy said. This wasn't the time to explain about her spec-only business model. Probably Lauren would never contact her about the trunk at all, and if she did—well, maybe it wouldn't hurt to do one commissioned project.

Back in the truck, Dirk chuckled. "Cabin

fever, nothing. Lauren came out here this morning because she wanted to check you out."

Macy felt her face heat up. Was this true? Were Alex and Lauren talking about Dirk and Macy right now, speculating, thinking of them as a couple?

BACK AT THE HOUSE, Gunnar met them at the door, looking eager, but less frantic than the first couple of times they'd gone to the ranch and left him alone inside. He was getting used to the new routine—only it wasn't a routine, Macy reminded herself. It was a temporary anomaly. Dirk didn't actually *live* here. Tomorrow, or the day after at the latest, he would go home.

"I'll make a second pot of coffee," she said.

"And I'll go get Taffy out of her room," said Dirk. "Then we'll be ready to do stockings."

Macy started the water boiling on the stove and spooned San Antonio Blend coffee into the French press. Dirk had told her how Miss Ida had regifted it to him after he'd checked on her, and they'd been using it ever since. It was good.

Dirk came down the hallway with Taffy in his arms, picked up the cookie tin and took it to the living room. He barely needed the cane anymore.

Just as Macy was pouring their coffee, the Christmas lights came on, shining out of the tree like tiny stars.

"Well, look at that!" said Dirk. "Just in time."

Macy hurried to charge her phone. "I'll find us some Christmas music," she said.

She opened Spotify, browsed for a bit and selected a bluegrass Christmas playlist. A fiddle and a banjo played "Joy to the World" as she carried the mugs to the coffee table.

Dirk was waiting for her over by the stockings, holding Taffy against his chest. She joined him. She suddenly felt shy, and he looked a little unsure.

"Animals first," he said.

They took down the animals' stockings and gave them their gifts. Gunnar was fascinated by his crinkle squirrel toy, and Taffy went right to work on her stuffed felt mouse, biting and clawing it with all four paws.

Dirk lifted down Macy's stocking and handed it to her. "Merry Christmas, neighbor," he said.

There was something knobbly inside her stocking, or several somethings. Macy sat down and emptied it on the sofa.

It was a set of small wooden figures, simply carved, but distinctive and beautiful. A man, a woman, a baby. A sassy-looking horse. A dog, curled up on his side with a kitten on his back. Even a peacock.

She stood them up on the coffee table and stared.

"It's a Nativity set," said Dirk. "I just thought, you know, since you didn't have one… I know some of those animals probably weren't present at the birth of Christ, but…"

"You *made* this?" she asked.

"Yeah."

"When did you even have *time*?"

He put his hands in his pockets and shrugged. "Here and there. When you took Gunnar for walks, and after you went to bed at night."

"Where did you get the wood?"

He pointed to the firewood tub. "Seasoned hardwood, just right for carving."

"It's wonderful," she said. "I love it. Thank you."

She set the figures on a high shelf, in front of a boxed set of Narnia books, where Taffy couldn't reach them and Gunnar's wagging tail couldn't knock them down.

"I had no idea you could carve," she said.

"Oh, yeah," he said. "You're not the only one who's *crafty*."

He rubbed his hands together and gave her a sidewise glance and a sly smile. She laughed. For a second she felt so good, and he looked so funny and sweet, that she almost wanted to hug him.

"Now yours," she said. She took his stocking down and handed it to him.

He reached inside and took out a book, covered in worn green cloth and embossed with gold letters.

"'*North of Boston*,'" he read aloud. "'Robert Frost.'"

His eyes met hers over the top of the book.

Now it was her turn to feel awkward. "Yeah, I didn't make your gift myself. I know you said you weren't big on poetry. But I think you'll like Frost."

"This looks old and valuable," said Dirk. He opened it up, scanned the opening pages and said, "Macy, is this a first edition?"

It was a first edition, and worth a lot of money.

"I want you to have it," she said.

He held her gaze a long moment. Then he laid the book on a shelf, stepped over to her and took her hand.

His touch felt something like an electric shock, only much more pleasant, and at the same time terrifying. Macy couldn't breathe. Those bright blue eyes were fixed on her, so grave and tender that she couldn't bear it, and yet she couldn't look away.

His gaze dropped to her lips.

Part of her was shouting, *What is happening?* But the rest of her was drawing toward him like iron filings to a magnet. She wanted to kiss him, and nothing else mattered.

His lips were unbelievably soft. A morning's worth of stubble rubbed against her chin, like fine sandpaper. She laid her hands on his chest, feeling hard muscle beneath the flannel and waffle weave.

Then his arms went around her, pulling her close. His cane clattered to the floor as his hands cupped her face.

It was a peacock scream that separated them. They both jumped, and Dirk, with his bad leg, started to topple, but Macy held on to him. For a moment it looked as if they might both fall down, but they managed to keep their balance. They clung to each other, quietly laughing.

"Maybe you'd better sit down," said Macy. She put her arm around him, like she had that first day before he'd gotten his cane, and grabbed his belt. He put his arm around her shoulders.

"What would I do without you?" he asked.

Together they made their way to the sofa. Dirk eased himself to the chaise, then gently tugged Macy down with him.

"Kiss me again," he said, and she did.

THE POWER STAYED on for most of the remainder of Christmas Day. Dirk and Macy snuggled under the quilts together, and kissed, and ate cookies, and kissed again, and finished watching *Pride and Prejudice*, and kissed some more.

He was so big and solid and safe and warm. She loved being close to him. He was a luxury, an indulgence, like the rich shortbread, spritz cookies and jam thumbprints in Miss Ida's cookie tin. She was dimly aware that she couldn't go on this way, that there had to be accounting sometime.

But that was a problem for another day.

CHAPTER SEVENTEEN

DIRK WOKE UP the day after Christmas feeling pretty good about things. Snow was coming down again, in big puffy flakes, but the temperature was in the upper twenties and rising. His ankle had recovered enough for him be able to rotate his foot without too much discomfort, and his head felt just fine.

Best of all, there was a woman in the next room who made him feel things he'd almost given up on ever feeling again. A strong, smart, competent woman, with a sweet smile and deep, thoughtful eyes and creamy-smooth skin, who'd curled up next to him under a patchwork quilt, and kissed him again and again, in the very spot where he was lying right now.

He lay there awhile, in no hurry to get up. It was enough—more than enough—to stare out the window and marvel at it all. Taffy was curled up right against his side under the quilt, a fuzzy little knot of comfort. He cupped his hand over her, and she purred.

When he heard Macy stirring, he got to his feet and started folding his bedding. His right foot was able to bear more weight today, and the swelling was way down.

By the time Macy came down the hall, he had the fire built up and the coffee brewing, and his packed duffel bag was resting beside the French door. Gunnar padded over to him, tail wagging, and greeted him like an old friend.

He reached down to rub Gunnar's head, smiled at Macy and said, "Morning."

"Good morning," said Macy.

She was wearing a long ivory-colored sweater over skinny jeans that made her legs seem to go on for miles, and her hair fell in honey-colored waves almost to her waist.

"I didn't know your hair was so long," he said. "I've never seen it all the way down before."

"What?" She looked down at her hair and touched it awkwardly. "Oh, yeah. I usually wear it up."

There were so many things left to be learned about her. He wanted to jump right in and get started, wanted to pull her close to him and kiss her, and run his hands through that shiny gold hair of hers. But there was something a little guarded in her manner this morning, and he knew he'd better hold back. This was an intensely private woman who had a bad history with pushy men, and he was in her home. He needed to let her know he wasn't going to crowd her, that he respected her space. And as soon as it was feasible, he needed to get back to his own house. As his oma used to say, houseguests and fish start to stink after three days, and he was on day four.

"The power hasn't gone out since yesterday afternoon," he said. "And it's supposed to get up to the forties by three o'clock. So I ought to be able to get out of your hair after feeding cattle this morning."

Her face was too neutral to read. "Are you sure you'll be all right on your own?" she asked.

"Oh, yeah. Alex is going to come over with his chainsaw and bring Nathaniel to help haul and stack wood. We've been texting about it. He thinks the three of us should be able to get the tree cleared and a tarp stretched over the hole in the roof in a matter of hours."

"Good. And he'll be able to assess the damage and help you make a plan for repairs."

Dirk pushed the plunger down in the French press and poured Macy a cup of coffee.

"It must be nice, having another rancher

so close by," she said. "Especially one with construction skills."

"Yeah, he's a good neighbor," said Dirk. "So are you."

As compliments went, it was a little bald, but the best he could do. He felt as young and green as a teenage boy.

She smiled, ducked her head and took a sip of coffee.

Don't come on too strong. Give her room to breathe.

It went against every instinct he had to rein himself in, but he did it. After breakfast, they fed the house animals and went out to the four-wheeler.

The snow had a different feel to it today. Wetter, slushier. The sky cleared before they finished feeding cattle, and the ice in the water tanks wasn't as thick as it had been yesterday. Everything seemed to have an extra shine on it somehow.

Back at the house, he loaded his stuff onto the ATV.

"What are you going to do about Hoss?" Dirk asked. "Try to hunt up his owners, or turn him loose and trust him to find his way back home?"

"If he could be trusted to find his way

home, I think he'd have done it that first night," said Macy. "I'll leave him here and walk over to Lot Six later today to see if that's where he belongs."

"His people had better get a good fence put up for him. He's shown himself to be quite a traveler, crossing the creek onto my place and back again."

"Well, you know what they say," Macy said with a smile. "Good fences make good neighbors."

He smiled back. He had that Robert Frost book tucked inside his duffel bag, ready to read when he got home. He'd taken a peek already and was hopeful about his chances of making sense of it. Frost's poetry looked pretty readable, not too dense or fancy.

Dirk stowed Taffy inside his jacket pocket like he had the first day, then climbed onto the ATV. Macy got on behind him, and he drove them back to the ranch.

He parked by the laundry room porch again. Macy helped him unload the four-wheeler and take his stuff inside the house. The living room looked about as bad as it had before, but not much worse, and the walls were still standing, so there was that.

"It's awfully cold," Macy said. "Are you sure you're going to be okay?"

"Yeah. Taffy and I'll camp out in the master bedroom until we get that tarp over the roof. There's a fireplace in there, so we'll be warm enough. And the cold isn't supposed to last much longer anyhow. We're supposed to have a high of seventy-two on Thursday."

He shut Taffy in the bedroom, then drove Macy back to her place one last time. He sure did like the feel of her sitting behind him with her arms wrapped around his middle. He was going to miss this—but not, he hoped, for long.

"WELL, WE MADE it through the Extreme Winter Weather Event," Macy said. "I'm sorry it was so rough on you."

Dirk had parked the ATV at Macy's back deck one final time, then gotten off to walk her the remaining ten feet to her back door. It was, Macy thought, a fine piece of Southern gallantry.

After all that kissing and cuddling on the sofa yesterday, she hadn't known what to expect from Dirk this morning. Would he give her knowing looks? Awkwardly try to distance himself? Or try to pick up where they'd left off?

He'd done none of that. He'd behaved exactly as he had before they'd kissed—which was good, because things needed to go back to how they'd been then.

"I'm glad it happened," said Dirk. "Otherwise I never would have gotten to know you."

Her heart started to pound. She told herself this was mere Southern gallantry, too, but she didn't believe it. He looked and sounded like a shy teenager.

"Well, it looks like the power is back on to stay, and there's no more snow in the forecast," she said lightly. "We can all get back to our regularly scheduled programming."

"I don't want to."

She could hear her pulse throbbing in her ears now. Those bright blue eyes of his were fixed on her with a level, sober gaze.

She saw him swallow. "It almost seems like a step backward to ask you on a real date now, but…may I take you to dinner?"

For one wild instant she almost said yes. She could feel the word on her lips, eager to be said, but she froze, and pushed it down.

"I don't know where or when yet," he went on. "We'll have to wait to see how things go with roads clearing and restaurants opening up again. But I'd imagine we should be able to figure something out by this weekend."

Still she didn't speak. The silence had lasted too long now. Dirk's eyes turned wary, and his jaw went stiff.

"Listen, Dirk," said Macy. "You're a great guy. And what happened between us was… fun. But we have to understand what it really was."

"Explain it to me," he said. "What exactly was it?"

"It was the effect of forced proximity under stress. Two unsociable cranky people in a confined space under trying conditions, having to work together and cooperate in order to survive. It produced an illusion of emotional closeness. That's all it was. And it's over now."

The words sounded horrible and cold. She wanted to unsay them. But there was no going back. This was what she wanted, or at least what she'd decided, and she was sticking to it.

"No," said Dirk. "I don't believe that, and I don't believe you do either. You're just saying it because you don't want to risk getting close to someone again."

He was right, of course. She was afraid of how quickly she'd gotten close to him, how good it had felt, holding him and kissing him, how much she wanted him even now.

But when she'd escaped from Andrew, she'd vowed never to forget, and never to let feelings override good judgment again. There were things worse than being alone.

"Look, I get it," said Dirk. "You don't want to get burned again. You let your guard down once and you got sucked into a soul-crushing relationship with a domineering man. But I'm not that guy. I won't treat you that way. I—" He swallowed again. "I care about you, Macy. And I think you care about me, too."

She turned away from him. "I'm sorry if I gave you a false impression."

A long silence followed, broken at last by a low whine. Gunnar was standing on the other side of the glass door, wagging his tail, looking from one to the other of them, clearly sensing the tension and wanting them both to come inside.

Macy's throat swelled, and her eyes stung. "Goodbye, Dirk," she said.

She went into the house before he could reply, and locked the door behind her.

A BRIGHT BLAZE crackled in the fireplace, warming the master bedroom of the old ranch house. In the ten months since Dirk had moved into the house, he'd gone into this room a total of maybe three times, bunking instead in the room that had been his when he was a boy. Same room, same twin bed, same worn sheets.

But not anymore. The master bedroom was going to be his headquarters for the next several weeks, or however long it took to get the living room roof rebuilt, the drywall replaced and the kitchen up and running again. After that, the whole house was getting a major overhaul—not a remodel, because he couldn't afford that, but a thorough decluttering and reorganizing. This whole bachelor-shabby thing of his had gotten way out of hand. It was high time he grew up and put his house in order, in more ways than one.

It had taken the better part of four hours for Dirk, Alex and Nathaniel to clear the fallen tree limbs from the living room, shovel out the snow and get the tarp stretched over the roof. Trash pickup was still a few days off, but Dirk had already taken a lot of sodden drywall and broken crockery to the end of the driveway, along with the wreckage of Granddad's old chair.

Now he was getting his new bedroom situated. He'd already set up a small drop-leaf table and a wooden chair near the fireplace to serve as a temporary dining area, dug out some old MREs from his military days, and brought all his water jugs and pitchers in from the kitchen. Taffy's litter box was in the master bathroom.

The comforter on the bed was covered in dust, and the sheets smelled funny. Dirk stripped them all off and made the bed with some fresh sheets out of his oma's cedar trunk at the foot of the bed, along with a couple of her patchwork quilts.

He ran his fingers over the top quilt. It had a churn dash pattern, like the one he and Macy had snuggled under together at her house on Christmas Day.

His stomach felt like it had a lead weight inside it. All the work he'd been doing, clearing tree limbs and stacking wood and cleaning house, had only covered over the ache.

The effect of forced proximity. An illusion of emotional closeness. That's what Macy had called the thing that had happened between them. The memory of the words stung him. He'd opened his heart to her, and she'd blown him off. And he'd taken it, and come home to his empty house.

What else could he do? He understood

why she was scared to get involved with him. She'd only just escaped from a mean bully of an ex. Dirk wouldn't be that. He wouldn't put his desires above hers, wouldn't try to push her into something she was afraid of. She wanted her space, and that was exactly what he would give her.

Taffy was sitting on her little haunches in front of the fireplace, blinking at the flames. Dirk hobbled over to the hard-backed wooden chair and sat down with a sigh. He wouldn't need the cane much longer, which was good, because he had a lot of work ahead of him. First thing tomorrow, he'd get under the house and fix those busted water pipes. Until that was done, he was going to be living off MREs, rehydrated with water from the pitchers, and taking tactical showers—basically a thorough wipe-down with heavy-duty body wipes. He'd lived a lot rougher in the Army, and he could manage.

Taffy toddled over and started climbing his jeans with her claws.

He scooped her up and held her to him. The ache deep inside him eased ever so slightly. It sure made a difference, having even one living creature in the house with you. Those days after Fletch had died and before Taffy showed up had been rough.

"We're home, Little Bit," he said. "I know it's cramped right now, but this is only temporary. We're going to fix that hole in the roof, and clear out all this trash and make this place real nice. We're going to be all snug in here, just you and me."

The words sounded a lot more cheerful than he felt. He missed Macy's woodstove and sectional sofa, her patchwork quilts and home-canned foods. He missed seeing Taffy climb the Christmas tree. He missed Gunnar's goofy affection and sweeping tail wags.

Most of all, he missed Macy—her conversation, her brisk competence, the feel of her in his arms, her lips against his.

Well, time would help him with that. Those memories would fade and not hurt him so much, and he wouldn't be making any new ones with her, because he wouldn't see her anymore—at least, not once he'd taken care of one last thing.

CHAPTER EIGHTEEN

MACY CARRIED ALL the flattened moving boxes from the work room floor to the trunk of her car, stepping carefully across the garage floor to avoid all the peacock droppings. Hoss was perched on the Kia's luggage rack, his tail trailing down the windshield.

She shut the trunk door and looked around the garage with distaste. In only four days, her shining clean garage had undergone a horrible transformation. She couldn't take the moving boxes to Goodwill until the roads were drivable, but she could get the mess-making peacock returned to his rightful home.

A few minutes later, she had Gunnar on his leash, and the two of them were walking down Gander Slough Road.

The kids on Lot Seven were outside, playing in the snow. In the past four days, they'd managed to make two sturdy snow forts and half a dozen snowmen.

The young couple who lived on Lot Six were

at their front gate, removing frost wrap from the rosebushes planted there. Macy had seen them from a distance before on her walks but had never spoken to them.

"Hello," she said. "My name is Macy Reinalda. I live down the road from you, on Lot Eight."

She'd planned that introduction ahead of time. It was the first part of a brief, factual speech, the main thrust of which was that she had a peacock at her house that she suspected was theirs.

The woman smiled. "Oh, hi! It's so nice of you to stop by. We've seen you and your dog lots of times, but we never wanted to bother you. You always seemed pretty focused on your walking. I'm Jill, and this is my husband, Kevin."

"Nice to meet you, Macy," said Kevin. "That's a good-looking dog you've got there. What is he, a mastiff?"

"Actually, he's part Rottweiler, part golden retriever."

Kevin and Jill both laughed over that, and wanted to know what Gunnar's name was and where Macy had gotten him, which led to an explanation of their own dog's origin— a shelter in Omaha—and their speculations as to his breeding. Then Macy was hearing about how they'd always wanted to live in the country, and raise their own vegetables, and keep chickens and ducks and maybe a steer or two, and how there was so much to do, and so much to learn, and how they weren't sure where to start because they didn't want to mess up, and they didn't actually have any chickens yet, but they'd answered an ad for free-to-a-good-home peafowl, and now they had two peahens and a peacock, but the peacock had gotten out of the enclosure before the storm and hadn't come home, and they were afraid he'd frozen to death.

Macy's original speech was past salvaging, but she seized this opportunity to get to the heart of the matter.

"I have your peacock," she said. "That's why I stopped by."

Jill pressed her hands to her mouth. "You have Reginald? Is he okay?"

"He's fine. He showed up Thursday night after the snow started. I put him in my garage, and I've been feeding him cat and dog food and kitchen scraps."

Macy was being hugged. "Oh, thank you, thank you!" Jill said in her ear. "Thank you for saving him. I've been so worried."

"You're welcome," Macy said into Jill's parka. "I'm sorry I couldn't let you know I had him. I wasn't certain whose peacock he was, and I didn't know how to contact you to ask if yours was missing."

Jill released Macy and pulled out her phone. "I'll give you my number right now. We really ought to have each other's contact information anyway. We're neighbors, after all."

The contacts section of Macy's phone was…sparse. Her real estate agent in Brooklyn, Reyes Boys Construction, the fabric store in Limestone Springs where she'd taken her sewing machine to be serviced—those were the sort of people or entities whose numbers she kept on hand. Jill was the first purely social contact she'd added, in…she didn't know how long.

"It was so good of you to look after Reginald," said Kevin. "He must have made a terrible mess in your garage."

"Ah, well," said Macy. The polite thing would be to deny this, but she didn't know how to do that convincingly.

"When can we pick him up?" Kevin asked.

"How about this afternoon, after I finish my walk? I'd say let's do it now, but Gunnar's been so cooped up the last few days, I think he could use the exercise."

"We'll be here," said Jill. "Just call or text me when you get home, and we'll come right over. And thanks again."

Macy continued down Gander Slough Road, past Lots Five, Four and Three. All her neighbors were busy with outside chores today—feeding animals, bringing firewood to the house, filling in low spots in their driveways—and they all looked cheerful about it. They waved at Macy, or called out greetings.

Between Lot Three and Lot Two was an area so overgrown that Macy couldn't see ten feet into it. Somewhere back there, close to the Serenidad Creek, was the old Masterson house, with its enormous pillars, iron scroll-work, multiple porches and ornate cupola. She'd never seen it in person, but the pictures Dirk had taken that first day for his little sister had been unforgettable. If he hadn't taken them, he never would have come across Gunnar in his tangle of barbed wire, or fallen down the creek bank or gotten hurt. Macy never would have hauled him up, or taken him to her house. The two of them wouldn't have made up after their quarrel, or eaten popcorn together in the firelight, or burrowed down together under warm quilts, or kissed. She wouldn't have this emptiness in her heart right now.

What was wrong with her? She hadn't minded being alone before Dirk came along. She'd treasured her solitude, relished it. She had to get back to that pristine isolation and self-sufficiency.

The overgrown wooden tangle of the Masterson lot ended abruptly at Lot Two. A bearded man with long gray hair was outside with his dogs; he waved at Macy as she walked by.

After passing Lot One, she turned right on Petty Road. About a quarter mile down, she came to a battered little house with a red front door. A white-haired woman in cowboy boots was in the horse pasture out front.

The woman smiled at her. "Well, hello there! I was wondering if you'd be out and about today. It's always a pleasure to see you and your dog out walking."

Macy hadn't realized that her neighbors had paid so much attention to her and Gunnar and their walks.

"Thank you," she said. "I'm always happy to see your beautiful horse."

The horse was a palomino pinto, with a golden body spotted with white, a white mane and tail and an alert intelligence in her brown eyes.

"She is a pretty one, isn't she?" the woman said. "Her name is Peaches. Doesn't she look like a bowl full of peaches and cream? My husband bought her for our granddaughter to ride, but I lost him years ago, and my son and his family moved away. I don't really ride anymore myself, so Peaches stays in her pasture most days. I suppose I ought to sell her to someone who'd ride her, but I can't bring myself to do it. What's your dog's name?"

"Gunnar."

"Hey there, Gunnar. Are you a good boy? You sure look like a good boy. Do you folks live around here?"

"Yes, in Masterson Acres."

"Masterson Acres! I remember when that was all ranch land and the family still lived in the old house. Did you folks make it through the storm all right?"

"Pretty well. How about you?"

"Oh, yeah, just fine. A couple of neighbor boys came over beforehand to set me up with plenty of firewood and make my house all snug."

"That was nice of them," said Macy.

"Yeah, Alex and Dirk always look after me. They're good boys."

"Alex Reyes? And Dirk Hager?"

"That's right. You know them? They grew up around here. Their families go way back in this county. My name's Ida Jeffries, by the way, but everyone calls me Miss Ida."

"Nice to meet you, Miss Ida. I'm Macy Reinalda."

By now Macy was resigned to a long chat, and so was Gunnar. He plopped his haunches down and stared at Peaches while Miss Ida asked Macy where she was from, how long she'd lived in Texas, what kind of dog Gunnar was, which lot Macy lived on, whether she was married or had kids and if she had any other pets.

When she learned that Macy used to ride, she said, "Oh, you'll have to come back and ride Peaches sometime."

"That's nice of you to offer," Macy said.

"I'm not saying it just to be nice," said Miss Ida. "I'm saying it because I mean it. It would be a kindness to Peaches, and to me. She doesn't have another horse to visit with, and I'm sure she gets bored never leaving this pasture. It makes me sad sometimes, seeing her here all alone, and thinking about my husband, and my little granddaughter across the world in Australia." Her eyes glistened, and she blinked hard. "I'm sorry," she said with a shaky laugh. "I didn't mean to go off like that."

"I'll do it," Macy heard herself say. "I'll come back tomorrow and ride Peaches."

What was she *doing*? Committing her time, forming a *relationship*, on the spur of the moment, based on a few minutes' conversation. There were a million things to consider and she'd skipped over all of them. Who knew where this might lead?

Miss Ida beamed at her through her tears. "Why, thank you, Macy. I look forward to seeing you then. And now I guess I'd better let you get on with your walk so Gunnar can get his exercise."

Macy and Gunnar continued down Petty Road. Macy was still so stunned by her own rashness that it took her a while to realize she was passing Dirk's land on the right now. She could see the windmill where she'd driven the truck for four mornings to break ice. What was Dirk doing right now? Was he thinking of her?

Stop it.

She turned again at Darnell Road. This was her usual walking route, but it felt different today—partly because of her new familiarity with the Masterson Place and the Hager Ranch, and partly because of all the interaction with neighbors. Being isolated during the storm must have put everyone in a garrulous mood.

Near Dirk's front gate, she suddenly stopped. That big, handsome evergreen, way back from the road on a little hill—that had to be the cedar tree Dirk had talked about, the one that used to be strung with Christmas lights when he was a boy. It must have looked spectacular, all lit up. No wonder he loved it.

He'd already taken some of his trash out to the road. The plastic cans held sad-looking soggy drywall, next to the torn-up upholstered chair she'd seen in Dirk's living room. It had a nice shape, big and boxy. She could imagine it paired with a wing chair like the one she had in her work room, with a little round table in between. Not in her house, maybe, but in Dirk's, over by the front windows in the living room.

She started walking again, fast. *What are you doing? You rejected the man not three hours ago. Stop trying to mentally furnish his house with your combined stuff.*

She made it to the edge of Dirk's property without seeing him. No one was out at the Reyes place either, at least not that she could see. Alex's property apparently ended at the creek, like Dirk's did, with Lot Nine on the other side. Macy turned back onto Gander Slough to complete her circuit.

At two hundred acres, Lot Nine was the biggest of the Masterson Acres lots. Macy had seen the family before—man, woman, teenage son—but they weren't outside today.

And then she was back at her own driveway. She went inside and texted Jill that she was home.

Jill and Kevin came to pick up their bird, bringing a fruit basket and a loaf of freshly baked zucchini bread as a thank-you gift, and a large dog crate to transport Reginald. They apologized profusely over the mess Reginald had made of Macy's garage, and Kevin insisted on coming back to personally pressure wash it, and to wash Macy's car. When Jill found out about Macy's upholstery business, she said she had a wonderful old comfy sofa with torn, stained seat covers, and that she'd be thrilled if Macy would make some slipcovers for her.

After they'd gone, Macy dropped onto her own sofa with a sigh. Her walking routine, usually a time of solitude and reflection, had turned into a social activity. The sanctity of her home was growing more compromised by the day. And tomorrow she had an appointment to ride a chatty neighbor's horse.

She hardly recognized herself anymore.

THE NEXT MORNING, Macy cleaned house with a vengeance. Four days of subfreezing temperatures and intermittent power had left their mark. With the woodstove seeing constant use, its firebox was full of ashes and cinders, and a fine dusting of ash covered its surface, its platform and the floor around it. A pile of dirty wet towels, used to soak up tracked-in snow, had accumulated around the back door. Dirk's sheets had to be washed, the blankets and quilts put away. The room where Taffy's food and litter box had been kept needed a good cleaning.

"There," she said aloud, once order had been restored. "That's more like it."

She had to regain her excitement over the little house that was so perfect for her and her dog. But the sound of her voice only made the house feel emptier.

It wasn't empty, though, not really. She had Gunnar. But Gunnar wasn't much help, moping around disconsolately looking for Dirk and Taffy, sticking his nose in the Christmas tree or behind the books on the lower shelves in search of his kitten friend. Now he gave Macy a reproachful look, walked over to his ottoman and flopped down with a sigh.

She wandered over to the shelf where the crèche stood. How long had Dirk spent carving those little figures, in stolen minutes while she was showering or walking Gunnar, or after she'd gone to bed? They were simply made, not detailed, and yet so full of personality. The horse was dignified but comical. The dog and kitten made her throat ache.

Suddenly, Gunnar gave a great joyous bark. He was standing at the back door now, looking through the glass and waggling his tail and entire rear end with all his might. Macy walked over to the door—

And saw Dirk driving the four-wheeler, coming her way.

He wore his cowboy hat low on his head. She couldn't see much of his face, only the mouth and jaw, but they were Dirk's mouth and jaw, and she'd have known them anywhere, and the set of his shoulders and chest.

Her heart gave a quick throb of pure pleasure. Dirk was here. She stood there, frozen, while Gunnar frisked about, making happy little yippy noises.

Rather than driving right up to the deck, Dirk parked the four-wheeler about fifty feet out from the back of the house, got off and started walking around with his cane. Macy steeled herself, trying to force her heartbeat to slow down, and walked outside.

Gunnar shot out the door and ran straight to Dirk. Dirk smiled, knelt down and gave him a pat.

"What are you doing here?" Macy asked.

Dirk looked up at her. "I'm here to build that fence."

Only now did Macy notice the rolls of fencing wire and metal posts in the cargo area of the four-wheeler.

"Oh," she said. "That's very thoughtful of you, but—"

"Never mind telling me all the reasons I don't have to do it," said Dirk. "I don't care. I said I would, and I will. Don't worry—I won't kiss you again."

He got back to his feet and glared at her, as if daring her to try to stop him from making that fence.

"Is it something I can help with?" she asked.

His expression softened. "Oh, yeah. It'll go faster for sure with two sets of hands."

He went back to the four-wheeler and started unloading materials and tools. "This is a T-post. It's called that because it looks like a T from the top. You drive it in with this T-post driver, and fasten your fencing to these little barbs along the side. This here—" he picked up a block-and-tackle-looking thing "—is the come-along. It's got a ratchet lever winch. You use it with the fence stretcher to get the fence panels stretched out all nice and even. I brought four-foot welded wire for your fence. It ought to hold up fine. We're not going to do anything fancy here, just drive in the posts and run the wire. I have some connector pieces that'll make it so's we don't have to use any wood posts for the corners. In a few hours, we should have a nice yard for Gunnar to run around in."

They got to work.

Dirk set the corner posts first, then ran

some wire between them to show where the line posts should go. Macy took turns with him, using the T-post driver. It was jarring, bringing the stout metal barrel down on the steel post again and again, but it made a satisfying ringing sound, and the posts sank quickly in the snow-soaked ground.

All this time Gunnar ran around delightedly nearby, or sniffed at the four-wheeler, or lay in the sunshine. The snow had all but gone, leaving behind patches of soggy yellow grass, and the air was mild enough for Dirk to shed both his coat and his flannel shirt.

"Did you get Hoss returned to wherever he came from?" Dirk asked as he wrapped wire fencing around a T-post.

"I did. He came from Lot Six, like I thought. The people were very happy to have him back. Nice young couple. They want to raise chickens and ducks."

"Miss Ida used to keep poultry when I was a boy. Ducks, chickens, even some turkeys for a while. Used to sell the eggs at the farmers' market, and the turkeys for holidays. Still has the chickens, but she's given up the rest."

"I met Miss Ida yesterday while I was walking Gunnar," Macy said. "She told me how two neighborhood boys got her set up with plenty of firewood before the storm. The boys turned out to be you and Alex."

Dirk chuckled. "Miss Ida has known Alex and me all our lives. I reckon we'll always be boys to her. She's good people. Grew up in this area, and has probably forgotten more about country living than most folks ever knew."

He told her about his boyhood on the ranch—riding fence with his granddad, rounding up the cattle with the hired cowboys, cutting and baling hay.

"We mostly used the Masterson place for hay," he said. "We'd grow wheat for early grazing, then move the cattle off, let it grow up and bale it the last half of the year. The best spot for hay was just to the west of your place. It's all lowland there."

"Lot Nine?" she asked. "The two-hundred-acre part?"

"Yeah. The reason they made that lot so big is because most of it is floodplain. Back when the land first went on the market, I was hoping no one would buy that part, and then maybe the price would come down enough that I could afford it myself. But no such luck. Those Hansens bought it, and built their house right up on the highest part, and what they're going to do with the rest of it, I can't imagine."

They worked together to fasten the fencing wire to the T-posts, and hung two gates, one in the back and one in the side.

"Thank you for doing this," Macy said. "It's going to be so nice to be able to put Gunnar in the yard and know that he can't run off."

"That's all right," said Dirk. "It's nothing but a few hours of work."

"For you it is, because you know what you're doing. For me on my own, it would have been a different story."

He was quiet awhile. Then he said, "'Before I built a wall I'd ask to know What I was walling in or walling out, And to whom I was like to give offense.'"

She looked up sharply. "You've been reading Robert Frost," she said.

"I have. You're right—it's good stuff. That one about mending fence is a lot to chew on. Why did he and his neighbor even have a fence, if all they were raising was trees? Trees don't stray onto someone else's property."

"Maybe it's about boundaries," said Macy. "Knowing without any ambiguity where your place leaves off and your neighbor's begins."

"Yeah, I reckon you're right. In a way, fences are just formalities. If a thief wants to steal your cattle, he can cut your fence. If a trespasser wants to go into your pasture, he can slip between the strands. Horses can jump over all but the tallest fences, if they're motivated enough. Cattle can knock down posts. Coyotes and hogs can go under. Mending fence is part of a rancher's life. It's a never-ending job, because something is always happening to mess up the fence. And if the land gets sold, the whole thing can be torn down in a single afternoon."

He gave the wire one last twist and smiled at her. "We'll make a nice sturdy fence for Gunnar, anyway. Keep him from running off and getting himself tangled up in barbed wire."

When they'd finished, Macy helped Dirk take his tools and leftover materials through the back gate and load them onto the ATV, which was parked just on the other side of the fence.

"You have any plans for the rest of the day?" Dirk asked.

Was he just making conversation, or trying to ask her out again? Either way, she had an answer ready.

"I do," she said. "I'm going to Miss Ida's to ride her horse."

Dirk's face softened into a surprised smile.

"Are you really? Well, that's mighty neighborly of you."

He reached between the fencing wires and gave Gunnar a farewell pat. "I'll be on my way, then."

"How much do I owe you?" Macy asked.

His smile vanished. "I'm going to pretend you didn't say that," he replied.

"Come on, Dirk. I can't just let you donate materials and labor to me. I've got to pay you."

"Alrighty, then. I'll send you an invoice, just as soon as you bill me for four days' worth of room and board during the storm."

She shook her head. "That isn't the same thing, and you know it."

He waved his hand toward the four-wheeler. "The materials are all used. And my labor isn't for sale—at least not to you."

He got onto the four-wheeler, pulled out the choke and turned the key. The engine turned over and started to thrum. He was leaning forward, his arms spread to reach the controls. She wanted to climb on behind him, and rest against that strong broad back, and hold on, the way she'd done all those other times. She wanted to ride all over his land with him, and then go back home together to their cat and their dog.

"Thanks again," she said over the engine noise.

He raised a hand to her in a silent farewell and drove away.

CHAPTER NINETEEN

WHEN MACY WENT to town to pick up her sewing machine the following day, she saw people dressed in a wild assortment of winter and summer attire—flip-flops and down jackets, sweaters and cutoffs, cargo shorts with cowboy boots and hoodies. A day after the end of the Extreme Winter Weather Event, the temperature was in the sixties, and the residents of Limestone Springs appeared to be doing their best to adjust.

The silver-haired woman working behind the counter at Sew Many Things gave Macy a cheerful smile as she took her credit card. Her name tag said Renée.

"I haven't seen you before," she said. "Are you new to the area?"

Macy was growing accustomed to people's friendly curiosity. "I just moved to Masterson Acres not long ago," she said.

"Oh, then you know my son-in-law Tony,"

said Renée. "He and his brother Alex built all the houses out there."

"They did a beautiful job," Macy said.

As she was signing for payment, Renée said, "That's a heavy-duty machine you have there. Professional quality. Do you quilt?"

"Yes, but I do all my quilting by hand. I mostly use my machine for upholstery projects."

"Ooh, upholstery! How fun! Do you have a business card? We're always having customers ask for referrals to someone who does reupholstery and slipcovers."

"I don't," Macy said, then, surprising herself, she added, "but if I get any made, I'll bring some in to leave here."

She wheeled her machine toward the door on the special hand truck she'd bought specifically for moving it around, but before she could make it outside, a thin woman with short blond hair stopped her.

"Excuse me, but I think I've seen you before," the woman said. "Do you live in Masterson Acres and have a big black dog?"

Goodness. Was the social interaction never going to end?

Macy put on a smile. "Yes, I do."

"My name is Pamela Hansen," the woman said. "I've seen you out walking—and if I'm not mistaken, I saw you riding a horse yesterday on Gander Slough Road."

"That's right. I'm Macy Reinalda. I live on Lot Eight."

"We're right next to you, on Lot Nine."

"Oh, the two-hundred-acre lot," said Macy. "What are you going to do with all that land?"

Pamela's smile faded. "That's a good question. We moved here because of our son Tim. He's thirteen—such a smart kid, but…well, we're worried about him. He's kind of an underachiever, and he'd rather play games online than do anything real. He's involved in I don't know how many role-playing games, where the different players all have characters, and they write scenes where their characters do things. I've read some of the writing he's done for them, and it's really good, but it doesn't seem healthy for his only social interaction to be with people he never sees, or characters who don't exist at all."

Macy felt a bond of sympathy with introverted, underachieving Tim, but she understood his mother's concern.

"The one thing all his role-playing characters have in common," Pamela went on, "is horses. They're all medieval knights, or warriors in a fantasy setting. So we thought if we moved to the country, maybe he'd have an opportunity to learn to ride, or work on a ranch or something. But I think we may have bitten off more than we can chew. We just found out what the taxes are going to be on our property if we don't do something agricultural on it, and it's more than we can afford. If we had some sort of livestock, it would be different. But my husband and I both have full-time jobs. We can't become farmers or ranchers overnight. We wouldn't know how. And we can't just start buying large animals to put on our land without knowing how to take care of them."

Macy thought of the great ratite bust that Dirk had told her about—all those city people trying to raise ostriches and emus without knowing what they were doing. Pamela was right to be wary.

"Have you tried getting to know some local ranchers?" she asked. "Maybe they could advise you."

Pamela sighed. "They probably could. But we'd barely moved in when we ran afoul of one of the ranchers close to our place. I'd be scared to even ask for help now."

"Which rancher was it? Alex or Dirk?"

"The one with the blue eyes and the angry mouth."

Pamela put on a fresh smile. "Well, I shouldn't keep you. I just wanted to say hello."

"It was nice to meet you," said Macy. "I hope you figure out something to do with your land."

And your son, she silently added.

She loaded her machine and her hand truck into her car. Just as she was closing the trunk, she had an idea of her own.

AFTER SEVEN HOURS of fruitless plumbing repair, Dirk was muddy, cranky and sore. He'd started out by replacing all the pipes that were visibly cracked. After waiting for the PVC cement to dry, he'd turned the water on, only to discover other, smaller cracks farther down the line where the water hadn't reached the first time. So he'd replaced those pipes, and waited for the PVC cement to dry, and turned the water on again, only to find still more cracks even farther down the line. Now here he was, covered in muck from crawling around under the house, tired, frustrated, out of PVC pipe, and no closer to having running water than when he'd begun. He'd have been better off ripping out *all* the pipes and starting fresh.

When he got the text from an unknown number, his bad mood was forgotten in an instant.

This is Macy. I need to see you.

His knees almost gave way, and he sat on the porch steps, staring at the words. The busted plumbing and wasted hours didn't matter anymore. Macy wanted to see him.

Sure, he typed back. I can be there in ten minutes.

A little rash, considering the state of his clothes, but he didn't care. He'd spent four days camping in her living room. She'd seen him first thing in the morning, precoffee. Now was no time to fuss about his appearance.

Her reply came quickly. How about if I come to you?

Fine by me, he answered. Better and better. More time to spruce himself up.

He told her the gate code and hurried inside to the master bedroom as fast as a sore ankle would let him.

Taffy was lying in the exact center of the bed, a little dab of cat on the brightly colored quilt. "We've got company coming," Dirk told her.

He stripped off his clothes and reached

for his body wipes. By the time the Kia Soul came down his driveway, he'd removed the worst of the mud smears from his face and arms and was buttoning up his nicest cotton shirt.

He met her on the front porch. She had her hair down again. It shone bright gold in the sunlight. The sight of her coming his way, looking so determined, made his hands shake. He stuck them in his back pockets.

"You got the tree limb out of your house," she said as she reached the steps.

"Yeah, I did. Alex and Nathaniel came over and we got 'er done."

"Good." She paused a moment, like she was thinking that took care of the small talk, and now she could come to the point. She looked all lit up inside. "I've been thinking a lot, and I want to run something by you."

"All right."

She waved an arm toward the front pasture. "Here you are, a seventh-generation rancher, trying to keep your place running. You can't get reliable help, and you can't do all the work yourself. Meanwhile, not a mile away from where we stand are nine households' worth of newcomers, people who've dreamed of living in the country, but don't have the practical knowledge to do it right. They're willing to work, but they need someone to show them how—someone like you, and Alex and Miss Ida. You have so much wisdom to share, and the newcomers are so eager to learn. Dirk, what if you started an internship program? You could teach the newcomers how to build fences, and ride horses, and take care of cattle, and raise poultry, and in return you'd get some free labor. What do you think?"

What did he *think*? She was smiling at him, eager and excited, expecting him to be excited, too, like she'd just handed him something wonderful. And here he was, like an idiot, slowly realizing that she wasn't here for *him*. She was here for her idea.

Her ridiculous, wrongheaded, harebrained idea.

"That's what you came here to say?"

His voice sounded harsh in his own ears, and his face must have matched it, because her smile faded away.

"You—you don't like it?" she asked.

Her disappointment only made him angrier. What right did she have to be disappointed? He was the one who'd put himself on the line with her, and been rejected. He was the one whose very way of life was in danger of disappearing altogether.

"Like it? Like the idea of teaching a course in country living to a bunch of folks who aren't from here?"

"Of course they aren't from here. That's the point. If they were from here, they wouldn't need help. Most of the original cowboys weren't from here either. They came from back East, because they needed a fresh start. Your own family wasn't from here to begin with."

"Yeah, well, that was a long time ago, and we've paid our dues. These new folks haven't. Macy, do you even hear yourself? You're asking me to take everything I know, everything my ancestors learned with their blood and sweat and tears, and hand it on a silver platter to the very people who bought the Masterson place out from under me."

"One of those people is me," she said, her voice chilly.

"Yeah, I know. I thought you were different, but you're just another outsider, coming in and telling folks who've lived here all their lives how to manage their own affairs."

She let out an exasperated sigh. "That's not—Dirk, don't you see? Like it or not, the newcomers are here to stay. Sooner or later, you're going to have to come to terms with that. If you want to save your ranch, you're going to have to adapt to a changing world."

A rush of heat flooded his face. "That's right, explain it to me. Poor Dirk Hager! He's just another benighted Southerner, toiling away on his failing ranch, too dumb to realize that what he really needs is an internship program! That'll solve all his problems!"

"You're not being fair."

"No, *you're* not being fair. You expect me to do all this adapting and changing, and be willing to take a chance and trust people, when you refuse to do the same."

"What are you talking about?"

"I'm talking about us, Macy. You and me. That's why I thought you wanted to come over, because you'd decided I was worth the risk. My mistake."

Her face froze. He waited for her to speak, but she didn't.

"I think you'd better go," he said.

"Yes," she said softly. "I think I'd better."

MACY SAT ON her slipcovered sofa in her tidy living room in her perfect little house, staring at her elegant lights-only Christmas tree and feeling absolutely miserable. She had her silence and solitude back, but they didn't feel peaceful anymore. They felt pinched and empty and cold.

She missed Taffy, scampering across the floor after her little felt mouse toy, clawing her way up the tree. She missed Dirk, stringing popcorn with those strong capable hands, mending the fire in the wood-burning stove, frying bacon in her kitchen. She missed feeding cattle with him in the mornings and relaxing with him at night.

She'd spent the past year of her life pursuing perfect freedom and solitude, and Dirk had ruined it for her.

Or maybe it had been an illusion all along. Maybe you couldn't insulate yourself from other people to the point where they couldn't ever hurt you anymore. Maybe you had to go on rubbing up against other people—helping them, being helped, giving, taking, offending, forgiving. It was messy and risky, but there was no getting away from it.

Which was pretty much what she'd said to Dirk after he'd rejected her internship idea. It was funny how set he was against outsiders, when he was so loyal and giving to the people he considered his, like Alex and Miss Ida… and, now, with her. Clannish, that's what he was—which really meant he wanted to protect his own. And his clannishness could be expanded to include new people. She'd seen that for herself. Beneath that tough exterior, the man was incredibly tenderhearted.

You expect me to do all this adapting and changing, and be willing to take a chance and trust people, when you refuse to do the same.

That's what he'd told her. It was infuriating... and true.

He'd opened his heart to her, and she'd pushed him away...for what? For an airtight sense of security that came from not risking anything.

And she didn't want that anymore.

She wanted him.

And right now he was all alone at his cheerless house with its caved-in roof and no running water, with only his kitten for company—while she was surrounded by beauty and comfort, but couldn't enjoy it without him.

She'd been gazing at her Christmas tree without really seeing it, but suddenly she sat up straight. She had an idea for how to bring back some of the security and joy he'd felt as a child.

She thought fast. Could she really pull this off? It was the sort of thing that called for extensive planning, but she didn't have time. She would have to wing it.

She would need several boxes of exterior Christmas lights, some sort of long-handled hook and a really big ladder.

DIRK WAS IN no sweet frame of mind when he went to Darcy's Hardware Friday morning to buy more plumbing supplies. What he learned there did not improve his mood.

"What do you mean, you don't have it?" Dirk asked.

Bill Darcy held out his hands in a helpless gesture. "I mean I don't have it. I am clean sold out of PVC pipe."

"Well, when are you going to get more in?"

"I honestly don't know. We usually get deliveries on Fridays, and we got one this morning, but we sold out within an hour, and now our suppliers are cleaned out, too. Most everyone in the state is repairing busted plumbing right now, and there aren't enough supplies to go around. I talked to the owner of the Ace Hardware over in Schraeder Lake, and he said he had folks driving in from Houston trying to buy out what he had left."

Dirk clamped his jaw tight. Everything was going to pot today. This never would've happened if they hadn't had so danged many people in the state to begin with.

"All right, then," he said. "I'll check in with you next Friday."

He turned to go, then stopped in his tracks.

Right down the aisle from him stood a big bearded man in a black cowboy hat. He'd gotten rid of the chaps and spurs, but he had on some sort of long oilcloth coat.

It was his non-cousin Roque.

The two of them stood there staring, like two gunfighters facing each other in an empty street at high noon.

Then Roque spoke. "Hello, Dirk."

Dirk nodded. "Roque. How are you?"

"Hanging in there. You?"

"Can't complain."

An awkward silence fell.

"Okay then," said Roque. "Take care."

"Yeah, you, too."

Well, Roque had survived the winter storm, anyway, and looked none the worse for wear. No reason to worry about him—not that Dirk had been worried, of course.

Then a voice behind him said, "Pardon me."

Dirk turned and saw a long-haired man who looked to be in his sixties. "I couldn't help but overhear you talking to Bill just now," he said.

"I've got plenty of PVC and CPVC in the sizes you need, and plenty of elbows, couplings and tees, out at my place."

A black market of plumbing supplies? Dirk supposed it was to be expected. "How much are you asking for them?" he asked.

The guy waved a hand. "Buddy, you can have 'em. They're left over from when I built my house, and now they're just taking up space in my workshop."

"Seriously? Thank you. That's mighty kind of you."

"Well, I've had a good year. And country folks have to stick together, don't we?"

"Yes, we do." Dirk stuck out his hand. "My name's Dirk Hager."

The man's face broke into a broad grin as he shook hands. "Well, I thought you looked familiar. I'm Walt Franklin. I knew your dad. We were state troopers together."

"Walt Franklin! I remember you. How long has it been? Fifteen years?"

"At least." Walt's smile faded. "I was sorry to hear about your dad, Dirk. He was a good cop."

Dirk swallowed hard. "Thank you. So what brings you to this area?"

"Retirement. I grew up in the country, and

always wanted to get back to it. I bought my-self a nice little twenty-acre spread over on Gander Slough Road."

"You live in Masterson Acres?"

"That's right. You know it?"

"Know it? My family's ranch backs up to it! Which lot are you on?"

"Two."

"Just north of my east pasture, then. We share fence line."

"Well, how about that? I won't have to give you directions, then. You can come on over to the house to pick up that pipe whenever you like. I'm heading straight home from here."

He clapped Dirk on the shoulder. "I'd love to catch up, but I'm sure you're eager to get that plumbing job finished. We'll have a beer soon, talk about your dad. Sound good?"

"Sounds good."

As he walked back out to his truck, Dirk was annoyed to find his eyes stinging.

CHAPTER TWENTY

MACY RAN HER gaze up, up, up the trunk of the tree to the very tip. It looked a lot bigger up close, and it had already looked pretty big from a distance. The lowest branches were higher than her head, and the diameter at the widest part was surely not less than twelve feet. Even with a sixteen-foot ladder and a closet pole with a hook on the end, getting this giant evergreen strung with Christmas lights was going to be a major feat.

She opened the first box and started unwinding the string of lights. Five boxes had seemed like a lot in the store, but now she doubted it would be enough.

Oh, well. There was nothing for it but to get started.

The first strand went on easily enough, but made it only a few times around the tree before running out. Macy plugged the second strand into the first, caught the cable in the hook of the pole and kept going.

It was a warm day, but breezy, which made for an interesting time on the ladder, especially considering the unevenness of the ground. By the end of the second light strand, Macy was wondering why she had ever believed this was something she could do on her own, or at all.

That was when she heard the sound of a truck engine, followed by the mechanical whirr of the electric gate.

She didn't turn around. She was trying to work the light strand up and over an unruly branch. Behind her, the truck tires crunched onto the gravel drive and slowed to a stop.

"Macy?" asked Dirk's voice. "Is that you? What the Sam Hill are you doing up there?"

Her heart pounded. She knew how ridiculous she looked, but it couldn't be helped. "I'm trying to get these lights strung onto this tree," she said.

She gave one last lunge with the closet pole, nearly upsetting the ladder. The truck engine died, and the door opened.

"Macy! Get down from there before you fall and hurt yourself!"

He took hold of the ladder and held it steady as she climbed down. She avoided his eyes until she was on solid ground again. When she finally looked at him, she didn't see any anger in his face, only confusion—and maybe, just maybe, a little tenderness.

He looked from her to the tree and back again.

"Why are you putting Christmas lights on my cedar tree?"

"Because it's something you loved."

His expression was as confused as ever, but she could see a smile forming at the corners of his mouth. "And you thought you'd just come on down here all by your lonesome, with a ladder and a whatever-that-is, and get 'er done?"

"Well, your grandfather managed to do it before," she said.

"Yes, he did," Dirk said evenly. "Thirty years ago, with my dad helping him. The tree was a lot smaller then."

"Oh. Yes, I guess it would have been."

He put his hands gently on her shoulders. "Macy, what's this really about?"

Up until now, she'd kept reasonably cool, but now, with those bright blue eyes looking into hers, something fluttered inside her, and when she spoke, her voice trembled.

"Dirk, I was wrong to push you away before. I was scared. I'm still scared. But I can't stop thinking about you. And what I think is…you're worth the risk."

His mouth fell open a little. She saw him take a breath and let it out.

"Macy," he said, "I told you I wouldn't kiss you again, but you are not making it easy for me to keep my word."

"Well, I didn't make any such promise," she said.

She took his face in her hands and drew his mouth down to hers.

And then his arms went around her and pressed her to him like he would never let go.

THE SOFT WHITE glow of hundreds of tiny electric lights fell on Macy's uplifted, sweetly smiling face. "We did it," she said.

"We sure did," said Dirk.

It had been touch and go for a while there. That closet hook thing that Macy had brought from home had worked well enough for the bottom third of the tree, but after that they'd needed something with greater reach. For a while they'd both been stumped, but then Dirk had remembered all the PVC pipes and fittings right there in his truck. He'd fashioned a U-shaped hook out of a couple of elbows and a tee, fastened it to the end of a pipe and had a tool suited to the job. Macy had fed the light strands up to him on the ladder and he'd strung them on the branches. The five strands of lights were exactly enough to reach to the top of the tree.

While they'd worked, the sun had gone down, and now the lights glowed in the twilight.

"Thank you for this," Dirk said.

Macy shrugged. "You did most of the work."

"But you had the idea, and you made a start. A job like this...it isn't something one person can do alone. It's a job for a team, or a crew or a partnership. Like building a fence... or running a ranch."

She turned to face him, her eyes widening.

"Which reminds me," he went on, "I met someone today that I think would be a fine addition to that internship program of yours, on the teaching end of things. Walt Franklin, your neighbor over on Lot Two. I've been out visiting with him for most of the afternoon. He knows how to weld, and repair engines, and butcher a hog. And he's got a whole slew of grandkids that he thinks would love to learn how to ride horses and work cattle."

"You told him about it?"

"I did. He thinks it's a fine idea. *Country folks have to stick together,* is what he said. And I reckon that means all of us now."

"Seriously?" she asked.

"Seriously," he said. "I'm going to get in touch with the Hansens and see if they'd like to lease their land to me for grazing and hay. They could keep their ag exemption, and I wouldn't have to reduce the size of my herd. I could use your land to drive them through—if you're okay with that. You're kind of the key to it all, in more ways than one."

Her eyes stung, and her throat swelled shut.

"Heck, I might even give my cousin Roque a call," Dirk went on. "He may be from New Jersey, but he's not a bad horseman."

She put her arms around him and rested her head on his shoulder.

"This has been the best Christmas of my life," she said.

He laid his cheek against her smooth golden hair. "Mine, too."

Standing there in the west pasture, with the lights on the cedar tree twinkling in the breeze, and the stars coming out in the sky, and Macy in his arms, Dirk felt as if he didn't have anything left to wish for…even though his roof still had a hole in it, and his living room was a wreck, and he had yet to restore running water to the house.

"There's no one in the world I'd rather be

snowed in with than you, Macy," he said. "And you know what? *Snowpocalypse* was the right word after all. It was a snow revelation. That winter storm seemed like a disaster while it was happening, but it opened my eyes to some things, and I'm grateful for it."

"So am I," Macy said softly. "Now let's go get Taffy and ride the four-wheeler back to my place. I'm hungry, and your house doesn't have a working kitchen."

Hand in hand, they strolled toward the house. Now that the sun had set, a chill had crept into the air. It would feel good to snuggle under one of Macy's quilts, and watch Taffy climb the Christmas tree. It might even be cool enough to start a fire in the wood-burning stove.

One way or another, they'd stay warm.

* * * * *

Get 4 **FREE REWARDS!**

We'll send you 2 FREE Books <u>plus</u> 2 FREE Mystery Gifts.

FREE Value Over **$20**

Both the **Harlequin® Special Edition** and **Harlequin® Heartwarming™** series feature compelling novels filled with stories of love and strength where the bonds of friendship, family and community unite.

YES! Please send me 2 FREE novels from the Harlequin Special Edition or Harlequin Heartwarming series and my 2 FREE gifts (gifts are worth about $10 retail). After receiving them, if I don't wish to receive any more books, I can return the shipping statement marked "cancel." If I don't cancel, I will receive 6 brand-new Harlequin Special Edition books every month and be billed just $5.24 each in the U.S. or $5.99 each in Canada, a savings of at least 13% off the cover price or 4 brand-new Harlequin Heartwarming Larger-Print books every month and be billed just $5.99 each in the U.S. or $6.49 each in Canada, a savings of at least 20% off the cover price. It's quite a bargain! Shipping and handling is just 50¢ per book in the U.S. and $1.25 per book in Canada.* I understand that accepting the 2 free books and gifts places me under no obligation to buy anything. I can always return a shipment and cancel at any time by calling the number below. The free books and gifts are mine to keep no matter what I decide.

Choose one: ☐ **Harlequin Special Edition**   ☐ **Harlequin Heartwarming**
                  (235/335 HDN GRCQ)   **Larger-Print**
                                                                       (161/361 HDN GRC3)

Name (please print)

Address   Apt. #

City   State/Province   Zip/Postal Code

Email: Please check this box ☐ if you would like to receive newsletters and promotional emails from Harlequin Enterprises ULC and its affiliates. You can unsubscribe anytime.

Mail to the **Harlequin Reader Service:**
IN U.S.A.: P.O. Box 1341, Buffalo, NY 14240-8531
IN CANADA: P.O. Box 603, Fort Erie, Ontario L2A 5X3

Want to try 2 free books from another series! Call 1-800-873-8635 or visit www.ReaderService.com.

*Terms and prices subject to change without notice. Prices do not include sales taxes, which will be charged (if applicable) based on your state or country of residence. Canadian residents will be charged applicable taxes. Offer not valid in Quebec. This offer is limited to one order per household. Books received may not be as shown. Not valid for current subscribers to the Harlequin Special Edition or Harlequin Heartwarming series. All orders subject to approval. Credit or debit balances in a customer's account(s) may be offset by any other outstanding balance owed by or to the customer. Please allow 4 to 6 weeks for delivery. Offer available while quantities last.

Your Privacy—Your information is being collected by Harlequin Enterprises ULC, operating as Harlequin Reader Service. For a complete summary of the information we collect, how we use this information and to whom it is disclosed, please visit our privacy notice located at corporate.harlequin.com/privacy-notice. From time to time we may also exchange your personal information with reputable third parties. If you wish to opt out of this sharing of your personal information, please visit readerservice.com/consumerschoice or call 1-800-873-8635. **Notice to California Residents**—Under California law, you have specific rights to control and access your data. For more information on these rights and how to exercise them, visit corporate.harlequin.com/california-privacy.

HSEHW22R2

COUNTRY LEGACY COLLECTION

19 FREE BOOKS IN ALL!

Cowboys, adventure and romance await you in this new collection! Enjoy superb reading all year long with books by bestselling authors like Diana Palmer, Sasha Summers and Marie Ferrarella!

Get 4 FREE REWARDS!

We'll send you 2 FREE Books plus <u>2</u> FREE Mystery Gifts.

FREE
Value Over
$20

Both the **Romance** and **Suspense** collections feature compelling novels written by many of today's bestselling authors.

YES! Please send me 2 FREE novels from the Essential Romance or Essential Suspense Collection and my 2 FREE gifts (gifts are worth about $10 retail). After receiving them, if I don't wish to receive any more books, I can return the shipping statement marked "cancel." If I don't cancel, I will receive 4 brand-new novels every month and be billed just $7.24 each in the U.S. or $7.49 each in Canada. That's a savings of up to 38% off the cover price. It's quite a bargain! Shipping and handling is just 50¢ per book in the U.S. and $1.25 per book in Canada.* I understand that accepting the 2 free books and gifts places me under no obligation to buy anything. I can always return a shipment and cancel at any time by calling the number below. The free books and gifts are mine to keep no matter what I decide.

Choose one: ☐ **Essential Romance**
(194/394 MDN GQ6M)

☐ **Essential Suspense**
(191/391 MDN GQ6M)

Name (please print)

Address   Apt. #

City   State/Province   Zip/Postal Code

Email: Please check this box ☐ if you would like to receive newsletters and promotional emails from Harlequin Enterprises ULC and its affiliates. You can unsubscribe anytime.

Mail to the **Harlequin Reader Service:**
IN U.S.A.: P.O. Box 1341, Buffalo, NY 14240-8531
IN CANADA: P.O. Box 603, Fort Erie, Ontario L2A 5X3

Want to try 2 free books from another series! Call 1-800-873-8635 or visit www.ReaderService.com.

*Terms and prices subject to change without notice. Prices do not include sales taxes, which will be charged (if applicable) based on your state or country of residence. Canadian residents will be charged applicable taxes. Offer not valid in Quebec. This offer is limited to one order per household. Books received may not be as shown. Not valid for current subscribers to the Essential Romance or Essential Suspense Collection. All orders subject to approval. Credit or debit balances in a customer's account(s) may be offset by any other outstanding balance owed by or to the customer. Please allow 4 to 6 weeks for delivery. Offer available while quantities last.

Your Privacy—Your information is being collected by Harlequin Enterprises ULC, operating as Harlequin Reader Service. For a complete summary of the information we collect, how we use this information and to whom it is disclosed, please visit our privacy notice located at corporate.harlequin.com/privacy-notice. From time to time we may also exchange your personal information with reputable third parties. If you wish to opt out of this sharing of your personal information, please visit readerservice.com/consumerschoice or call 1-800-873-8635. **Notice to California Residents**—Under California law, you have specific rights to control and access your data. For more information on these rights and how to exercise them, visit corporate.harlequin.com/california-privacy.

STRS22R2

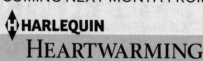
#443 HER FAVORITE WYOMING SHERIFF
The Blackwells of Eagle Springs
by Cari Lynn Webb

Widower and single mom Adele Blackwell Kane must reopen the once-renowned Blackwell Auction Barn—if she can get Sheriff Grady McMillan to stop arresting her on town ordinances long enough to save her ranch. Can love prevail in county jail?

#444 THE SERGEANT'S CHRISTMAS GIFT
by Shelley Shepard Gray

While manning the NORAD Santa hotline, Sergeant Graham Hopkins gets a call from a boy who steals his heart. When he meets the boy's mother, Vivian Parnell, will he make room in his heart for both of them?

#445 THE SEAL'S CHRISTMAS DILEMMA
Big Sky Navy Heroes • by Julianna Morris

Navy SEAL Dakota Maxwell is skipping Christmas—and not just because his career-ending injuries have left him bitter. But Dr. Noelle Bannerman lives to heal. And she'll do that with physical therapy...and a dose of holiday magic.

#446 AN ALASKAN FAMILY THANKSGIVING
A Northern Lights Novel • by Beth Carpenter

Single mom Sunny Galloway loves her job as activities director of a seniors' home—then Adam Lloyd shows up, tasked with resolving financial woes. They have until Thanksgiving to save the home. Can working together mean saving each other, too?

HARLEQUIN
PLUS

Announcing a **BRAND-NEW** multimedia subscription service for romance fans like you!

Read, Watch and Play.

Experience the easiest way to get the romance content you crave.

Start your **FREE 7 DAY TRIAL** at <u>www.harlequinplus.com/freetrial</u>.